Fifth Column

Book Five

The Lone Star Series

by
Bobby Akart

Copyright Information

© 2018 Bobby Akart Inc. All rights reserved. Except as permitted under the U.S. Copyright Act of 1976, no part of this publication may be reproduced, distributed or transmitted in any form or by any means, or stored in a database or retrieval system, without the prior written permission of Bobby Akart Inc.

This is a work of fiction. Names, characters, business, events and incidents are the products of the author's imagination. Any resemblance to actual persons, living or dead, or actual events is purely coincidental.

Other Works by Bestselling Author Bobby Akart

The Lone Star Series
Axis of Evil
Beyond Borders
Lines in the Sand
Texas Strong
Fifth Column
Suicide Six

The Pandemic Series
Beginnings
The Innocents
Level 6
Quietus

The Blackout Series
36 Hours
Zero Hour
Turning Point
Shiloh Ranch
Hornet's Nest
Devil's Homecoming

The Boston Brahmin Series

The Loyal Nine
Cyber Attack
Martial Law
False Flag
The Mechanics
Choose Freedom
Patriot's Farewell
Seeds of Liberty (Companion Guide)

The Prepping for Tomorrow Series

Cyber Warfare
EMP: Electromagnetic Pulse
Economic Collapse

Dedications

Every day, I wake up to a beautiful world filled with the undying love of my wife and the loyalty of our pups. Without them, none of my books would be possible. I wish every family could have what we have.

The Lone Star Series is dedicated to the love and support of my family. I will always protect you from anything that would disrupt our happiness.

Acknowledgements

Writing a book that is both informative and entertaining requires a tremendous team effort. Writing is the easy part. For their efforts in making *Beyond Borders*, book two in the Lone Star series, a reality, I would like to thank Hristo Argirov Kovatliev for his incredible cover art, Pauline Nolet for her editorial prowess, Stef Mcdaid for making this manuscript decipherable in so many formats, Sean Runnette and the folks at Audible Studios for producing the incredible narration, and the Team—Shirley, Denise, Joe, and Jim, whose advice, friendship and attention to detail is priceless.

A special thank-you to Kevin Baron and the team at *Defense One* for providing invaluable insight into the North Korean threat and how we'd defend against it. Also, thank you to Michaela Dodge, senior policy analyst at the Heritage Foundation, Center for National Defense, for her extensive background material on missile defense, nuclear weapons modernization and arms control.

Thank you all!
Choose Freedom!

About the Author

Bobby Akart

Bestselling author Bobby Akart has been ranked by Amazon as the #3 Bestselling Religion & Spirituality Author, the #5 Bestselling Science Fiction Author, the #7 Bestselling Historical Author and the #10 Bestselling Horror Author. He has written twenty international bestsellers, in forty different fiction and nonfiction genres, including the critically acclaimed Boston Brahmin series, the bestselling Blackout series, the frighteningly realistic Pandemic Series, his highly cited nonfiction Prepping for Tomorrow series and his latest project—the Lone Star series, which has already produced four #1 bestsellers.

Bobby has provided his readers a diverse range of topics that are both informative and entertaining. His attention to detail and impeccable research have allowed him to capture the imaginations of his readers through his fictional works and bring them valuable knowledge through his nonfiction books.

SIGN UP to Bobby Akart's mailing list to receive special offers, bonus content, and you'll be the first to receive news about new releases in the Lone Star series, updates on his other series, special offers, and bonus content. You can contact Bobby directly by email (BobbyAkart@gmail.com) or through his website:

BobbyAkart.com

Foreword

by Dr. Peter Vincent Pry
Chief of Staff,
Congressional EMP Commission

Executive Director, Task Force
on National and Homeland Security

The recent escalating war of words and actions with rogue nations like North Korea and Iran has given rise to a new sense of urgency about threats we face—especially the existential threat that is a nuclear electromagnetic pulse (EMP) attack. I am pleased to write this foreword for author Bobby Akart as he continues to inform his readers, through his works of fiction, about the EMP threat, both man-made and naturally occurring.

With the Lone Star series, you will learn about the potential of nuclear-armed satellites flying over America daily in low Earth orbit, positioned to collapse our power grid, destroy our way of life, and possibly kill up to ninety percent of Americans.

The Congressional EMP Commission warns North Korea may already pose a worldwide threat, not only by ICBM, but by satellites, two of which presently orbit over the United States and every country on Earth.

A single satellite, if nuclear-armed, detonated at high-altitude would generate an EMP capable of blacking out power grids and life-sustaining critical infrastructure.

Yet, after massive intelligence failures grossly underestimating North Korea's nuclear capabilities, their biggest threat to the U.S. and the world remains unacknowledged—nuclear EMP attack.

The EMP threat continues to be low priority and largely ignored, even though on September 2, 2017, North Korea confirmed the EMP Commission's assessment by testing an H-Bomb that could make a devastating EMP attack.

Two days after their H-Bomb test, on September 4, Pyongyang also released a technical report "The EMP Might of Nuclear Weapons" accurately describing a "super-EMP" weapon generating 100,000 volts/meter.

North Korea's development of a super-EMP weapon that generates 100,000 volts/meter is a technological watershed more threatening than the development of an H-Bomb and ICBM because even the U.S. nuclear deterrent, the best-protected U.S. military forces, are EMP hardened to survive only 50,000 volts/meter.

My colleague EMP Commission Chairman William Robert Graham warned Congress in 2008 that Russia had developed super-EMP weapons and most likely transferred that technology to North Korea allegedly *by accident*, according to Russian generals.

The result of this newly discovered relationship between Russia and North Korea is that the DPRK now has the technology to win a nuclear war. At the very least, a North Korean EMP attack could paralyze the U.S. nuclear deterrent and prevent U.S. retaliation, perhaps even by U.S. submarines at sea that cannot launch missiles without receiving an Emergency Action Message from the president.

However, the warning signs have gone largely ignored. Although North Korea, Russia, and China have all made nuclear threats against the United States recently, in the case of North Korea and Russia repeatedly, most analysts dismiss the war of words as *mere bluster* and *nuclear sabre rattling*, not to be taken seriously.

In the West, generations of leaders and citizens have been educated that use of nuclear weapons is unthinkable and the ultimate horror. Not so in Russia, China, and North Korea, where their nuclear capabilities are publicly paraded—missile launches and exercises are televised as a show of strength, an important part of national pride.

Then there is the issue of an EMP attack. An electromagnetic pulse attack would be perfect for implementing Russia's strategy of "de-escalation," where a conflict with the U.S. and its allies would be won by limited nuclear use. It's their version of "shock and awe" to cow the U.S. into submission. The same kind of attack is viewed as an acceptable option by China and North Korea as well.

An EMP attack would be the most militarily effective use of one or a few nuclear weapons, while also being the most acceptable nuclear option in world opinion, the option most likely to be construed in the U.S. and internationally as "restrained" and a "warning shot" without direct loss of life.

Because an electromagnetic pulse destroys electronics instead of blasting cities, even some analysts in Germany and Japan, among the most antinuclear nations, regard EMP attacks as an acceptable use of nuclear weapons. A high-altitude EMP ("HEMP") attack entails detonating a nuclear weapon at 30–400 kilometers altitude—above the atmosphere, in outer space, so high that no nuclear effects, not even the sound of the explosion, would be experienced on the ground, except the resulting EMP.

An EMP attack will kill far more people than nuclear blasting a city through indirect effects—by blacking out electric grids and destroying life-sustaining critical infrastructures like communications, transportation, food and water—in the long run. But the millions of fatalities likely to eventually result from EMP will take months to develop, as slow as starvation.

Thus, a nation hit with an EMP attack will have powerful incentives to cease hostilities, focus on repairing their critical infrastructures while there is still time and opportunity to recover, and avert national extinction.

Indeed, an EMP attack or demonstration made to "de-escalate" a crisis or conflict is very likely to raise a chorus of voices in the West against nuclear escalation and send Western leaders in a panicked search for the first "off ramp."

Axis of Evil and the entire Lone Star series are books of fiction that are based upon historical fact. The geopolitical factors in this series leading up to a potentially catastrophic collapse of America's power grid are based upon real-world scenarios.

Author Bobby Akart has written several fiction and nonfiction books with the intent to raise awareness about the threats we face from an EMP, whether via a massive solar storm or delivered by a nuclear warhead. While many books have been written about the results of nuclear war and EMPs, few have tackled the subject of using satellites as a means of delivering the fatal blow, until now.

The Lone Star series is written to be thought-provoking. It will be a reminder to us all that, as Bobby says, you never know when the day before is the day before. Prepare for tomorrow.

Dr. Peter Vincent Pry
Chief of Staff
Congressional EMP Commission
Executive Director
Task Force on National and Homeland Security

About Dr. Peter Vincent Pry

Dr. Peter Vincent Pry served as chief of staff of Congressional Electromagnetic Pulse (EMP) Commission (2001-2017), and is currently the executive director of the Task Force on National and Homeland Security, a Congressional Advisory Board dedicated to achieving protection of the United States from electromagnetic pulse (EMP), cyber warfare, mass-destruction terrorism and other threats to civilian critical infrastructures, on an accelerated basis. Dr. Pry also is director of the United States Nuclear Strategy Forum, an advisory board to Congress on policies to counter weapons of mass destruction. Foreign governments, including the United Kingdom, Israel, Canada, and Kazakhstan consult with Dr. Pry on EMP, cyber, and other strategic threats.

Dr. Pry served on the staffs of the Congressional Commission on the Strategic Posture of the United States (2008–2009); the Commission on the New Strategic Posture of the United States (2006–2008); and the Commission to Assess the Threat to the United States from Electromagnetic Pulse (EMP) Attack (2001–2008).

Dr. Pry served as professional staff on the House Armed Services Committee (HASC) of the U.S. Congress, with portfolios in nuclear strategy, WMD, Russia, China, NATO, the Middle East, Intelligence, and Terrorism (1995–2001). While serving on the HASC, Dr. Pry was chief advisor to the vice chairman of the House Armed Services Committee and the vice chairman of the House Homeland Security Committee, and to the chairman of the Terrorism Panel. Dr. Pry played a key role: running hearings in Congress that warned terrorists and rogue states could pose EMP and cyber threats, establishing the Congressional EMP Commission, helping the commission develop plans to protect the United States from EMP and cyber warfare, and working closely with senior scientists and the nation's top experts on critical infrastructures, EMP and cyber warfare.

Dr. Pry was an intelligence officer with the Central Intelligence Agency, responsible for analyzing Soviet and Russian nuclear strategy, operational plans, military doctrine, threat perceptions, and developing U.S. paradigms for strategic warning (1985–1995). He also served as a verification analyst at the U.S. Arms Control and Disarmament Agency responsible for assessing Soviet arms control treaty compliance (1984–1985).

Dr. Pry has written numerous books on national security issues, including *Blackout Wars*; *Apocalypse Unknown: The Struggle To Protect America From An Electromagnetic Pulse Catastrophe*; *Electric Armageddon: Civil-Military Preparedness For An Electromagnetic Pulse Catastrophe*; *War Scare: Russia and America on the Nuclear Brink*; *Nuclear Wars: Exchanges and Outcomes*; *The Strategic Nuclear Balance: And Why It Matters*; and *Israel's Nuclear Arsenal*. You may view his canon of work by visiting his Amazon Author page.

Dr. Pry often appears on TV and radio as an expert on national security issues. The BBC made his book *War Scare* into a two-hour TV documentary *Soviet War Scare 1983*, and his book *Electric Armageddon* was the basis for another TV documentary *Electronic Armageddon* made by National Geographic.

Epigraph

"They will charge with resolve to thrust a sword through the enemy's heart like lightning."
~ DPRK State Television on the newly created Lightning Death Squads

*****

A nation can survive its fools and even the ambitious, but it cannot survive treason from within. An enemy at the gates is less formidable for he is known and he carries his banners openly. But the traitor moves among those within the gate freely, his sly whispers rustling through all the alleys and heard in the very halls of government itself. For the traitor appears not the traitor. He speaks in the accents familiar to his victims and he wears their face and their garments, and he appeals to the baseness that lies deep in the hearts of all men. He rots the soul of a nation. He works secretly and unknown in the night to undermine the pillars of power. He infects the body politic so that it can no longer resist. A murderer is to be less feared.
~ Cicero, 42 B.C.

*****

The Fifth Column in America consists of all those in the Deep State and elsewhere such as academia, politics, and the media who worked for a soft coup against President Trump, who have spread falsehoods to undermine his presidency, and who are actively working to impeach him.
~ Michael S. Rozeff

*****

Drain the swamp!
~ Donald J. Trump, 2016

Preface

The Post-modern Fifth Column: The Deep State

Author's Note to the Reader:

The following is not required reading in order to continue the Lone Star series; however it will provide you a valuable understanding of the threats to our nation, from within. If you choose to skip over the preface to find out who was on the receiving end of the sniper's bullet, may I encourage you to return to this preface at a later time.

Thank you and enjoy.

The year was 1942, and it marked the beginning of an era in which a centuries-old geopolitical strategy morphed into today's modern political warfare. America had been blindsided at Pearl Harbor, and feelings of patriotism were running high. The nation rallied together as scores of young men volunteered to fight, and families helped one another fill the void left behind—both in the home and the workplace.

To say that a monumental event like a worldwide military conflict would have a profound impact on a population is certainly a given. The Second World War, which caused an enormous number of deaths, saw the European continent divided as armies attacked one another. When the war ended, much of Europe was in ruins and the rest impoverished.

The end result was a transformation of Europe politically, socially, and economically in the immediate postwar years and for decades to come.

The same was true in America although the battlefield remained abroad. The war resulted in an appreciable change in the role of women in American society. During the war, the number of women in the workplace rose by fifty percent. Millions of families, seeking to maintain a two-earner household, flocked to the cities to work in the military defense industry.

This vast migration resulted in higher divorce rates, housing shortages, and challenged school systems unable to deal with the postwar baby boom. The family dynamic changed, and the country's view on social issues of the time began to change as well.

Politically, the New Deal of President Franklin Roosevelt gave way to the Fair Deal of his running mate, President Harry Truman, who took office upon President Roosevelt's death in April of 1945. An era of huge government spending was ushered in, which resulted in higher and higher levels of taxation.

With more government spending came a larger bureaucracy, and the burgeoning federal government began to take root in America. The larger the federal bureaucracy, the more out of control it became. Soon, as many limited government, constitutional conservatives like to say, the inmates began to run the asylum.

Enter the deep state, the modern-day equivalent of the fifth column.

The use of the term *fifth column* dates back to 1936 during the Spanish Civil War between anarchist-communists and conservative-nationalists. The conflict lasted for three years in the lead-up to World War II and was indicative of the struggle between democracy and fascism throughout Europe.

The nationalist general, on the eve of his assault on Madrid, Spain's capital, told a news journalist that his strategy involved his four columns of troops, which would attack the city, and a fifth column, a group of unlikely supporters within the city, who worked to undermine the government from within. This fifth column, a group of sympathetic government workers, committed acts of sabotage on the government that employed them in order to aid the advancing troops. Madrid eventually fell, and the war was brought to an end.

The concept of using opponents who were not necessarily loyal to a cause but were also an opposing party of a common enemy was not a new one. Early Sanskrit writings dating back to the fourth century BC espoused the basic premise:

The enemy of my enemy is my friend.

Following the Siege of Madrid and the subsequent fall of France in 1940, which many at the time blamed on a pro-German fifth column within the Parisian government, a series of articles began to run in the media. One such article in *Life* magazine warned of *Signs of the Nazi Fifth Column Everywhere.*

In a speech given to the House of Commons in 1940, Winston Churchill promised to *put down fifth-column activities with a strong hand.* The *New York Times* reported on *the spasms of fear engendered by the success of fifth columns in less fortunate countries.*

The western nations of the world became beset by fears of enemy infiltration of their governments, and the fears continued after World War II, especially in America. This leads us to a United States senator who was often vilified but who may have been on the right track— Joseph McCarthy, republican from Wisconsin.

Senator McCarthy became famous for his investigations into communist subversive techniques in the U.S. within our media, Hollywood, and the government. He was a student of history who warned America of the *First Red Scare*, a period following World War I in which concerns over radical political agitation in American society coupled with the spread of communism and anarchy within the American labor movement fueled fears of an undermining of the U.S. government.

The so-called *Second Red Scare* occurred after World War II and lasted through 1956. Fears of fascist, Communist, and subversive activities against the American way of life permeated the nation's psyche. During the McCarthy era, many Americans were accused of being communists or socialist subversives, agents of the Soviets, or generally treasonous.

The fifth column was resurrected once again as those operating within our government came under McCarthy's scrutiny. Over time, however, McCarthy was attacked by the press as a demagogue, accused of making reckless and unfounded accusations against everyone from high-ranking government officials to members of the media, including in Hollywood.

Now, fast-forward to the headlines of 2018. Accusations of Russian collusion with a political campaign without basis in fact. Counteraccusations of a deep-state apparatus that works against an administration's policies. The players include the media, the nation's intelligence agencies, and the FBI.

The definition of McCarthyism via Wikipedia is the practice of making accusations of subversion or treason without proper regard for the evidence. I would submit to you, my friends, that the efforts of those within the United States government who are advancing false narratives without evidence are just as guilty of McCarthyism as the famed senator was alleged to have been.

Further, with the exposure of the deep-state apparatus in the United States, the tool once known as the fifth column is more powerful than ever. It is so deeply rooted into our federal government that it may be impossible to dislodge. And, as we've seen by the actions of high-ranking FBI officials and others, activities of this new fifth column can be more impactful than the onslaught of the world's most powerful armies.

Today, we must ask ourselves. *Where does noble opposition to your political foes end and treasonous collaboration to undermine our government and the will of the people through the electoral process begin?*

Part One

One Long Day

Chapter 1

January 16, 2023
Klondike High School
Patricia, Texas

Manuel Holloway feared no man. Desensitized as a teen to the concept of death as he played video games like *Call of Duty*, his days in the United States Army hardened his soul even further. But all semblance of feeling within his heart was sucked out the day one of his recruits and trainees in Afghanistan detonated the bomb strapped to his chest, killing dozens and taking Holloway's eye. Filled with anger after being denied the ability to continue in military service, Holloway became a murderer, a killing machine who had found his niche in the universe—*a post-apocalyptic world.*

He was reunited with recently anointed General Kyoung-Joo Lee, formerly a commander in North Korea's Lightning Death Squad and now in charge of the entirety of the invasion forces within the continental United States and Texas. Combining their brilliant strategic minds, the commandos broke through the border security maintained between Texas and New Mexico, quickly making a hole large enough to allow their forces to invade the new nation, together with tens of thousands of refugees.

Holloway's strategic preplanning provided the means to plow through the undermanned Texas border patrols and quickly move undetected to this desolate part of West Texas, where they regrouped.

The Klondike High School outside Patricia, Texas, was the perfect facility to house the commandos as they reunited for the next stage of their mission. There was plenty of cover for the dozens of shiny new Ford pickup trucks stolen in Lubbock. The classrooms allowed the commandos the opportunity to rest in a shelter far superior to the caves at Carlsbad Caverns in New Mexico. And the operable showers with hot water in the school's gymnasium provided Lee's men the opportunity to wash off the stench of living like animals for weeks.

Holloway and Lee walked quietly through the dimly lit hallways. The school was darkened to practice light discipline, preventing discovery from the Texas military helicopters, which were abuzz to their west. As they found their way through desks and chairs stacked haphazardly through the corridors, Holloway glanced into each room. Despite the low light, he could make out the silhouettes of the steely-eyed commandos staring back at him. They couldn't be seen nor heard, but the intensity of their resolve could be felt.

Occasionally, a glimpse of moonlight peeked through a classroom window, revealing the sclera of the commando's eyes, the protective outer layer known as the *white of the eye*. The eyes were said to be the windows to one's soul. Holloway saw glimpses of white, but mostly, he saw the darkness behind them, much like his own.

There was a difference between Holloway and the men whom he was growing to admire. It was commitment. Despite the oppressive nature of the DPRK's totalitarian regime in which they had lived, these men were fiercely loyal to North Korea and the Kim dynasty. They were prepared to lay down their lives as they followed General Lee's orders, as if the orders came directly from the mouth of Dear Leader himself.

In the coming days, a wave of commandos would spread across Texas, seeking to destroy infrastructure, commandeer military and civilian assets, as well as instill the fear of God in the minds of all who would stand in their way. When their mission was accomplished, under the command of General Lee, they would move on to the next strategic target in the war with America, leaving behind bedlam and death.

Holloway had a different design for his future. He was an opportunist, not unlike tens of thousands like him throughout North America who were seeking financial gain from the collapse. In normal times, there were always those who took advantage of a crisis to advance their political, social, or economic agenda. *Never let a good crisis go to waste.*

For Holloway, the crisis created an opportunity for advancement. The perfect catalyst to allow him to fulfill a dream of wealth, power, and pride of ownership in which he was respected. He would assist General Lee and his commandos in fulfilling their mission. In the meantime, Holloway would advance his cause centered around *me, myself, and I.*

Chapter 2

January 16
Klondike High School
Patricia, Texas

Holloway escorted Lee to the faculty lounge, which was located in the center of the high school. The windowless room was one of the few that was illuminated. Each of the men remained surrounded by their top lieutenants at all times, eagerly awaiting orders from their respective superiors. However, as the two men got settled onto the sofas in the lounge area, they unscrewed the caps on two aluminum bottles of Budweiser, which were covered in a graphic depicting the Statue of Liberty on the side.

"Give me your tired, your poor, your huddled masses," said Lee with a chuckle as he offered a toast to Holloway. Both men laughed at the irony.

"I'm impressed with your knowledge of American hypocrisy," Holloway added with a hint of snark. Once a red-blooded, patriotic American, he'd lost his way over time.

"Outside, please," instructed Lee with a wave of his arm. Soon the room had emptied and the door was closed, leaving the two commanders alone together.

Holloway stood and retrieved a couple more beers from the refrigerator. The supplies he'd procured from the convenience store warehouse in Lubbock had yielded *Bulls and Buds*, as Holloway had joked when he made reference to his favorite beverages—Red Bull and Budweiser.

The men unscrewed the tops of the second round and immediately relaxed, a posture they rarely took in front of the soldiers. Commanding respect of their troops required maintaining a certain decorum when around their men. This was a rare opportunity for the two unlikely allies to converse as equals, a level of status much coveted by Holloway.

"*Geonbae!*" Holloway said with a smile as he offered his beer to toast Lee's. The aluminum bottles clanked together.

"Very good, Holloway. Cheers to you as well!"

"General, your command of the English language is much better than the few words I know in Korean."

"I've spent the last decade instructing my men to blend in to American society. Between living in Canada and teaching the commandos conversational English, I've become fluent."

"Well, General, it serves you well."

Lee studied Holloway and took another drink. His voice deepened as he asked, "Will you?"

"Will I what?" Holloway was confused.

"Will you serve me as well?"

Holloway laughed, leaned back in his chair, and propped his feet on a small table in front of them. His brown leather boots were covered with dirt, which left a slight cloud in the air as they hit the table.

"I prefer to look at our relationship as one of mutual respect and collaboration," started Holloway. "General, my fight is not one of ideology or patriotism for a particular country. I've been a man without a cause for many years, other than my own self-interest, of course."

"My men fight with you," interrupted Lee. Holloway sensed a point being made by Lee, and he wanted to be muted in his response. Under other circumstances, this type of conversation would turn heated, and someone would be killed. Holloway, by virtue of the fact that he was still breathing, typically won the arguments.

"Yes, some of them were your men, but loyalties, like military missions, change. Over time, the former commandos who stand with me are loyal, but they are also free to make their own choices. I guess you could say they've become Americanized. Freedom has overcome their sense of loyalty to a nation they hardly remember."

Lee was also being cautious and chose his words carefully. "They were trained to become, and always remain, members of the Lightning Death Squads. They are now being called upon to do their duty. They must honor Dear Leader's orders."

"They are, General, but in a different way than you envision. The men under my command will undertake the same types of activities to accomplish your goals in Texas, but when the mission is over, they will be free to leave with you, or they will choose to remain with me. You see, they've had a taste of life as free men. It is now ingrained within them."

Both men finished off their beers, and they set the empties in the center of the table at Holloway's feet. Four stoic bottles of Budweiser stood proudly with the image of the Statue of Liberty on each. Lee fiddled with the bottles, lining them up so that they stood side by side, creating a mural-like display.

He stuck his chin out and nodded his head slightly. Holloway surmised that Lee had expected the conversation to go this way. The next words out of Lee's mouth would determine if the two commanders would be at crossed purposes going forward, or not.

"I have many men, with more on the way," Lee began to state his position. "These men have been trained to respect their superiors. Our nation and its people only respect the iron fist. I will allow you to continue operating independently from my men, but you must agree to lend the appearance of falling within my strategic command. Otherwise, I will appear weak. Signs of weakness will sow discord within the ranks and doom our mission."

Holloway was pleased to hear this, but he offered a caveat. "I agree, General. For so long as I, and my men, are treated with respect, we'll advance your cause. When the time comes for you to move on, we may or may not remain behind. Personally, I'd like to find a nice big ranch out here and live out my days in semiretirement."

Lee stood and extended his hand to Holloway to shake. In turn, Holloway stood, and the two men reached an accord. Lee would exhibit his ability to command, but Holloway would be autonomous, having his way with West Texas and the Panhandle.

This called for another round of Buds.

Chapter 3

January 16
CIA Headquarters
Langley, Virginia

Billy Yancey's mind began to wander as he received a briefing from two CIA analysts and the military liaison from the Pentagon. He'd been suffering from a lack of sleep for days, opting on a couple of occasions to sleep on a cot brought into his office suite at the George Bush Center for Intelligence.

The business of orchestrating regime change around the world was slow, and its importance was secondary to Washington's attempts to gain control of the U.S. populace in the aftermath of the EMP and nuclear attacks perpetrated by the *Axis of Evil*.

Yancey had been ordered by the director of the CIA to take on additional duties as it related to the domestic challenges. Specifically, he was tasked with following up on reports of an influx of North Koreans in the wake of the attacks. Yancey was an expert in the use of false flags, subversion techniques, and propaganda to bring about regime change. He'd personally orchestrated covert missions to topple governments, similar to sending Duncan and Park into North Korea to assassinate Kim Jong-un.

Because of his expertise, it was natural to call upon him to assess the potential of a ground attack on American soil that used insurgency tactics. Normally, his first assessment revolved around the attackers' goals.

What did they hope to accomplish?

If the DPRK forces had infiltrated the U.S., was their intention to inflict additional damage and hardship on the American people? Now that the country was knocked to its knees, were they attempting to deal a final death blow to the back of the head?

These questions swirled in his head as the analysts flipped from one slide to another on the large screen mounted on the wall at the end of his office. The evidence of a potential DPRK foray into America was mounting. Interestingly, the reports from his moles in the Texas military at Fort Hood, loyalists to America who were instructed to toe the line as Austin took control under Montgomery Gregg's direction, were that the North Koreans had played a role in the breach of the Texas border with New Mexico.

If that was true, it meant that the prize highly coveted by President Harman's chief of staff, Texas, was also the object of the DPRK subversive activity. At this stage, the information regarding the North Korean commandos' involvement in the breach was kept within the confines of his office. Yancey would have to decide how to play it.

Do I notify the White House? What about my fellow Texans who are standing directly in the line of fire?

As was true of everyone within the deep state, self-interests played a large part in the exchange of information.

Yancey turned his thoughts back to the analysts.

"We have reports of an attack in Roswell, New Mexico, and St. Louis, Missouri," continued one of the analysts. "A military patrol in Memphis, Tennessee, came upon a group of Korean men near the Mississippi River bridge crossing into Arkansas. Their activities were described as *reconnaissance.*"

Yancey became engaged in the meeting. "Does the president's martial law declaration deal with Korean nationals? Are there any provisions for taking them into custody, you know, for their own protection?"

"It's my understanding that a protection order is being considered," replied the military liaison. "The president is worried that comparisons will be drawn to the Japanese internment camps during World War II."

"Can we begin taking them into custody for curfew violations or some other trumped-up charge?" asked Yancey.

"Sir, the problem is that the prisons, for humanitarian reasons, are releasing their populations," offered one of the CIA personnel. "The prison system doesn't have the manpower nor the food and medical supplies to warehouse millions of incarcerated Americans. I doubt internment is an option."

The three analysts began to discuss the various scenarios among themselves when Yancey's phone buzzed in his pocket. He pulled it out and his eyes squinted as he read the display.

1S1K

One shot, one kill, the sniper's motto.

Yancey shuddered as he closed his eyes. He recalled the words of General George S. Patton—*Do your duty as you see it and damn the consequences.*

Those words allowed him little comfort.

Chapter 4

January 16
The Armstrong Ranch
Borden County, Texas

Sook had never been in love. Her entire life had been devoted to helping her family survive in a world she thought she'd never escape.

The Kim regime, officially known as the Democratic People's Republic of Korea, was anything but democratic. The Kim dynasty spent over half a century coalescing the North Korean people socially, ideologically, and with loyalty to their Dear Leaders. Everyone was required to adopt the same thoughts, whether it be their military-first approach to government or the Kim's *juche* philosophy.

Juche meant, literally, self-reliance, a concept that was embraced by precious few Americans. However, within the context of North Korean life, *juche* ideology emphasized the DPRK's political, economic and military self-reliance. While the philosophy encouraged their citizens to be self-reliant and the masters of their own destiny, in practice, it meant after the government took its cut.

In North Korea, the citizens worked at the pleasure of the state, and for so long as one obeyed the orders of the state and its hard-line military minions, you were allowed to live your life. Life, however, was always enjoyed under a shroud of fear and amongst those who'd quickly report your improprieties to the government in order to gain favor or an elevation in societal status.

For that reason, Sook had never sought to engage with men in a romantic way. She was distrustful for one, and as part of a Christian family in a nation that persecuted people for their religious beliefs that ran contrary to *juche*, she'd feared for her family's safety.

The day she and her father had saved Duncan from the frigid waters near their fishing village, Sook had immediately recognized his rugged, handsome features. Floating unconscious and struggling to breathe, as he was close to death from hypothermia, Duncan had struck Sook as a man who was a fighter. A man who'd do anything to survive. A man very much like herself.

Her father had always jokingly referred to his daughter as *being a man in a woman's body*. She worked hard. She shunned any boy's advances. Plus, she routinely practiced martial arts in order to protect herself from the predatory North Korean soldiers.

On that fateful day when they'd discovered Duncan, her mind had raced as she assessed the risks of taking this foreign stranger aboard their fishing skiff and then bringing him to their home. She could have dropped him at the feet of the local military officer and gained favor, as so many others would've done. That, however, would have resulted in a more gruesome death for Duncan.

Her father had agreed that God had put them in the position to save Duncan, and that was what they would do. Using her nursing skills and supplies she'd obtained while working with the United Nations humanitarian workers, she'd nursed Duncan back to health and, in the process, fell in love too.

Sook was unfamiliar with the glamorization of love stories written in novels or portrayed in movies. The love that developed between her and Duncan was real and could've easily been made into a romance movie had circumstances been different.

She'd saved him from certain death in that river. He'd helped her escape the tyrannical rule of Kim Jong-un and protected her from the military as they made their way to freedom. They'd both helped one another as they fought their way across the Southwest to reunite with Duncan's family.

Moreover, despite the fact she was a North Korean, a country who'd just initiated a war against her beloved's home, she had been welcomed with open arms by everyone at the Armstrong Ranch. No judgment. No hesitation. Pure, unconditional love.

All of these things ran through Sook's mind as she raced back to her first love for one more hug and kiss. She respected his decision to protect his homeland. She would never stand in the way of his core beliefs. Sook would miss him while he was away, and long for his return. But she would never openly show her fear of losing him to the horrors of war.

"One more kiss for good luck!" she shouted as she rushed back to his side.

Sook crashed into Duncan, and he wrapped his arms around her. It comforted her, and for a brief moment, the fear of losing him was gone.

They spun around in a circle, holding one another, kissing again, until suddenly, Duncan broke his embrace and fell to both knees in front of her.

Sook's eyes darted around, unsure what was happening. Espy had arrived with the Humvee, and he abruptly opened his door and stood on the side rails, his face awash with uncertainty.

She looked down into Duncan's eyes as he loosened his grip on her waist. He stared back and then welled up in tears. He reached into his jacket, grabbed at his chest, and then he smiled.

"Sook, I had big plans for this morning. I wanted to take you on a quiet, romantic ride around the ranch. I had a spot picked out where we could sit on a rock together and look out across West Texas as the sun rose into the sky."

Duncan revealed a ring box that had been tattered and smudged with age. He opened it and revealed the contents to Sook. It was his grandmother's diamond engagement ring.

She covered her mouth with both hands as tears streamed down her face. Her mind raced, but her mouth did not.

"Sook, I've learned there is only one true happiness in this life, and that is to love and be loved. Being loved by you has given me a strength and courage I've never known. I have an inner peace when I'm with you, and I ache when we're apart."

Duncan became more emotional, laughed, and wiped the tears from his face. Sook was touched by the outpouring of emotions, something she'd never seen from the men in her life. She removed her hands from her mouth and touched Duncan's cheeks. They were warm, and his tears were still flowing.

"Sook, I want us to spend the rest of our lives together. Will you do me the honor of marrying me?"

Sook started laughing nervously and once again covered her mouth. As a child, she'd dreamt of a moment like this. It was a vision that had faded from her consciousness as she grew older. Now, kneeling before her was the only love she'd ever known, and he was professing his undying love for her.

Yet she couldn't speak. The words wouldn't come out of her mouth. All she could do was cry and laugh and nod her head up and down so fast that the tears flew off her face and joined Duncan's as they flowed down his cheeks.

Duncan quickly stood, kissed Sook all over her face, and looked into her eyes. "Does that mean yes? Will you marry me?"

The nodding increased in speed, and she finally was able to shout to all who could hear—yes! "Yes, I love you, and I will marry you!"

Chapter 5

January 16
The Mansion
Austin, Texas

"Madam President, we need to get you into the bunker or, at the very least, the command center," insisted Adjutant General Kregg Deur.

"Kregg, I appreciate your concern, but it's just a border breach," said President Marion Burnett. "It's not like they're dropping bombs on our heads. I've got work to do, and I can't run into hiding every time there's some semblance of an uprising."

"I understand, but can you at least come to the command center for the day until we know what we're dealing with here?" asked Deur.

"Nope. That's settled. Please, tell me what the heck happened out there."

The president found her way to the head of the conference table and settled into the dark saddle brown, tufted leather chair. As Deur and his aides prepared to start the briefing, President Burnett impatiently swiveled back and forth in her chair.

She'd spent most of her days dealing with the food crisis spreading across Texas. Despite all of their efforts to obtain food resources from abroad, it still wasn't enough. Unrest was growing in the major cities, especially Houston and San Antonio. She'd ordered the military into those two cities to quell the riots and protect businesses from looting.

This had an adverse effect on those directly impacted by the military's presence. Several occurrences of violent clashes between her troops and the citizens had been reported to her. She'd admonished her military department not to get heavy-handed, but they'd quickly pointed out that citizens were using guns to attack the Texas National Guard personnel.

President Burnett had always stood against the use of military forces on American soil and vowed her principles wouldn't be compromised once Texas declared its independence. As she waited on Deur, she thought back to those early days when she'd breathed a sigh of relief that the Texas power grid had been spared from both the direct effects of the EMP and the cascading failure of the Western and Eastern Interconnection synchronous power grids. Texas had dodged a bullet and used the occasion to declare their independence from the United States.

She didn't second-guess her decision to make the bold move of secession. She did, however, underestimate the ancillary impact that the loss of power around North America would have on Texas. Food was only one aspect of her daily challenges. The hundreds of thousands of starving and dying refugees beyond their borders was another.

"Okay, Madam President, here is our up-to-the-minute status report," began Deur. "Early this morning, just before sunrise, an assault upon our checkpoint near Hobbs, New Mexico, was initiated by armed gunmen. The first of our soldiers to die were manning the gate. Emboldened by the attack, refugees apparently broke the chain-link gates and forced their way through."

"How many of our people were present?" she asked.

"We don't have an exact number yet, but typically there are three units of four plus officers and civilians used to process the paperwork of displaced Texans."

"Go ahead," instructed the president.

"The following is based on assumption and speculation," said Deur.

The president sat up in her chair and raised her hand, indicating Deur to stop. "What do you mean?"

"Madam President, we've based our reports on civilian refugees who were taken into custody following the breach. Ma'am, all of our troops were killed."

President Burnett stood up and slammed both hands on the conference table. "What? How could all of them be taken out? By armed refugees? This stinks to high heaven, Kregg. It sounds like Wichita Falls all over again."

"We can't rule out the possibility of covert involvement from Washington, Madam President. It's also being reported that military-style vehicles were used in the breach. Not armored, however. Namely, M35 personnel carriers, from the descriptions I've received in the reports."

The president fell back into her chair. She reached for her coffee, thought better of it, and pushed it toward her chief of staff. "What else?"

Deur continued with the bad news. "The roving patrols that were added in recent weeks reacted as quickly as possible to the breach. As they departed their posts, multiple instances of incursions by the refugees took place all along our West Texas border."

"Do you have an estimate of how many refugees entered Texas?" she asked, dejected.

"By our rough calculations, as many as twenty thousand crossed into the country," replied Deur. He stepped back a couple of feet, apparently expecting an outburst from the president.

President Burnett bottled up her anger and continued to ask questions. "Have you stopped the bleeding?"

"Come again?" asked Deur.

She raised her voice out of frustration. "Have you secured the dang border?"

"They are doing that now, Madam President. The fences are being repaired. Troops have been dispatched from Fort Bliss and—"

"Why not from Lubbock?" asked the president.

"Camp Lubbock is designed to be a reactionary force, and the unit there is expected to defend the population areas, you know, towns and cities. The military units focus on border security."

President Burnett leaned back in her chair once again and looked around the room. She suddenly realized her vice president, Montgomery Gregg, wasn't present. During the chaotic morning, she'd forgotten he'd taken a few days away to spend with his wife at his ranch outside San Angelo.

"I really need my top military advisor," said President Burnett, who unintentionally disparaged Deur, her longtime associate and adjutant general. "Has Monty been notified? Have you called him back to Austin?"

Chapter 6

January 16
The Gregg Ranch
West of San Angelo, Texas

"When did this happen?" asked Vice President Montgomery Gregg. He switched the satellite telephone into his left hand. He reached for his wife, who'd reluctantly turned around when he'd requested her to wait. He managed a slight smile but received a scowl in return. As he listened to his aide describe the situation at the West Texas border, he studied his wife's closed-off body language. It saddened him to see Candice this way. He hoped he could find a way to bring her around for the sake of their marriage.

He tucked the phone between his chin and shoulder, then reached out to pull her closer. At first, she hesitated, then finally succumbed to his wishes. Then his chest exploded in pain. In those milliseconds as his brain comprehended what had happened, Gregg knew he was about to die.

Gregg's body flew backwards, away from his wife, and he landed flat on his back. His brain couldn't comprehend the agony his body suffered from the trauma as the bullet tore into him and exploded through his back.

"Monty! Monty!" screamed his distraught wife as she crawled through the dirt to his side.

His brain's blood supply began to diminish as he struggled to remain coherent. When the human body nears death, it tends to die from the top down as the brain fails. During those precious seconds, the human mind loses its sense of self and begins to wander.

As the wave of blood-starved brain cells spreads out, memories, ability to speak, all feeling disappears. One wonders why so much emphasis is placed upon a dying person's last words. It's because the brain has determined those last utterances to be the most important of a person's life.

Sometimes the dying reassured a loved one by promising them life will be okay without them. Other times, they confirm their love. Some request a promise be kept. In that moment, Gregg muttered the words that plagued his mind the most at that moment.

Gregg's eyes closed, and he whispered, "Tell Armstrong. It was Yancey."

*****

His wife's eyes grew wide in horror. Despite being married to a military man, she'd been shielded from the throes of war. Her husband rarely discussed the dark side of the death caused by military conflict, and she would immediately change the channel on the television when gory scenes were delivered via the news without warning.

She was frantic, unable to comprehend what had just happened. She shook her husband and clawed at his clothing in an attempt to revive him, but he was unresponsive. His eyes, devoid of life, stared into the morning sky.

His final words. What were his final words?

The most painful goodbyes were the ones that were never said, never explained, or never heard. Monty had spoken to her, but she couldn't comprehend his words.

"What?" asked Mrs. Gregg. Then she began screaming frantically for help. "Somebody help us! Please help!"

Their ranch hands and two members of Gregg's security detail finally arrived to comfort her. Mrs. Gregg's nightgown was covered in her husband's blood, as her housecoat had fallen open, abandoning any sense of modesty. She clutched for her husband's shoulders, but the men pulled her away.

Several seconds later, Gregg's prone body, bleeding out on the ground, was surrounded by men in suits, speaking into radios and frantically searching the surrounding hillsides for the source of the single gunshot.

"I'm sorry, Mrs. Gregg," said one of the agents, who'd checked Gregg's pulse. "He's dead, ma'am. We need to get you inside."

Distraught, she wailed and lost her strength. With the assistance of a female member of the security team, she managed to make her way back into the house. The walls were closing in on her, and she suddenly felt trapped and alone.

Barely coherent, she was led into her bedroom, where she reached out into the empty space, trying to find her husband. Then she touched her clothing and looked at her bloody hands. She frantically patted her chest and stomach, wondering if she had been shot too.

Eventually, she returned to reality, and after some prodding, she finally agreed to remove her blood-soaked clothing and put on a loose-fitting flannel gown. She plopped into a chair in the corner of their dark, empty bedroom.

Since their arrival in Texas, her husband had frequently been gone, tending to the business of the new nation. When he was home, he slept in another room, as had become the case over their last several years in Washington. Mrs. Gregg stared at their bed as a wave of sadness came over her once again. They'd drifted apart in recent years, but now she missed him more than ever.

"My medicine, please," she said as mental shock began to overtake her. She pointed toward the bathroom, and the security agent retrieved a small tray of medications. "Ketalar, please."

Ketalar had been given to her at Raven Rock when she was experiencing bouts of depression and panic attacks. It was a fast-acting antidepressant also used in conjunction with anesthesia. Oftentimes compared to a tranquilizing hallucinogenic like LSD, Ketalar was abused by some as a recreational drug.

She'd hidden the medication from Monty because he considered the need for an antidepressant drug to be a sign of weakness. Yet he completely understood when his troops suffered from post-traumatic stress disorder and combat fatigue.

The use of the medication had been symbolic of the turn their marriage had taken, in which Montgomery Gregg treated his soldiers one way and his wife another. But despite his shortcomings, his lack of attentiveness, and oftentimes gruff attitude, she'd loved him.

And now Montgomery Gregg—decorated war veteran, four-star general, and the first person in history to hold cabinet-level positions in both the United States and a foreign country—was dead.

Chapter 7

January 16
The Armstrong Ranch
Borden County, Texas

"Are you kiddin' me?" shouted Palmer from the front porch of the ranch house. She bounded down the stairs and sprinted toward the happy couple. Sook turned toward her new sister and immediately beamed. Her smile said it all. "Did you really? You popped the question!"

Sook ran to Palmer with her left hand in the air to show off her engagement ring. The two women hugged one another just as Miss Lucy emerged from the house, wiping her hands on her apron before pulling it over her head to hang it over the railing. She paused to shout to the guys inside.

"Major! Boys! I think your brother has some news!"

Within seconds the entire Armstrong family stood in front of the house, congratulating Sook and Duncan. Tears of joy covered their faces as a rare moment of celebration washed over them. After a few more minutes of hugs and handshakes, Duncan explained about the phone call Espy had received.

"Y'all, I'm sorry, but I've got to go. Duty calls."

Major moved closer to Duncan and put his hand on his shoulder. "What's happened, son?"

"Espy got a call a few moments ago from Camp Lubbock. The border checkpoint near Hobbs has been attacked. We've also been told the fences to the north and south have been breached."

"Attacked by who?" asked Riley, who was not surprisingly still teared up from the emotional moment.

"I don't know yet," replied Duncan, although he had his suspicions. He patted his father on the hand and walked toward Sook. "I'm so sorry that I have to leave like this."

Another tear rolled down her cheek, but she nodded. "I know. I will see you later."

"I promise, Sook. Do you have a saying in Korean that means good luck?"

Sook wiped off her tears and smiled as she stood a little taller. Proudly, she responded, "I am a Texan now. I say saddle up, cowboy!"

The group burst out in laughter, and everyone gave Sook a family bear hug that caught her off guard somewhat. Duncan saw the startled look on her face and raced in to the rescue.

"Hey, guys, don't you squish my betrothed!"

After everyone gave him a last set of good-luck wishes, Riley retrieved Duncan's rifle, and he joined Espy at the Humvee.

"I'll drive," said Duncan. "You've got some calls to make."

Duncan gave his family a final wave and tore down the packed-dirt driveway with the military-grade Goodyear Wrangler tires kicking up dirt and rocks in the process.

After they hit the road and sped northward toward Lubbock, Duncan instructed Espy to make the call to the Texas Quick Reaction Force regional headquarters at Camp Lubbock to gain more information.

Corporal Esparza, the aide assigned to Duncan when he'd become commander of the TX-QRF for this part of West Texas and the Panhandle, had an innate ability to switch from casual acquaintance to mentally tough soldier. As Duncan's aide-de-camp, he'd be a constant companion and protector. As a result, he had been introduced to the Armstrong family and was easily accepted within the group.

Espy's training with the Screaming Eagles of the 101st Airborne Division out of Fort Campbell, Kentucky, was invaluable to Duncan. The 101st was known for its air assault operations coupled with special ops that gave it a reputation as the most potent and tactically mobile unit of the U.S. Army.

The TX-QRF was designed to fulfill its name—react. Capable of mobilizing on short notice, the teams under Duncan's command would be called upon to address any situation that threatened Texans or the country's critical infrastructure. Espy's experience would be called upon as Duncan faced these challenges.

"Commander," started Espy as he transitioned from new friend to corporal, "our unit is mobilized and awaiting orders."

"What kind of support are we getting from Bliss and Hood?" asked Duncan.

"Fort Bliss is responding with reinforcements at the border fences," he replied. "They'll plug the holes and regain control of the refugees streaming into Texas. Logistics teams are on the way to effectuate repairs to the perimeter fencing while new National Guard units will replace those who were killed at the Hobbs checkpoint."

"How many?"

"All of them, sir," replied Espy. "I believe the detachment numbered twenty-two active-duty guardsmen and four civilian border patrol workers.

"This was supposedly done by refugees?" Duncan began to doubt the narrative.

"Yes, sir, although we will have the opportunity to interrogate some of the refugees. Fort Hood has been tasked with mopping up the ten thousand plus refugees who broke through the fence and scattered across the oil fields like cockroaches when the lights are turned on."

Duncan thought for a moment and recalled his mission, which was to protect Texans and respond to crisis situations. "Okay, the first order of business is to cordon off Lubbock to prevent these refugees from entering the city. I think we have to consider them to be armed and dangerous."

"All of them, sir?"

"Listen, I don't have any directive from Austin or Fort Hood concerning our rules of engagement. You and I are both military men used to some competent authority delineating the when-where-how of a battle. The world has changed, at least for now, and I have to determine what constitutes civilized warfare."

"Sir, what about unarmed refugees?"

"Naturally, we'll be facing unarmed mobs whose level of hostility is unknown. If we take on hostile fire, then our personnel should shoot to kill. If our defensive positions are stormed by an out-of-control hostile crowd, then I have no problem using force to turn them back. Espy, we're not operating in a law enforcement capacity or as the riot-control police. We're soldiers defending our homeland. That necessarily requires the use of lethal force."

They were riding in silence for the final stretch of highway into Lubbock when the phone rang. Espy took the call and listened intently to the information being relayed to him.

"It's Fort Hood on the line," he whispered as he cupped his hand over the satellite phone. "They're interrogating refugees."

Espy turned his attention back to the phone as Duncan pulled up to the front gate at Camp Lubbock. A line of vehicles was awaiting entry, and Duncan honked his horn out of frustration to get the attention of the guards.

"Okay, I'll pass that along to Commander Armstrong," said Espy as he signed off the call.

As the guard approached, Duncan looked over to his aide. "What?"

"Sir, there were reports of North Korean gunmen leading the assault. They were driving U.S. military transports and all-terrain vehicles."

The guard tapped on his window, but Duncan ignored him.

"North Koreans? Confirmed?"

"Yessir."

Duncan set his jaw and gritted his teeth. He rolled his window down, flashed his military ID, and barked at the soldier, "I'm Commander Armstrong. Get these vehicles out of my way, now!"

Chapter 8

January 16
The Mansion
Austin, Texas

Montgomery Gregg would not necessarily have been President Burnett's first choice as vice president of Texas, but circumstances had dictated a marriage of convenience. For years, when she was a rising star in Texas political circles, she'd quietly floated the idea of secession to like-minded thinkers both within and without political circles in Austin. As the concept gained traction after the U.S. presidential election of 2008 and the near economic collapse in the latter part of that year, she began to incorporate the rally cry *Texas strong, Texas free* into her political campaign rhetoric.

As the mainstream media began to recognize her status as an up-and-comer within the Republican Party in Texas, they showed their fangs and set about to tear her down. The politics of personal destruction was a favorite tool of all political persuasions, and generally speaking, the public accepted the rhetoric as part of the game.

But the media's use of destroying politician's careers was problematic in many respects. For one, the mainstream media was decidedly liberal with very few exceptions. Accordingly, the target of their ire was typically conservative politicians and causes. President Burnett had gotten the full brunt of this when she ran for governor the first time.

As attendees began to chant *Texas strong, Texas free* at her rallies, the media began to imply racism and xenophobia from her words.

She had to combat the onslaught of fake news with counterattacks against the media and Washington in general. Her tactic struck a nerve with Texans, and her popularity exploded.

There was one group with whom she hadn't garnered favor—the United States military. Patriotic by nature, and bound to the United States Constitution by oath, the hundreds of thousands of military personnel stationed in Texas were a forgotten aspect of President Burnett's grand plan of seceding from the U.S. at some point.

The formation of a new country involved a lot of moving parts, most of which went beyond the political machinations required to accomplish the purpose. The logistics of establishing a new form of governance, law enforcement, and providing for the country's citizenry in a time of crisis was complex.

Just as the realities of dealing with the impressive military forces stationed on Texas soil had hit President Burnett, Montgomery Gregg arrived on the scene to save the day. Most of the commanders at Fort Bliss and Fort Bragg were elevated in rank thanks to Gregg. They were good soldiers and loyal to him.

When it came time to secure their allegiance to the new Texas Constitution, President Burnett took comfort in knowing Gregg could make that happen.

Every president has their levels of expertise. In U.S. politics, it used to be an unspoken requirement that the president have some type of military background to effectively act as Commander-in-Chief of the armed forces. Over time, especially following the Vietnam War, a military background could be seen as an impediment to the job.

When President Burnett's chief of staff had entered her office several minutes ago to inform her of Gregg's death, she became physically ill. She needed Monty Gregg, as he was the glue that held together the fragile relationship between her young administration and the Texas military, which had been secured through negotiations with Washington. If she lost the support of the military, she'd likely lose Texas.

A firm rapping at the door brought the president out of her

melancholy state of mind. It was time for her to cowboy up, as they say.

"Come in."

Adjutant General Deur entered her office. "Madam President, with all due respect, we need to have a very frank discussion about the circumstances we're facing."

"Sit down, Kregg," she said and motioned toward a chair. While she appreciated Deur's dedication to looking after her self-interests, the drama wasn't helping her process the events of that morning.

"Madam President, I'll be succinct in my concerns," said Deur. "First, we've had a major breach at our West Texas border, orchestrated by gunmen armed with fully automatic weapons, resulting in nearly twenty thousand people infiltrating our country. Second, not only were some of the refugees armed, but it appears from our intelligence gathering they were assisted by North Koreans. These are possibly trained soldiers based upon their successes against our military personnel. We suffered all of the casualties. There were none on their side except unarmed, innocent civilian bystanders.

"Third, said North Koreans entered driving relatively new U.S. military vehicles. I'm not talking about the government-surplus trucks people used to buy online at IronPlanet.com. These vehicles, as described by the detainees, appear to be used by our—I mean current U.S. military forces.

"Fourth, it's apparent the Hobbs checkpoint was attacked from our side of the fence too. Under interrogation, captured Americans recalled the shooting taking place from the Texas side of the border, followed by a military convoy entering and attacking from New Mexico. This is a clear indication of a coordinated assault, which requires advanced communications, command and control, and most importantly, a plan.

"Finally, within an hour of the breach, our vice president, a military general, was killed by a single sniper bullet, which, according to our people, must've traveled at least a mile before hitting him in the center of the chest. This was not some whack-a-do with a hunting rifle, ma'am. This shot could only be achieved by a highly trained marksman."

Deur, who'd been nervously speaking very fast, took a deep breath before stating his assessment. "Madam President, this simply cannot be coincidental, and I believe you are in grave danger."

President Burnett contemplated her adjutant general's words. All of these facts were known to her, but this was the first time she'd put them together as part of a cohesive set of events. Foremost on her mind was securing the border.

"Kregg, I need your honest opinion now," she began. "What is your take on the reaction of the commanders you've come into contact with at Fort Bliss and Fort Hood?"

"Positive and without reservation, ma'am," he replied. "To a man, they expressed sadness over the loss of Vice President Gregg, but they are soldiers and seem committed to doing their duty to protect Texas."

"I want to meet with the top brass of each military base as soon as possible. Let's allow sufficient time for the border fencing to be mended and control reestablished."

"Madam President, are you suggesting a meeting with all of them at once, here in Austin?"

"Yes, why wouldn't we?"

"Ma'am, we've not established a continuity-of-government plan for Texas. The prospect of our nation coming under attack hasn't been at the forefront of our transition meetings. If we are at war, or under attack, a plan needs to be established in case … you know …" Deur's voice trailed off before he said the words—*in case you're killed.*

President Burnett got the point and realized here was yet another detail of forming a new country that needed to be addressed. She nodded her acknowledgment and began to give him direction. "Point taken, Kregg. Let me think about this, and I also have to name a new vice president. As soon as we're done here, I'll bring in the attorney general to discuss my options."

"Yes, ma'am."

The president continued as Deur began to take notes. "We need to assign additional military resources to our main checkpoints, and until further notice, we will not process any new applicants attempting to return to Texas. I'm sorry for displaced Texans who are still beyond our borders, but in light of the circumstances, we need to hunker down.

"The North Korean aspect of the breach troubles me. I was warned of this possibility but, quite frankly, didn't see it coming to fruition. Now that it has, I'm beginning to question who orchestrated this attack. We have people within Texas working against us. They assisted in the assault on the Hobbs checkpoint, and obviously someone within the state assassinated Monty.

"I agree with you regarding coincidences. We need to find out who is behind this and flush them out of the darkness."

Deur interrupted with a series of questions. "Who can we trust? What if there is someone within our military apparatus still loyal to Washington?"

"Valid questions, Kregg. But they're questions I don't have answers to. This is why I need to shut down our borders and then meet with all the military. I may not be a soldier, but I can sure as heck look someone in the eyes and tell if they're lying."

Deur nodded his agreement and finished his notes after the president issued a few more minor orders. "Anything else, ma'am?"

President Burnett shrugged. "I don't think so at this time. I need to contemplate the who and why. Then, I need someone, an outsider, whom I can trust wholeheartedly to get to the bottom of Monty's death and help us make sense of it all."

Deur stood to leave, and the president reached onto her desk for her Texas Rangers coffee mug. After taking a sip of coffee, she slowly rotated the mug in both hands, staring at the five-pointed blue star with the red *T* superimposed over it.

CHAPTER 9

January 16
Camp Lubbock
Lubbock, Texas

Duncan studied the map on the wall as his squad leaders awaited his instructions. He'd just received a report from command and control at Fort Bliss that a large mob was moving due east along Highway 62 toward Seminole. Another had infiltrated Levelland to the west of Lubbock, broken into homes and businesses, and assaulted residents before the locals began to open fire upon them. Several hundred people had been killed during the fighting.

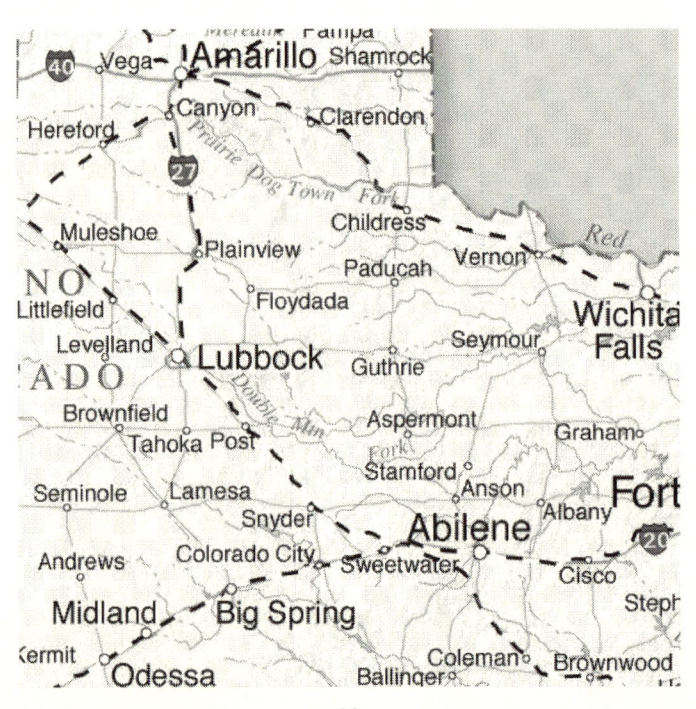

"Okay, we've got our hands full," began Duncan. "The military will focus their efforts on rounding up the refugees, which means air assets like helicopters will be unavailable to us. We are gonna be short on manpower until this crisis dies down. My orders are to maintain our units in Abilene for now and operate with a skeleton team here at Camp Lubbock. Our priorities are to close off access along the major roads into the city and respond to hot spots in the outlying areas as needed."

"Sir," began Espy, "we have our units deployed to West Lubbock already to assist local law enforcement. May we use our existing MPs to remain at Camp Lubbock?"

Duncan turned to his men and propped his right leg up on a chair as he twirled a Sharpie through his fingers. "How many are on duty?"

Espy quickly responded, "Twenty-eight, sir, on a rotational basis. We can incorporate double shifts if we think there's a credible threat to Camp Lubbock."

Duncan sighed. This was part of the reason he wanted to retrieve his TX-QRF teams from Abilene for the next several days. Quelling uprisings in these small towns of West Texas would leave Camp Lubbock and other parts of the city without adequate protection. He was already feeling stretched too thin.

"Corporal, instruct the base command to a sixteen-hour daily shift, split up by four-hour rest periods. It will be difficult for them in the near term, but no more difficult than those of us in the field. We've got to pull together until order is restored."

One of his lieutenants raised his hand. "Sir, I understand the rules of engagement you've established. Like you, I've served in the Middle Eastern theater, where it was near impossible to tell a bogie from a good guy. When we come in contact with what appears to be a local or unarmed civilian, are we to engage, sir?"

"Whadya mean by engage?" asked Duncan.

"You know, ask for identification," the lieutenant replied.

"I understand," Duncan said as he furrowed his brow. "Show me your papers, right? Here's my opinion. Everyone in Lubbock, and most likely in the surrounding communities, knows what's happened.

For a period of time, in order to protect them from outsiders and armed refugees, we're going to need identification to confirm who they are. If they resist, try your best to explain. If they become belligerent, then relieve them of their weapons and possibly take them into custody with the assistance of law enforcement."

"Yessir."

"Listen, I'm not a policeman. I'm a soldier. I identify the enemy and I kill them. Like you, that's how I was trained, and that's what I do best. That said, I've never imagined that in my lifetime the enemy possibly would be Americans like we were once. The bottom line is this. Those who cooperate will be treated with respect. As for the others, well, as General Mad Dog Mattis said, *Be polite, be professional, but have a plan to kill everyone you meet.*"

"Oorah," shouted the former members of the U.S. Marine Corps who were now under Duncan's command.

As Duncan gave his men their marching orders, suddenly Espy burst through the door, holding the phone in his outstretched arm.

"Commander, it's for you. Vice President Gregg has been killed."

Chapter 10

January 16
The Armstrong Ranch
Borden County, Texas

Major slowly walked from the ranch house to the barn, where Lucy stood holding their horses. He'd received a phone call, and as he talked, he unexpectedly removed his hunting rifle and walked into the house, leaving a puzzled Lucy standing alone. When he returned, he was carrying his new Daniel Defense DD5V1 rifle.

"Is there a reason to break out the heavy artillery?" said Lucy, referring to the AR-10 long gun.

"That was Duncan on the phone. Monty Gregg was assassinated earlier today."

Lucy's mouth fell open before she covered it. "How? Where?"

Major folded down the foregrip, which he'd attached to the accessory rail on the barrel, and removed the magazine containing the 7.62 millimeter rounds and slipped it into his jacket pocket. The magazine protruding from the rifle prevented it from fitting into his saddle's scabbard.

Always the gentleman, Major assisted his wife onto her horse just as Pops had taught him to open a door for a lady. The simple act of kindness and respect eventually gave way to the new feminism, which considered the gesture an insult. That wasn't the case in West Texas.

"Apparently, he was at his place northwest of San Angelo when a sniper shot him center mass in the chest," started Major as the frown on his face deepened. Because of the suspicions he and Duncan shared about the Kim Jong-un assassination attempt, Major privately considered Gregg's death by a sniper bullet to be a form of karma.

Nonetheless, he deserved the respect afforded a former military man and vice president of their new nation. "He was shot right in front of his wife."

"Oh my, that poor woman!" exclaimed Lucy as she looked at Major. He sensed that she imagined what Mrs. Gregg was going through, and fear entered her mind, wondering if that could happen to her husband.

"Very sad, and mysterious," continued Major. "Duncan didn't have a lot of details other than the shot traveled in excess of a mile and that it had to be someone like himself to pull it off."

"How did he react to the shooting?" asked Lucy. "I mean, there was no love lost between them."

"Cold as ice. Unemotional is the best way I can describe it. Our son understands the game. He used to be part of it. The only thing he said was it crossed one of the names off his list. There is still one more."

"That Yancey fella?" asked Lucy.

"Yep."

They rode toward the barnyard to check on a calf Preacher had helped birth last night. Lucy wanted to gather eggs for pickling.

"What will Marion do about a new vice president? This has to leave a big hole in her administration."

Major nodded as he slowed his horse's gait. The ramifications of Gregg's death were far-reaching. "From the standpoint of the government, Marion will need to appoint a successor, who, I imagine, has to be confirmed by the Senate and the House just like under the U.S. Constitution. From my brief conversations with her on the transition process, it appeared that her attorney general focused on taking the provisions of the Constitution that were adopted by the Founding Fathers and made them a part of the Texas laws."

"Who will she choose?"

Major shrugged. "I have no idea. Gregg was tight with the military and had been a creature of Washington for many years. He knew his way around politicians and commanded the respect of the new Texas armed forces. His shoes will be hard to fill."

"Dear, why would anyone want him dead? Other than our son, of course."

Major subconsciously looked around and then turned his face toward the sky. Not too long ago, America's advanced intelligence apparatus might've picked up Lucy's words through some kind of satellite surveillance. He chuckled because the thought sounded far-fetched, but you never knew for sure.

Major eventually responded, "Duncan has a theory, and if it's true, we might be in for trouble."

"*We* as in Texas, or *we* as in the ranch?" asked Lucy inquisitively.

"*We* as in Texas. Duncan is on his way to deal with a situation in Seminole, but he said the reports he's receiving from Fort Hood state North Koreans were involved in the attack on the checkpoints early this morning. Further, Gregg was shot within an hour of the initiation of those attacks. Plus, it appears the North Koreans were driving U.S. Army vehicles."

"Major, would President Harman be so bold as to invade Texas when she's got a mountain of problems to deal with? Shouldn't she focus on her own problems instead of stirring up new ones?"

They had arrived at the barnyard, and several ranch hands were milling about, so Major pulled his horse to a stop to finish the conversation. "I don't know anything about President Harman other than my opinion that she was soft on national defense and seemed to focus entirely on spending us into oblivion, not that it matters anymore. I can assume, however, Gregg's defection from her cabinet to the vice presidency in Texas put quite the burr in her saddle. It was pretty disrespectful on Gregg's part, but he obviously saw an opportunity when it presented itself."

Lucy adjusted herself in the saddle and stretched her back, which had been bothering her. "Would she order Gregg killed?"

"I don't think so, but you know how things operate in Washington. Presidents don't run things. Shadow governments do."

"Duncan was right about the Koreans, wasn't he?"

Major nodded. "I believed him from the beginning. He's not one to embellish a story. He doesn't have to. His experiences are more real than a novel or a movie. The question really becomes—who do the North Koreans work for? Washington or Pyongyang?"

Chapter 11

January 16
Patricia, Texas

In a politically and economically volatile world, energy security became an increasingly important aspect of a nation's governance. As modern times were ushered in with the development of fuel-driven machinery, developed nations became dependent on the production of electricity to compete economically and to satisfy its citizenry on the domestic front. The stable and secure flow of electricity became an imperative for all national governments as the twentieth century was ushered in, both for basic household needs and for industrial progress.

Given this critical role electricity played in the economic success of the United States, it was natural that rogue nations and bad actors, who were either jealous of America's place in the world or hostile to the freedoms and ideals upon which she stood, would look for a way to knock the greatest nation on earth to its knees.

Advanced technology provided these bad actors a myriad of options to destroy America's power grid. Initially, it was the discovery of the electromagnetic pulse, a byproduct of nuclear warfare uncovered during the nuclear testing of the fifties and early sixties.

Next, the wired world dominated by internet activity presented a portal into every power-generating system for armies of computer hackers, some working for a nation-state, or so-called patriotic hackers who were not state-sponsored, but who acted on their behalf as part of a perceived patriotic duty.

Cyber attacks became an integral part of asymmetric warfare after the start of the twenty-first century as a means to disrupt a nation's power supply in advance of a conventional military attack. Russia was notorious for successfully using this tactic.

North Korea's EMP attack upon the United States was a variant of the Russian use of cyber warfare. After collapsing the Eastern and Western Interconnection power grids, the DPRK's imbedded commandos, together with additional forces making their way to North America, would take out additional critical infrastructure such as communications, transportation, and as many of the other fourteen essential services relied upon by Americans as possible.

The failure to destroy the Texas power grid was not anticipated by the North Korean war planners. After the EMP bursts were partly successful, the nuclear bombs flying in both directions should have finished the job. Yet Texas stood strong against the worst military conflict in the history of mankind.

However, General Lee and his Lightning Death Squads would not be deterred. They were trained in the art of sabotage and insurgency. In Lee's mind, what couldn't be destroyed by bombs or keystrokes on a computer could still be rendered inoperative by bullets and knives.

The planned attacks on the Texas power grid were to be old-school operations involving speed, cunning, and precision. They required fearless men who were prepared to die for Dear Leader in order to accomplish their mission. The key to success was preplanning, the coordination of movement to ensure surprise, and the tenacity of his men.

Holloway had rolled out a large map of Texas on top of the geography teacher's desk. He retrieved his notes from the ERCOT substation in Wink and referred to them as he pointed to the circles made by a black Sharpie on the map.

As a state, Texas was the crown jewel of America's energy production. It had been the leading oil-producing state, producing more than a third of the country's crude oil. The twenty-nine petroleum refineries within its borders accounted for more than thirty percent of the total U.S. refining capacity. Texas led the nation in wind-powered generation capacity and was also the largest producer of lignite coal, which powered roughly fifty percent of the coal-fired plants producing electricity.

This energy self-sufficiency was one of the key reasons political leaders like Marion Burnett believed Texas could secede from the United States and quickly become a viable nation on its own. But energy production was only half of the equation. The electricity generated by these varied sources must be distributed to government facilities, businesses, and households through the power grid—a complex system of electricity substations, transformers, and power lines.

Most grids were interconnected for reliability and cost efficiency. Consumers demanded a steady flow of electricity at the lowest possible cost. In order to satisfy consumer demands, larger and larger interconnected networks were created so that outages in one area could be supplemented by others.

However, this desire to please the demanding consumers of America created a vulnerability. When a severe blackout occurred in a large area, additional burdens were placed on the working components of the power-generating systems asked to pick up the slack. If the failure overwhelmed the system, then a cascade of failures across a larger part of the grid occurred.

When the EMP had struck the coastal regions of the U.S., the cascading failure had occurred throughout the interconnected grid. Within the ERCOT system of Texas, a similar system was established and, thus, was vulnerable to a cascading failure on a smaller scale.

Visually, one could see the high-power transmission lines connecting homes and businesses to a power-generating station somewhere. But the hub of the activity, the source of control of that power, was a substation. At the substations, the high-voltage electricity that ran through those power lines and ultimately to the end user had to be reduced in its level of power—from high voltage to low.

For purposes of terrorist attacks, or Lee's mission in Texas, the substations were the target. Generally, these substations scattered throughout the ERCOT power grid remained unattended, relying upon SCADA for remote supervision and control. SCADA was an acronym for *supervisory control and data acquisition*, a marvel of computer technology that created the ultimate method of delivering electricity efficiently at the lowest cost. The SCADA systems, however, were also highly vulnerable to cyber attacks.

Lee was out of EMPs, and the North Korean cyber army known as Bureau 121 had most likely been destroyed by the nuclear warheads delivered by an assumed American counterattack. The unprotected power substations, when destroyed, would throw the Texans into darkness with the rest of North America.

"Here's what the guy at the substation told me," began Holloway. "According to a Department of Energy report, there are two substations in Texas that are most likely to cause a statewide blackout if taken down."

Lee looked at the map and counted the circles. "Which two? There are eighteen marked on this map."

"He didn't know, and he said it was a closely guarded secret within ERCOT," replied Holloway. "He identified the eighteen largest distribution substations around the state that are nearest their power-generating plants."

"Did he tell you how to destroy them? How do we make them stop functioning?"

"We strike them simultaneously, destabilizing the grid and causing a blackout across Texas."

"I understand that, but what do we do specifically to make that happen?" asked Lee.

"There's a substation to our south near Midland," replied Holloway. "Let's take your key people there now and do some surveillance. The best way to plan your attack is to study what you're attacking."

Chapter 12

January 16
Seminole, Texas

"Come on, Corporal, pick up the pace!" shouted Duncan out of frustration as he rode in the passenger seat of his Humvee. An hour ago, Camp Lubbock had been notified that armed men had stormed several homes in Seminole, Texas, looting them for their food and, in some cases, killing the occupants. Local law enforcement had been decimated by defections, and the skeleton crew in place was quickly overwhelmed, prompting the call to the TX-QRF.

"Sir, I can go faster, but we'll leave the troop transports and the support vehicles behind," replied Espy.

Duncan ignored Espy's response and studied a map of Seminole obtained from his father's old offices at Company C headquarters in Lubbock. The town was due east of the Hobbs checkpoint, which had been breached, and was the first logical source of armed conflict.

With a relatively small population of just under seven thousand, there were no strategic military or government assets to defend in Seminole. Duncan had no idea how people in the small town were faring as a result of the collapse, but they deserved to be protected.

The reports of the gunmen also reaffirmed for Duncan that the refugees were, in fact, armed and dangerous, as he'd surmised. The distress calls coming from the Gaines County Sheriff's Department made no mention of North Korean infiltrators, but Duncan would be on the lookout for them nonetheless.

The most direct route to Seminole covered over eighty miles, rendering the hour-and-a-half drive for the convoy far from *quick reaction*, as his unit's moniker implied. After today's mission was completed, Duncan would make a point to enlist helicopter support or, better yet, have several choppers assigned to Camp Lubbock for his benefit.

As they approached the intersection of US Highway 62 and CR 104, where they were to rendezvous with local law enforcement, Duncan studied the layout of the town one last time. Seminole was bisected by Main Street, which ran north to south, and the continuation of Highway 62, which ran from the Hobbs border checkpoint to the center of town. The residential areas were laid out in a series of perfect, cross-hatch streets. If they could determine how far the refugees had penetrated into the town, his unit could go house to house if necessary.

But first, they'd need to put out any fires, so to speak. Hopefully, the local cops would provide up-to-the-minute information on hot spots to address.

"Look, there's a county patrol car," announced Espy.

Up ahead, a white Chevy Tahoe stood waiting with its emergency lights flashing on its roof and grill. A single deputy stood next to the open driver's side door. He was speaking into a microphone that was stretched through the opening.

Espy parked the truck, and Duncan was the first to emerge to greet the deputy.

"You folks have arrived just in time. I'm Deputy Jerry Diaz with the Gaines County Sheriff's Office. Most folks call me Deputy Jerry."

"Commander Duncan Armstrong, sir," said Duncan as he stretched out his hand to shake the young man's. "Deputy Jerry, tell us what you know so far."

"I can only refer to these people as a herd," he began. "We didn't have any warning from the military about them comin' our way. The checkpoint at Highway 62 and the border is just about twenty miles to the west. I don't know for certain when they broke through, but they arrived at the Walmart on 62 around noon or a little after. The store had closed some time back and boarded up their windows and doors. I mean, the shelves were pretty much bare, but these people didn't know that. They broke down the barricades and ransacked the place."

"How do we get there from here?" asked Duncan.

"It won't matter 'cause they've moved on," replied the deputy. "Most started going door-to-door in the residential neighborhoods around Forest Park. The residents, at least the ones that are still in town, locked their doors and refused to answer. Eventually, the lack of a response wasn't enough for these people."

"What happened?"

"Well, the ones with guns forced their way inside, shot our folks, and then took what they wanted. Those without guns used anything they could find, from knives to hammers, as a weapon to attack our residents. In some cases, our armed neighbors fought them back and even killed a few. Either way, it has turned our neighborhoods into a war zone."

Duncan rubbed his temples as he considered his options. This would be extremely dangerous for his men. Door-to-door searches in closely packed residential areas could result in taking on fire from scared, nervous homeowners. It would be the same type of nerve-racking operation he'd led in the Middle East on multiple occasions.

He exhaled and then began his assessment. "How many men do you have available to assist?"

"Eight, including myself," replied Deputy Jerry. "Right now, all of them are protecting the Seminole Hospital and the area surrounding the Wyndham Hotel. I mean, I have to tell ya, most of these people look like they're on their last leg, you know what I mean? They're not armed. They're barely alive. They just need medical attention and a place to stay. And food, of course."

Just as Duncan was about to ask his next question, Deputy Jerry's radio squawked to life.

"We've got a ten thirty-one, shots fired, Oswalt Pharmacy, seven-oh-one Hobbs Highway. Multiple gunmen. Possible hostage situation."

"Deputy Jerry, advise your dispatch that we'll handle this one," ordered Duncan, who quickly turned his attention to Espy and his lieutenants. "Do this quickly, Corporal. Gather the men and divide them into two groups. Those who've had combat experience in Afghanistan or Iraq will come with us. Those guardsmen who've remained stateside, send them to relieve the law enforcement personnel at the town's hospital and the nearby hotel."

Espy left and began his task, so Duncan immediately turned to Deputy Jerry to give him instructions. "We're gonna deal with the active-shooter situation first. In the meantime, I'm sending our armored vehicles and a strong military presence to relieve your fellow LEOs guarding the hospital and hotel. I'll need them to rally with us at, um—how far do you believe the refugees have pushed into town?"

"The pharmacy is the farthest I've heard reports on," replied the deputy. "If you're looking for a place to circle up, we could use the Texas Department of Public Safety at the corner of *Main and Main*, as we like to say it. It's a couple of miles straight down 62 at the center of town and only a few blocks from the pharmacy."

"Perfect!" exclaimed Duncan. "Call your dispatch and tell them the plan. We'll get organized and split up into two groups. My group will follow you to Main and Main to deal with the active shooter, and afterwards, we'll clear the neighborhood."

As Espy made the personnel assignments, Duncan recalled the Dora residential district of Baghdad. Amid the smashed-up and bullet-riddled storefronts, Iraqis had attempted to make a life for themselves under the constant threat of gunfire and improvised explosive devices.

In the center of this chaotic neighborhood was a U.S. combat outpost with the designation of Gator. Located in a gutted medical clinic with the word *swamp* scrawled across the window of the outpost's command center, the *swamp* became an appropriate metaphor for the lawlessness and the constant pandemonium that pervaded their surroundings in Dora.

The mayhem was caused by insurgent, hard-line Sunni militants who occupied some of the residences. Labeled a *no-go neighborhood* by Duncan's commanders, the streets remained dangerous for the residents, the merchants, and the American military personnel.

After a Sunni suicide bomber drove an explosives-packed car into a nearby Iraqi police station, a plan was developed to clear the residential community of the dangerous militants. Many of the Sunnis were armed with AK-47s, and trained snipers waited for an opportunity to shoot to kill a U.S. service member.

Duncan's unit was ordered to clear the neighborhood of the militants. It was a tense, perilous task to go door-to-door and confront local residents. Each unit consisted of the soldiers, who were constantly scanning their surroundings, a local leader who was familiar with his neighbors, and an interpreter, who assisted in gathering information from the residents about possible militants hiding nearby.

The process was methodical and plodding, but eventually the soldiers assigned to Combat Outpost Gator cleared the area of insurgents, and Dora became a source of pride for what remained of the U.S. forces' time around Baghdad.

As he prepared to lead his men into the unknown, Duncan mumbled to himself, "Gators, swamp, Dora, and now Seminole. Am I in Florida?"

Chapter 13

January 16
Seminole, Texas

A crowd of uniformed police officers mingled with Duncan's men from the TX-QRF in the parking lot of the Texas Department of Public Safety. It wasn't battalion strength, but it certainly provided Duncan enough warm bodies to get the job done. The sheriff was the last to arrive on the scene and immediately drew the attention of his deputies. Without introducing himself to Duncan, he addressed the group.

"Listen up, people. We don't have any time to chitchat here. We've got at least two gunmen holed up at the pharmacy with Mrs. Oswalt and Mrs. Wright from next door. I don't know what their demands are, how many people are inside, or if anyone has been injured. We're going to turn this operation over to those fellas from Lubbock and let them take the lead."

The sheriff nodded to Duncan, who stepped forward to lay out his plan. "As you know, my men have taken control of perimeter security around the Seminole Hospital District. I need six deputies to step forward to work with my teams in clearing the neighborhood from Main Street westward toward Forest Park. Please, I need those of you who patrol that area regularly and are most familiar with the residents who live there."

For a moment, the deputies looked at one another, unsure what to do.

The sheriff urged them on. "Come on, people. We don't have all day here." This prompted some movement, and four men and two women stepped forward to assist Duncan's teams.

"Thank you," said Duncan. He motioned for Espy to join his side. "All right. This is Corporal Espy. He is going to pair you up with four of our guys. You're gonna start at Main Street, and each team will be assigned a street to clear."

Espy raised his arm and spoke up. "I've got team leaders for each of the streets from Avenue B through Avenue G. These men have extensive experience in Iraq and Afghanistan in patrolling neighborhoods far more dangerous than this one. That said, everyone needs to keep their head up and eyes open. Deputies, we need your assistance in differentiating between locals and refugees. Study their eyes, body language, etcetera. Although the homeowner may open the front door, that doesn't mean there isn't a gun pointed at their head from behind that same door."

"Okay, thank you, Corporal," interrupted Duncan. "Everyone team up and move out. Time's a-wastin'."

The deputies, with Espy's assistance, found a four-man unit from the TX-QRF to work with and immediately set foot down Main Street to begin the task of apprehending the refugees. The deputies retrieved zip-tie restraints from their patrol cars as well as their riot gear for protection.

Duncan walked up to the sheriff, who was standing with Deputy Jerry. He noticed a resemblance.

"Thank you, Sheriff, um," Duncan began as he squinted in the bright sun to view his name badge, "Diaz. I'm Commander Duncan Armstrong stationed at the newly created Camp Lubbock."

Sheriff Diaz noticed Duncan comparing the two name badges and introduced himself. "A pleasure, Commander, and yes, we are related. This is my son, Jerry."

"Deputy Jerry," the younger man added. "Since I was a kid playing cops and robbers, and Dad was sheriff, I got the nickname Deputy Jerry."

"Not a terrible nickname, considering," said the sheriff.

"Why's that?"

Deputy Jerry continued. "Well, most kids wanted to play cowboys and Indians, but I was always the Indian. Indian. Diaz. Get it? It got old, you know?"

"I can imagine," replied Duncan. He was anxious to get started. "The four of us can ride together in my Humvee. I have six men left to assist. How can we get close to the building without being seen?"

"The best way is from behind, along Avenue A," replied the sheriff, pointing catty-corner across the street. "The buildings along that stretch are basically prefabricated metal with a brick façade. The problem, as you'll see, is there is only a single plate-glass window in front and the glass entry door. Getting eyes inside the pharmacy is near impossible."

"What about a rear entry?" asked Duncan.

"Just a single steel security door."

Duncan grimaced as he motioned for the sheriff and his son to get into the truck. Espy had completed his duty assignments and instructed the remaining men to follow in an open-bed four-door Humvee with a fifty-caliber machine gun mounted on top. It was a vehicle designed to show any hostiles the TX-QRF unit meant business.

They made their way down the deserted street toward the back of the pharmacy. As they did, Duncan learned more about the situation.

"Your dispatcher mentioned over the radio that shots had been fired."

"Yes," the sheriff began. "Dr. David Wright has been an optometrist here for decades. His wife works as his nurse and office manager. According to Dave, she'd gone to Oswalt's for some gum and a Dr. Pepper when he heard a scream. He ran to his front door and saw two men shooting at the pharmacy entrance door. The glass shattered, and the men stepped inside. He reached our dispatch on his portable ham radio."

"Do you have eyes on the front of the building?"

"Yes. I've got a patrol car parked across the street with two deputies waiting for my instructions. I told them not to engage or do anything to spook the shooters. Commander, I don't know how many hostages might be inside the building although I doubt it's very many. Over time, Oswalt's began to run out of medications and their shelves became bare. Folks around here don't have much to trade, and their money is considered worthless. I really don't know why either of them open up shop every day. I'm guessin' it's 'cause they've got nothing else to do."

Duncan arrived at the back of the building and parked the truck. "Corporal, quickly. Grab some duct tape and cover that peephole in the pharmacy's back door."

Espy reached behind the seat and retrieved a grimy roll of the multipurpose wonder of the world. He muttered as he exited the vehicle, "There's nothing that love and duct tape can't fix."

"I wish that were true, Corporal," added Duncan, who then turned his attention back to the sheriff. "We're not gonna be able to force this issue. Let me walk around the front of the building and take a look. I think the only solution to this standoff is talking about the options with the gunmen."

"I'll have to trust you on this, Commander," began the sheriff. "We've never had a hostage situation like this other than the time Jason Roberts held his girlfriend and kids hostage with a knife. He finally stood down when she agreed to marry him."

"She married a guy who held her and her kids at knifepoint?"

"Nah, she lied, and he fell for it."

Espy returned from the back door and stood outside awaiting orders.

Duncan asked a few more questions. "What's the layout like inside?"

"Pretty straightforward," replied the sheriff. "Along the front wall is a long countertop immediately to the left of the entry. There's a cash register, and behind the counter are things like cigarettes, batteries, you know, pickup items. Then the pharmacy itself is in the back, elevated above the floor level. It's locked up during the day, but a guy could easily climb over the counter. Other than that, there are probably six or eight rows of shelves that run from front to back full of, you know, stuff."

"Tell me about the two women held inside," said Duncan.

"That's the thing, Commander. These old ladies are fixtures in the community. They're both in their early seventies and dainty as can be. They're probably frightened out of their minds."

"Okay, thank you, Sheriff. Here's what I need you to do. I'm going to position Corporal Espy on the left front corner of the building, and I'm gonna take the right corner. Is that closest to the entrance?"

"Yes."

"Deputy Jerry, I need you to watch the back door. If only one comes out with a hostage, shoot him if you have a clear shot. Don't hesitate unless you're unsure of your line of fire, okay?"

"Okay."

"Sheriff, make radio contact with your patrol car across the way," Duncan continued. "Tell them about our approach to the corners of the building. When they see that we're in position, tell them to leave."

"What? But—" stammered the sheriff.

"That's right, Sheriff. I want these gunmen to get the impression they're dealing only with one guy, me."

"Okay, will do."

The sheriff raised his deputies on the radio, and his son hustled into position. Duncan approached Espy and told him the plan.

"Okay, Espy, sidearms on this one. We'll be in close quarters inside, and we don't have the space to maneuver with our rifles."

Duncan reached into the pouches attached to his military-issue body armor and pulled out a pair of Dupont Kevlar-lined gloves. The black, tight form-fitting leather gloves were designed for frisking suspects while providing one hundred percent cut-resistant Kevlar protection from razor blades and knives.

"What's the plan for those?" asked Espy as they set their rifles inside the Humvee and locked the doors to the truck. Duncan didn't want the hostiles to escape past the young deputy and run off with their truck.

"These," replied Duncan as he deftly removed two knives from stitched-in pockets in his pants with a motion barely discernible to even a trained soldier like Espy. He rolled one of the blades through his fingers and offered it handle first to Espy.

"Nice."

"Yeah, they've served me well over the years," said Duncan. "They're made by United Cutlery. Seven inches of black-coated, high-grade stainless steel. The ring on the end of each knife makes it easy to pull in a fight and also cuts down on wind resistance when I let 'em fly. The black coating matches the Kevlar gloves, so I can mask them in my hands."

"Can you throw them both at once?" asked Espy.

"I have many times," replied Duncan mysteriously.

He began to lay out the plan for Espy, who approved. The guys moved in unison to both corners of the front of the pharmacy building. Once they made eye contact with one another, Duncan nodded to the deputy across the street, who started up his patrol car and slowly pulled away.

Duncan pressed his back against the red brick wall and inched toward the broken plate-glass door. He positioned his knives for a quick release and then focused on the muffled voices he could hear inside the pharmacy.

"The cops left, man. Maybe they didn't know we were in here or figgered we snuck out the back?"

"Let me see," the other attacker grumbled in a deep, baritone voice. "Come on, lady!"

The sounds of shuffling footsteps could be heard by Duncan as he carefully peered around the edge of the brick. A hulking figure was manhandling a frail woman wearing a white medical-style coat. She was barely able to stand as he dragged her along using his left arm while he held a rifle in his right.

"Sho' 'nuf," he said. "Have you checked the back?"

"Nah," replied the other. "There hasn't been any activity out that way since we busted in. I'm tellin' ya, that stupid cop that left had no idea we was in this place."

"Okay, then," said an older woman's voice from the back of the store. "Take the drugs and go. We don't have anything else to give you."

The hulk neared the front door to get another look. "Shut yo' mouth, lady! We'll go when we're good and ready. Now, check out the back, and I'll watch the front!"

"C'mon, granny," ordered the other man, and the sound of his working his way to the rear of the store could be heard by Duncan. The two men were separated.

Duncan crouched low and got Espy's attention. He held his left hand up and motioned for Espy to come toward the other side of the door opening. When Espy was in place, Duncan held up two fingers indicating two hostiles. Espy nodded.

Now he waited, trying to predict what was going to happen next. He needed the big man to turn his attention away from the door for just a second.

Come on, buddy. Distract him. I know you will because you're stupid.

Back-door bad guy fulfilled Duncan's wishes.

"Hey, somethin's wrong! I can't see out the peephole!"

Instinctively, the hulk spun around and redirected his attention to the rear of the store. As he pulled his captive with him, she lost her balance slightly, forcing him to use his efforts to lift her up. That was all Duncan needed.

In one simultaneous movement, Duncan changed his grip on the knife in his left hand to a stabbing position, and the knife in his right hand was repositioned to slash. He jumped from his crouch toward the big man, landed right behind him, and immediately buried the left knife at the base of his skull and sliced his throat with the other using his right hand.

The older woman's mouth gaped open, too frightened to scream, but Espy followed his instincts and jumped into place to cover her mouth before she gave away what had happened. Duncan nodded toward the door, and Espy removed the woman from the store to safety.

"Hey, did you hear me?" the man shouted from the stockroom door.

When his partner didn't answer, back-door bad guy came back into the middle of the pharmacy, unaware that he was on his own and being stalked by Duncan.

Duncan returned his knives to his pants pockets and drew his sidearm. The remaining assailant would be on guard now, most likely pointing his weapon at his hostage. Duncan couldn't allow the man the luxury of that precious couple of seconds as he release his knives in his direction. Only the split-second travel time of a bullet would take him out. All Duncan needed was a clear shot.

Law enforcement officers were trained to deal with a situation like this one. They were advised to keep the assailant calm, don't escalate the situation, and certainly don't take a risky shot that might get the hostage killed.

Duncan wasn't a cop. He was a trained killer. In his world, there was no such thing as hands up or I'll shoot. He acted as judge, jury, and executioner, but he was best at the execution part.

Slowly, walking heel to toe, he moved forward down the aisle lined with makeup and various women's sundries. The lone gunman had grown silent now, probably convinced that something had happened to his buddy. He finally broke the silence.

"I don't know who's in here, but I'll kill this old lady if you don't leave us be. I swear it! I'll shoot her dead right in front of her own drug counter."

Thanks, idiot, Duncan thought to himself as he picked up the pace to the end of the aisle. He raised his weapon and waited to listen for movement. They were stationary. Duncan rose slightly to see between the rows of hair coloring when he saw a man's legs in blue jeans standing still next to the pharmacy checkout counter.

Duncan removed a box of Clairol from the shelf and pulled out the plastic squeeze bottle. He needed a distraction, one that wouldn't cause an untrained gunman to pull the trigger. All Duncan needed was an opening.

He rose a little higher to get a better look through the shelves. The gunman, who was left-handed, held a rifle awkwardly away from his body in order to point the barrel at the side of his hostage. The man's finger was on the trigger, but his hand shook out of nervousness.

Duncan debated whether to talk the guy down. He had to know

his partner was dead or in custody. Maybe he'd give up without a fight.

He holstered his sidearm and opted for his knives as well. First, he wiped the blood off on his pants so the black matte finish could be hidden against his palms. He prepared himself for a quick strike.

"Your buddy's dead," Duncan announced himself with a growl as he stood and made his location known. "You wanna be next?"

"Hey, stay back! Ya hear me? Stay back, or I'll kill her!"

The man backed away from Duncan and stumbled into the counter filled with condoms. Somehow, he managed to keep the hostage between himself and Duncan.

"Nobody else needs to die today," said Duncan calmly as he raised his arms to show the man he was unarmed. At twenty-some feet away, the knives would be hidden against the background of the black leather gloves. "Listen, I get that you've been through a lot. I didn't think it was right to keep y'all locked out either. But it is what it is. There's no need to face the electric chair because you killed this nice lady. To be honest, you'll never walk out of here alive if you harm her at all."

"You can't make any promises to me, Army boy."

"Well, actually, I can, and you've heard one of them already," replied Duncan, maintaining his composure. "The first promise I just made you is that you'll die if you hurt her. The second promise I can make is this. Because I am the commander of the Texas military in this region, I have the authority to give you a pass today if you cooperate."

"You swear?"

"I swear on my huntin' dog's life, and any Texan will tell ya, there ain't nothin' more sacred than a man's huntin' dog." Duncan never had a hunting dog, and he made up the saying.

The man thought for a moment. "Yeah, I think I've heard that somewhere. Listen, this wasn't my idea. And I've never killed nobody. Those Korean fellas gave us these guns, no questions asked. When the fence opened up, me and that other guy just followed everybody through. It was the other guy who wanted the drugs. I was just hungry."

Duncan adjusted his grip, still waiting for an opening. But now he wanted the man alive to interrogate him about what had happened at the Hobbs checkpoint.

"See, you're innocent," lied Duncan, again. "Why don't you let her go, drop your weapon, and we'll get you something to eat while we talk about what happened at Hobbs. Okay? I mean, with that information, you've become valuable to me, and that washes away everything that's happened here today. Fair enough?"

The man hesitated; then he loosened his grip on the elderly woman, who spun away and ran down an aisleway to the entrance, where Espy quickly intercepted her. The hostage-taker carefully set his gun on the counter and stood with his hands in the air.

Duncan slipped the knives into their pockets and pulled his weapon to hold the man in place until he could get him cuffed.

"Corporal, get the deputy in here to take this man into custody."

"Yes, sir!" shouted Espy from the front door.

"In the meantime, spread your legs apart and put your hands on your head," Duncan ordered. As the man complied, Duncan grabbed the rifle from the countertop and quickly studied the AR-15. It was shiny stainless steel with no identifying markings. He'd never seen anything like it. "You say you got this from a Korean?"

"Yeah. Actually, there were a bunch of them. They were riding in Army trucks. You know, camo paint, the whole nine yards. I thought it was weird when the guy handed it to me, but I just rolled with it. I was glad to get into Texas."

"How many Koreans did you see?"

"I didn't count, you know," he responded. "Maybe forty or fifty."

Espy arrived with Deputy Jerry, who quickly pulled the man's hands behind his back and cuffed him.

"Whadya want me to do with him?"

"I don't care," replied Duncan. "That's between you and the sheriff."

As the deputy started to wrestle the man toward the front of the store, the assailant plead with Duncan, "Hey, man, you said I could get a pass!"

"You did," said Duncan dryly. "You're still alive, unlike your buddy up there."

CHAPTER 14

January 16
ERCOT Substation
Near Midland, Texas

Holloway, Lee, and four top lieutenants piled into a pickup and headed for the outskirts of Midland to view the ERCOT substation. Holloway might have been a murderous thug, but he was an astute, learned murderous thug.

When the attacks on the Metcalf Substation near San Jose, California, took place in 2013, he'd followed the story. Shooters had unloaded more than a hundred rounds of thirty-caliber ammunition into the radiators of transformers on the property. Thousands of gallons of oil had leaked, causing the electronics operating the substation to overheat and melt down.

Later in 2013, the Liberty Substation outside Phoenix, Arizona, had been attacked. Despite an alarm sounding for two days, the warnings had been ignored until an electrical worker was dispatched to determine the cause of the alarm. He'd found the fencing and surrounding razor wire pulled open, the security doors knocked down, and the station's computer cabinets vandalized.

Over the next several years, gunmen had attacked other substations around the U.S. in a manner similar to the Metcalf incident. Holloway recalled that not all of those had been successful. Accordingly, he would propose a two-step attack on each substation based upon detection concerns.

They pulled within a half mile of the substation at Midland, and Holloway stopped to observe the surroundings using his monocular. As had been the case with his prior surveillance opportunities, the substation was unmanned and unprotected.

"Let's go closer," said Holloway as he put the truck in gear and began his approach. "The other day, I had my best shooter take out the security cameras on the north side of the substation. We'll find out if they've been replaced."

The substation facility could best be described as a prison for transformers with lattice-style metal towers standing guard over the inmates. A single white concrete building stood in the middle of the facility. It was surrounded by tubular metal structures, the transformers, power lines and the aforementioned metal towers.

At one hundred yards away, Holloway stopped again and located the security cameras. The marksman had done his job well. The cameras had been torn from their mounting brackets and dangled in destroyed heaps from their wires. Comfortable that they could approach the fence undetected, Holloway drove forward, and the group unloaded as the setting sun began to take away their light.

The commandos spread out and walked along the fence, careful not to fall within the line of sight of an operable camera. They spoke among themselves, looking intently at the workings of the substation and periodically exchanging ideas during the process.

While they compared notes, Holloway laid out the suggested

approach. "We'll deploy two trucks, with six men per truck, to each of the eighteen identified substations. Some of the men will act as perimeter security for the hit teams while the others will be given specific tasks."

"Why don't we shoot the transformers and leave?" asked Lee.

Holloway nodded, acknowledging the validity of the question, and replied, "Most likely, the transformers can be repaired or replaced given sufficient time. The eighteen substations the ERCOT engineer identified are only a fraction of the total. Replacement transformers are probably available to them."

"Okay, please continue," said Lee as he pointed to each transformer and counted them.

Holloway noticed his gesturing. "General, most of the substation facilities will be much bigger than this one. In some cases, there will be more buildings and possibly security patrols. I'm going to recommend that once our people are in place, they take at least a day, or maybe two, to conduct surveillance. In order to guarantee our success, each of these substations must be taken off-line."

"Of course, but my men are not afraid to die," said Lee.

"It's not their dedication that concerns me, it's making sure they are effective in their mission. There can be no shortcuts."

Lee nodded and waved his right hand toward his chest, indicating for Holloway to continue.

"We need to avoid weapons fire until the final step of the operation. Each of the teams will need to find axes, sledgehammers, or prybars to be used in destroying the computer equipment within the control structures. The Texans' ability to remove and replace damaged transformers is one thing. But to rebuild the computerized apparatus necessary to operate the substation is another."

"Some men will run perimeter security while others enter the buildings and wreak havoc," Lee proposed.

"Exactly, General. In all likelihood, those actions alone will be sufficient to take down the power grid. However, the second step of opening fire on the transformers will render the substation useless and beyond repair."

"Yes, I understand," said Lee. "What caliber of bullet is necessary to penetrate the steel?"

"The 7.62 millimeter NATO rounds are best," replied Holloway. "Are your men equipped with AR-10s or AK-47s?"

"AK-47s, but we consider them to be substandard," replied Lee. "As part of our agreement with the CJNG Mexican drug cartel to assist our men across the U.S. border, we purchased clones of the AK-47 rifle. They use the more powerful NATO 7.62 ammunition. They jam often."

The CJNG, an acronym for Cartel Jalisco New Generation, was part of the new violent associations of drug lords at war with the Los Zetas and Sinaloa cartels. With over forty armed cells spread throughout Mexico, the CJNG had managed to gain the upper hand on the older drug cartels by using more powerful weapons manufactured in their own facilities.

Trained by former members of the Colombian terrorist group FARC, the CJNG began building clandestine arms factories, which manufactured clones of the AR-15 and AK-47 platforms in both NATO 5.56 mm and 7.62 mm calibers. The weapons were sought after because of their power and their lack of factory markings or serial numbers.

"Substandard? Will they shoot straight?" asked Holloway.

Lee answered with a smug grin. "They worked at the border checkpoint."

Holloway nodded and led Lee back to the trucks. In turn, Lee summoned his men to return as well.

As the sun set over the horizon, Holloway leaned on the hood of the truck and considered their timetable. The Texans would be busy for days rounding up the thousands of refugees who had flooded into their territory. Because the intruders were on foot, it wasn't likely roadblocks would be set up yet. However, the caravan of military vehicles would be reported to the Texas authorities.

"General, tomorrow we should handpick your teams, assign them weapons, and determine their targets. In addition, we should conduct training sessions with the teams and their commanding officers to make sure each group has a clear understanding of the mission."

"Very good, Holloway. This can be accomplished in one day, don't you agree?"

"I do. The day after tomorrow, we send the teams to their targets and provide them two days for travel and perhaps two days for surveillance. Your ability to communicate with your commanders is the key to the success of this operation. On your orders, everyone will initiate the attack at once and then get out of there."

Lee patted Holloway on the back as he walked around to the passenger side of the truck. "What are your plans?"

"Lubbock is the first prize," replied Holloway. "General, what is next for you after the Texas grid is destroyed?"

"Our men will attack the oil refineries along the Gulf Coast before we join forces with our soldiers fighting in America. What will you do, Holloway?"

"Find a quiet, out-of-the-way ranch somewhere and retire."

Part Two

The Hits Just Keep On Comin'

Chapter 15

January 17
The White House
Washington, DC

Chief of Staff Charles Acton had become the most powerful man in Washington since the EMP attack collapsed America's power grid. Between keeping President Alani Harman's head in the game and juggling the recovery effort, he'd been granted unfettered leeway in decision making concerning domestic affairs and a seat at the table on all international matters.

More importantly, he'd become a gatekeeper for the president like never before. Nobody accessed the Oval Office without his approval or presence. As a result, he meticulously controlled the flow of information that crossed President Harman's desk.

This included the assassination of her former Secretary of Defense and thorn in Acton's side, Montgomery Gregg. He'd received information from his sources within the Texas administration, and because the news hadn't been made public yet, he was safe in keeping it from President Harman until he could digest the ramifications for himself. There would be a way to use the occasion of Gregg's death to his advantage, he just needed to think it through.

"Good morning, Charles," greeted the president as Acton entered the Oval Office. "My secretary said you needed to see me on an urgent matter."

"Yes, Madam President. You might want to sit down."

"Charles, I don't need any more drama. Isn't the collapse of America enough for one president to endure?"

"It is, ma'am, but there's progress on that front, which I'll tell you about after."

"After what, Charles?" asked the president, who reluctantly sat down.

"Ma'am, this hasn't been formally announced yet, but I have it on good authority that Monty Gregg has been killed."

"Wow, Charles. Are you sure?"

"I don't have all the details yet, but it's been confirmed to me by multiple sources."

President Harman spun around in her chair and looked to the telephone, which still did not work. She turned back around and looked at Acton. "I should call Austin."

"Not quite yet, Madam President. They've not called a formal press conference, and you don't want to be in a position of explaining how you know."

"Okay. My goodness. He and I didn't always see eye-to-eye, but he was a hero to this country, and his death is distressing."

Hero isn't the word I would have chosen.

"That's all I know at this time. When something official is released, I'll formulate our formal response."

"Good, thank you. Charles, why would they withhold the announcement? Has something else happened?"

Acton retrieved a side chair from next to the wall and pulled it up to the president's desk. "There have been some additional developments regarding Texas that might have an impact on our relationships with them and the United Nations."

"Go ahead."

"There was a serious border breach in West Texas near Hobbs, New Mexico. Anywhere from fifteen to twenty thousand American refugees streamed into Texas."

"Good for them," said the president with a chuckle. "How are they making out?"

"Hard to tell, as, once again, there is no reporting because the Burnett administration has clamped down on the media."

"How are you finding out these things?"

"Sources," replied Acton. Then he raised both hands and leaned back in his chair.

"I get it, plausible deniability," said President Harman. "I won't ask again."

Acton took a deep breath before proceeding. "I think we should make a formal request, through proper channels, of course, for an accounting of the refugees and confirmation that they are being treated well. If the Burnett administration refuses to comply, we should take our case to the United Nations."

"She'll just refuse to comply," said the president.

"Perhaps," began Acton. "However, international pressure brought her around regarding the UN airlift of relief supplies. It might work again."

"May I assume that *channels* refers to State Department to State Department?"

"Yes, but allow me to draft the outline of the proposal. My approach worked pretty well before."

President Harman rose out of her chair and walked to the window to admire a soft blanket of snow, which had fallen overnight. "What else, Charles?"

Under other circumstances, he'd try to encourage the president to get involved in more of the daily affairs relating to the recovery following the nuclear attacks. However, their working relationship was such that Acton was given carte blanche around the White House and Washington. He had become the de facto president.

"Nothing, Madam President. If something of consequence arises, I'll let you know."

CHAPTER 16

**January 17
Camp Lubbock
Lubbock, Texas**

Duncan had envisioned putting in a long day's work at Camp Lubbock and then returning to Armstrong Ranch to spend time with Sook and his family. At the end of day one, he requisitioned a cot for his office and placed a phone call to Sook to wish her goodnight. He crashed in his makeshift bunk, sleeping uncomfortably until he awoke like always, just before dawn.

He'd just returned from the latrine when he was greeted outside his door by Espy, who held two empty coffee mugs and an entire pot of black coffee.

"Espy, notwithstanding everything else you do, which is above the call of duty, delivering that pot of coffee should earn you a third stripe."

"That would be nice, sir," said Espy as he pushed Duncan's door open with his boot and stood aside as his commander entered his office turned home/office.

Duncan accepted a steaming mug of black coffee and took his first sip. He furrowed his brow and looked inside his mug as if he expected the brand name to be floating on the surface of the dark brew.

"I know, it's not Starbucks," apologized Espy.

"Espy, it's not even Folgers. Did they grow these coffee beans out back somewhere?"

"I don't know, but I can find out."

"I'm just kidding. So you wanna be a sergeant? I suppose I could make that happen, right?"

Espy laughed as he gestured toward a chair, seeking permission to sit. Duncan nodded and smiled.

"I suppose, sir, not that it really matters. I might get paid a little more, but there's nothing to buy with the money. I don't exactly have any free time to spend it, not that there's any entertainment to spend it on. You know, the world's kinda frozen in time. Nothing comes and nothing goes. We're all just waiting to see what happens next."

Duncan hadn't thought of it that way, but Espy was right. Even though Texans had avoided the apocalyptic world that had beset most of North America, life as they knew it had come to a screeching halt. A person's ordinary day might begin with the ringing of an alarm clock, followed by a shower, and breakfast while watching *The Today Show*. Then you hustled the kids off to school and went to work. Your job might be mundane, but it paid the bills, and at the end of the day, you could mentally check out and spend time with your family. Your busy day might include time at the soccer field or shopping or reading your favorite eBook.

All of those ordinary daily activities had come to a screeching halt despite the fact that the Texas power grid had been spared. Electricity provided Texans a sense of normalcy and safety. Police, fire, and health professionals were still at work. Transportation was still an option if you could afford the fuel. Some goods and services were available, for a price. Otherwise, Texans, like Americans, were in a holding pattern until their trusted politicians could fix this mess.

"Nonetheless, let's get you promoted," said Duncan. "Will you prepare the necessary paperwork for me to elevate you to the rank of sergeant?"

"I will, and while I appreciate it, it's not necessary, sir. The lieutenants already let me boss them around as if I'm you. It's kind of comical, actually. They do the dirty work that I used to."

"Where the axe meets the stone," quipped Duncan.

"Yes, sir."

Duncan looked at the paperwork on his desk and quickly shoved it aside. He wasn't interested in the administrative side of the job.

He'd allow his newly promoted sergeant to handle it. His primary concerns were troop readiness and rapid deployment.

"Well, the teams worked late into the night clearing the houses in Seminole. We turned all of the refugees over to Sheriff Diaz to hold until further notice. I think he plans to bus them to a nearby prison facility. I've requisitioned rations from Fort Bliss to keep them fed until they're moved."

"What about interrogations?" asked Duncan.

"I thought we'd send a bilingual team down there today to conduct interviews," replied Espy. "They can compile a report and advise me directly if anything pertinent arises, especially related to the Korean involvement in the border breach."

Duncan checked his watch. It was eight a.m. "Why don't you take care of those things and advise the lieutenants that I'd like us to meet as a group in the small conference room at ten. I need to pull a few things from the armory and make a quick call to the ranch."

"Yes, sir," said Espy as he topped off his coffee. He left Duncan's office and closed the door behind him.

Duncan had only spoken to Sook the night before, but he found himself wanting to advise his father of yesterday's events. While he had been conducting clandestine operations abroad, Duncan had tried to close his family out of his mind. The distractions of a worried father or a grieving mother would likely have resulted in his capture or being killed. It had hardened him emotionally, but all of that had changed the day he'd opened his eyes and saw Sook standing over him.

Since then, his family had become his priority, and he remembered that his father stored a wealth of information and experience in his mind. When he'd woken up that morning, he vowed to speak with him daily, not just to seek his advice, but to keep him abreast of what was going on beyond the borders of Armstrong Ranch.

After their twenty-minute conversation, in which he relayed his experience in Seminole and Major provided Duncan his opinion on the death of Vice President Gregg, Duncan headed to the armory to do a little *shopping*.

He hoped to get back to the ranch this evening, assuming, of course, there wasn't another crisis. With each trip to Armstrong ranch, Duncan planned on procuring weapons to be used in its defense.

Today, he was going to focus on home-defense weapons to be used by his parents, Sook, and his siblings. He made his way through the impressive array of weapons until he reached the shotguns. There were several to choose from, but one in particular caught his eye.

He pulled a Mossberg 590 Shockwave shotgun off the rack and studied its black Cerakote finish. Yesterday's use of his matte black knives reminded him that a homeowner had the upper hand on an intruder because they knew their way around the home in low lighting. The dark earth finish of the Mossberg Shockwave would not give away their position like some shotguns that had metallic finishes.

Duncan weighed the weapon in his hands. At just over five pounds, it was light enough for the women to use without growing weary, although he never envisioned his mother, Palmer or Sook growing weary in a gunfight to defend the ranch. As the big guy on the *A-Team* television show used to say, Duncan thought to himself, *I pity the fool who takes those three honey badgers on.*

He grabbed two of the Mossbergs and moved on. He wanted everyone at the ranch to begin using a backup sidearm stored safely in an ankle holster. Most attackers didn't expect the average person to be armed in this manner, so the element of surprise would be a help.

Duncan stopped at the handguns and studied his options. He picked up a Smith & Wesson M&P Shield compact chambered in nine millimeter. This small, lightweight handgun would match the calibers used by his family at the ranch in their other handguns. Despite its small size, it came with extended grip magazines, which would hold eight rounds. At just over a pound, this would make an ideal backup weapon. He opened the case and discovered the package included an ankle-carry holster.

Sold, he muttered to himself as he tried to determine the best way to carry four of those and the two shotguns. With the shotguns tucked under each armpit and his large hands gripping the hard-plastic handgun cases, he made his way for the exit of the armory. Just as he reached the desk of the young woman at the checkout cage, something caught his eye.

"Good morning, Corporal," said Duncan.

"Good morning, Commander," she responded jovially. She flashed a pretty smile, and her eyes looked down shyly at her desk. Duncan smiled at her flirtatious movements but was proud that he was engaged to the love of his life and didn't give this pretty girl a second thought.

"Corporal, what do you have there? Behind you, on the credenza?"

She got out of her chair and retrieved one of the boxes to show Duncan. He set his weapons aside.

"Sir, I'm calling this our new *Star Wars* gun. It's the TS12 bullpup shotgun. Do you wanna see?"

Duncan didn't respond and simply opened the box, revealing a unique, futuristic form of shotgun. Only twenty-eight inches long, including its eighteen-inch barrel, the weapon was very light in his hands at eight pounds.

"What's the magazine capacity?" he asked as he studied the weapon's features.

"Fifteen, sir. Twelve gauge. Did you notice it was semiautomatic?"

"I did."

"No pumping."

"Right," said Duncan as he avoided eye contact. He'd had enough of the corporal's flirting. "I'll take two of these. In fact, have someone deliver these to Corporal Esparza's office together with a thousand rounds of ammo for each weapon."

"Oh, I know Espy," she said. "I'll do it myself."

Duncan immediately thought of how Palmer and Espy had hit it off. While he'd never envisioned a fellow soldier dating his sister, the two were infatuated with one another, and he didn't plan on standing in their way.

"No, Corporal. You do your job very well right here. Summon a private to take care of it. Thank you."

Duncan turned and strode out of the armory.

Chapter 17

January 17
The Armstrong Ranch
Borden County, Texas

Major rounded up Lucy and Preacher to discuss his phone conversation with Duncan. It was an unseasonably warm day, so they met outside by the horse barn. Sook and Palmer were nearby grooming the horses, so Major moved the conversation a little farther away to keep them out of earshot.

"It's not that I care if the girls hear what I've got to say, but I don't want to unduly alarm Sook concerning the potential dangers our boy faces out there," Major explained as he led them over near the horse-training pen. "If he wants to keep her up to speed on his activities, that's up to him."

"Has he been in danger?" asked Lucy nervously.

"No, Momma," replied Major somewhat sarcastically. "Besides, I don't think he'd tell me if he was. I can only imagine how many times he's been shot at or near death. I do have a certain comfort level in knowing that those brushes with danger made him smarter and more careful."

"I agree with Major," said Preacher. "Your boy is smart enough to know you can't just bring a knife to a gunfight."

"Okay, if you two say so," said Lucy. "What did he say that's caused you to call us all together?"

"Two things," Major replied. "The North Korean presence has been confirmed from multiple sources. At least forty broke through at the Hobbs checkpoint, and countless others infiltrated West Texas where the fences were knocked down. In addition, they provided the refugees with high-powered weapons, including AR-15s."

"Why would they do that?" asked Preacher.

"I suggested it was because the North Koreans were going to either use the refugees as scapegoats for the attack on the Texas checkpoint or to make them a distraction to evade capture once they'd entered our country."

"What did Duncan think?" asked Lucy.

"He agrees and also thinks they have designs on something bigger," replied Major. "He pointed out that the dialect they were using, as heard by Sook, was native North Korean. That rules out a group of Korean Americans banding together, who would most likely be of South Korean descent."

Preacher removed his hat and ran his fingers through his hair. He had a puzzled look on his face. "You think these are real North Koreans? I don't know, boss. That sounds more like a movie than reality."

"It adds up, however," said Major. "Plus, Duncan said the coordinated attack on our border security indicates a level of command and control beyond a bunch of thugs or gangbangers lookin' to make trouble. And there's one more thing."

"What's that?" asked Lucy.

"He mentioned that one of the weapons they confiscated yesterday was completely clean of markings or serial numbers," replied Major. "I'd read about this before everything went crazy. The Mexican drug cartels were manufacturing their own AK-47s and AR-15s. Duncan thinks it's possible the cartels helped North Korean commandos enter the U.S. through the southern border."

"For what purpose?" asked Lucy.

"Maybe we're at war and don't know it yet," replied Major dryly.

His words hung in the air as Lucy and Preacher contemplated this new information.

"I don't know, y'all," said Preacher. "The three of us have talked about the possibilities of an EMP attack or even nuclear missiles flying over our heads, but I didn't think any country would have the ability to attack us on our own soil with a ground invasion. 9/11 doesn't count as an enemy attack either."

Major rolled his head on his shoulders to work out the kinks. "I can't disagree, Preach. But all the signs point to just that. With Washington's hands full trying to save the U.S. and initiate some semblance of a recovery effort, and our own obsession with keeping folks out of Texas, maybe the stars are aligned for something previously thought to be absurd, like invading us."

Major wandered over to the horse pen fence and propped his right leg on the bottom rung and leaned on the top rail with both arms. Lucy and Preacher followed suit as their conversation continued.

"How will this affect us?" asked Lucy.

Major responded, "Setting aside the North Korean issue for a second, Duncan said thousands of refugees broke through the fences and started heading into the country in all directions. We're a hundred miles away, but it's a matter of time before they could arrive here. When they do, it could be dozens or even hundreds bunched together."

"We can't shoot 'em all," said Lucy.

"True," said Preacher. "All we can do is try to warn them off. But, and we all have to agree upon this, if they try to climb the fences, I say we shoot 'em. We kinda said that before, but if they come at us and we're outnumbered—I mean, I'm sorry. It's us or them."

"Yes, I totally agree," said Lucy.

"Then it's settled," added Major. "Preach, will you spread the word about the potential for increased activity. Also, we need to increase our perimeter patrols. If a hundred people show up at the fences, a couple of our patrols on horseback won't be enough to turn them away."

"I'll try, boss, but we're stretched pretty thin as it is," said Preacher.

The three of them were startled by a voice from behind them.

"Sook and I will help with the patrols," said Palmer, who looked over to her future sister-in-law. "Won't we, Sook?"

Sook nodded her head and stood firmly with her hands on her hips. Her determined look drew a smile from Lucy.

"I don't know, girls," started Lucy. "I suppose we could pair each of you up with the guys. Cooper and—"

"No, Momma," interrupted Palmer. "Sook and I are a team, and we work best that way. Right, sister?"

Sook laughed and then regained her composure. She parroted Palmer's serious demeanor. "Yes, we are a team."

Major grinned and shook his head in disbelief. The Armstrong Army had just expanded.

"Preach," he began, "incorporate Team Girl Power into the perimeter patrol rotation. Daytime only, and their coverage area is restricted to the fence row bordering the Slaughter property and the east fence line."

"Daddy," whined Palmer, "there won't be any action over thataway."

Major raised his hand, and Palmer immediately stopped. "Young lady, that's the way it's gonna be, for now. Understood?"

"Yes, Daddy," said a dejected Palmer. Then she perked up. "When can we start?"

"How about today?" asked Preacher as he glanced at both Lucy and Major. "They can relieve the morning riders who are pulling a double shift. I can get them some much-needed rest and use them all night tonight."

"Fine by me," said Lucy.

"Us too," said Palmer. "Can that be our regular shift, at least for now?"

"Absolutely," said Major. "Now, you two skedaddle, but make sure your weapons are checked out and you've got fully charged radios. You two will be alone on the back forty. The terrain's rougher, and you've got to keep your eyes open."

Major continued to shout advice to the backs of Team Girl Power, who'd reached the front porch of the ranch house before he was finished. He turned to Lucy. "Are you sure you're okay with this?"

Lucy laughed. "If you'd tried to tell me no, I would've punched you in the nose instead of whining like your daughter. They'll be fine."

CHAPTER 18

January 17
The National Mall
Washington, DC

Unlike their previous meeting at this spot ten days ago, when the Reflecting Pool was mostly frozen and snow was falling over them, today the skies were clear, but the temperatures remained crisp. Also, power had been restored to the parts of Washington that provided essential services to the government.

Chief of Staff Acton rarely left the confines of the White House. Prior to the collapse, political insiders looking to advance their careers at the expense of others would track his every movement, looking for a discernible pattern in order to draw bizarre conclusions about his activities.

Now the White House was occupied by mind-numbed robots, responding to one crisis before moving on to another. Gone were the political hacks looking for an angle to curry favor or an opportunity for advancement, which in Washington-speak meant more power.

Also, the rabid press—which traversed the hallways of the West Wing, looking to break the next scandalous story—were also missing. Make no mistake, there were plenty of stories to break, only there was nobody in America interested in reading them.

Prior to the collapse, in America's hypersensitive, overly political atmosphere, every perceived slight became a source of front-page drama. If the story had legs, as they say, then it might survive the twenty-four-hour news cycle. Otherwise, one day's drama became old news by the time Lester Holt took to the airwaves at 6:30 that evening with the latest breaking news.

He checked his watch and noticed that Billy Yancey was five minutes late. His tardiness would typically send Acton into a tirade about whose time did Yancey think was more important—the right arm of the president or some spook who used to spend his days overthrowing governments.

Fortunately, Acton had become mesmerized at a sight that harkened back to days of old—kids were playing field hockey across the street on the JFK Hockey Fields. It was a reminder to him that despite the suffering across the nation, they were making progress.

The first step in the recovery effort was to restore the U.S. government. To do that, they needed to bring Washington, DC, back to life. This was happening slowly but surely, Acton made sure of it. As the relief supplies poured into Texas from abroad, Acton instructed the Department of Homeland Security to direct the bulk of the food and equipment to the DC area.

To operate a government, you needed people. Lots of people. Once order was restored and government employees could feel comfortable returning to the District, then the federal government could take the reins of the recovery.

The next step in the recovery effort was to control the chaos and mayhem in the cities. The martial law declaration was working with respect to the large cities. Surrounded and then isolated, residents were forced to calm down and succumb to the will of the military or face a certain death from starvation, disease, or the brutality of their neighbors. It was a form of tough love, but the technique was working.

The last step was to deal with the rural areas, the so-called *flyover country*. If one were to study a map of presidential election voting results by precinct, the vast majority of America would be seen as a sea of red. The congregation of blue precincts were found in the heavily populated cities on the two coasts and cities like Chicago and Detroit.

As much as Acton and the president were political polar opposites to the Americans living in flyover country, it was accepted that those citizens were generally more self-reliant and capable of holding on longer than the city-dwellers. Plus, as Acton pointed out often, they weren't the president's constituents.

Acton was politically astute and had the ability to look at the big picture. He was certain America would survive this heinous attack. Yes, there would be death and suffering, as well as a massive die-off of the population. But through the proper marshalling of recovery assets, those most likely to survive would owe their lives to the efforts of the federal government. It was an opportunity to change the political landscape in the United States forever.

There was just one hurdle to jump. One thorny issue that consumed his thoughts from the moment he woke up in the morning until he finished his nightcap before bed.

Texas.

Yancey's black Lincoln Town Car pulled up to the curb, and the rear window rolled down. He waved Acton over. Initially, Acton didn't like the change in routine. As Yancey's driver exited the car and hurried to open the door for Acton, thoughts of a double-cross and hidden microphones filled his mind. He'd be careful with his words today.

Yancey slid over on the bench seat, and Acton ducked his head to enter. There was another passenger in the backseat facing him. Acton hesitated, his eyes darting back and forth between Yancey and the mysterious newcomer. He almost backed out, but Yancey spoke.

"Please come in, Charles. There's somebody I'd like you to meet. She's a friend."

Acton reluctantly joined them, and the door was closed behind him by Yancey's driver.

"Who's this?" asked Acton nervously. He hated being blindsided, and he'd let Yancey know it at a more opportune time.

He quickly turned his attention to the leggy brunette who sat comfortably in the seat across from him. Her long hair was pulled to one side over a professionally tailored blue suit consisting of a jacket and a knee-length skirt. Her appearance had the usual effect on men who encountered her for the first time—disarming.

"My apologies for the cloak-and-dagger," said Yancey. "Charles,

I'd like you to meet Pauline Hart. She's deputy adjutant general in charge of clandestine affairs in Texas. It's a newly created position designed to mirror our CIA."

"Good morning, Mr. Acton," she said with a noticeable Southern accent.

Acton simply nodded, still processing the addition of the newcomer to the conversation. Yancey seemed to sense Acton's apprehension, so he continued.

"Charles, Pauline has worked with me for thirteen years. She has been inserted into several regime-change operations as a member of our diplomatic corps as well as being an operative in her own right. She's fluent in seven languages, including Spanish and Korean, and moreover, she's a native Texan who's well acquainted with her boss, Texas Adjutant General Kregg Deur."

"He's my brother-in-law," she added.

"Why does Texas need a spy agency?" asked Acton. He'd regained his composure and was prepared to vet the attractive former CIA operative.

"The government is getting on its feet, slowly," she began in her response. "Each department is patterning itself after the U.S. federal model, starting from the top down. The upper echelon of Austin's governmental officials are calling upon known quantities—friends and family, or those who come highly recommended—to fill the positions first."

"How did Deur know you were with the CIA?" asked Acton.

Yancey stepped in. "I instructed her to reveal enough of a resumé regarding her time in the agency to ensure she got the position. It worked."

"Deur is your family," challenged Acton. "How can we trust your loyalties?"

"He's my sister's family, not mine," she stated flatly. "I'm an American who happened to be born in Texas. I've risked my life for my country, and I'm appalled that they've tried to tear it apart."

Acton studied Hart for a moment and then turned to Yancey. "What role will she play?"

Yancey nodded. "For one, information. Pauline delivered Monty Gregg's schedule to me, together with his protection detail's information."

Acton stared at Yancey's eyes as he attempted to read the subliminal message being sent. He knew Yancey had ordered the hit on Gregg, and now he was revealing that he'd had inside help from this new addition to his clandestine team.

"What else?" asked Acton.

"As a result of recent events, there is an aura of mistrust running through Austin," replied Yancey. "Burnett is naturally paranoid that there's a bullet out there with her name on it. She's circled the wagons and has convinced herself that Washington might be behind the shooting, as well as the breach of their West Texas border."

"Why us?"

Hart sat forward in her seat. "Two reasons, Mr. Acton. One was the prior situation at the Interstate 44 bridge checkpoint. Vice President Gregg confided in President Burnett just days before his death. He told her trained operatives, likely U.S. military, were behind the attack."

"The second reason?" asked Acton.

"United States military vehicles were used to attack the border checkpoint at Hobbs, New Mexico. President Burnett is becoming convinced the U.S. was behind the attack."

Acton looked to Yancey. He was still going to choose his words wisely. He didn't like being tag-teamed by trained spies.

"The intelligence I was provided stated that North Korean soldiers were driving those vehicles, although the findings were inconclusive."

"We have confirmed that, sir," said Hart. "Based upon information received from an acquaintance of President Burnett's, the North Koreans may have traveled from as far west as Arizona to plan the attack."

"For what reason?" asked Acton.

"Unknown at this time, sir," replied Hart.

Acton sat back in his seat and stared out the window as the kids continued to play field hockey. He glanced at his watch, cognizant of the fact he'd been away from the White House for just over an hour.

"What are you two suggesting?" asked Acton. He wanted to hear the proposal out of their mouths not his. If ever confronted about this meeting, he would claim he was investigating rogue agency personnel on behalf of the president.

Yancey responded. "Hart is assembling a covert, non-sanctioned team to locate these Koreans and determine their intentions. If their intentions are to attack Austin to throw Texas in disarray, we'll do everything within our means to help or allow that to happen. Keeping our hands clean, of course."

"You're collaborating with the enemy," said Acton dryly. "You need to be careful, Billy."

"I prefer to call it a gentle assist or nudge against a common foe," replied Yancey. "Let me remind you, we created ISIS and arguably al-Qaeda too. When we ploughed billions of our dollars via the Saudis into arming the Mujahideen fighters in Afghanistan against the Soviets, al-Qaeda was born with our money. When we started funding Syrian rebels against Assad, we did so with full knowledge the rebels were dominated by extreme sectarian groups hell-bent on creating an Islamic State."

"Billy, still, this is different," interjected Acton. "We're at war with North Korea. They've used American soil to advance upon Texas. Rendering aid to the enemy won't sit well with anyone, Texans or Americans."

"Charles, this is how things are done," Yancey shot back. "Do you want Texas back or not?'

Yancey had backed Acton into a corner. He had to commit or look for a better option. Then the anger crept back into his mind. Burnett had betrayed America at a time when the nation needed help the most. She and the rest of Texas didn't deserve a heads-up or the assistance of Washington. Let them fail in order to teach other states a valuable lesson. This nationalistic approach to state government could not go unchallenged.

"Do it," said Acton as he pulled the door handle and escaped the close confines of the deep state's clutches.

Chapter 19

January 18
The Mansion
Austin, Texas

The early morning phone call from Austin caused a considerable amount of consternation for Lucy and Major. The sun rising in the east had barely shone through their bedroom windows when the satellite phone's combination of beeping and vibrating stirred them awake. Phone calls in the middle of the night to right after dawn generally meant some form of bad news, and their minds raced to concerns for Duncan.

After President Burnett's chief of staff quickly identified herself and the purpose of the early morning call, their attitudes changed from apprehension, to relief, to aggravation at being called so early.

Major signed off by saying, "I'll be there as quickly as I can." He placed the phone back on the counter and propped himself up against the headboard. He fiddled with the covers, pulling them up to his waist and folding the excess into one four-inch fold after another.

"Where and why?" asked Lucy as she rolled over and reached for his hands, forcing him to stop the nervous fumbling.

Major responded by squeezing her hand, and then he replied, "Quote—*several matters of utmost importance.*"

"What the devil does that mean?" asked Lucy before adding a little snark. "Doesn't her highness have plenty of minions to call upon without yanking my husband out of bed?"

Major chuckled and sighed. He didn't want to get his wife stirred up. Setting aside their cordial informal past as fellow ranchers and then close confidants, Major had been asked by the president of his country to meet with her immediately. You didn't say *no* to such a request, regardless of the ongoing apocalypse.

"Come on, let me grab some coffee and a few of those corn pones you made yesterday," said Major as he deflected her questions. A rustic cousin to corn bread, Lucy had created several baskets full yesterday to be enjoyed by everyone on the ranch. Major was surprised any were left, especially with the ravenous Riley always lurking about the kitchen.

He swung his legs out of the bed and looked through his closet for attire that was a cut above his usual blue jeans and plaid western shirt. After a moment of indecision, he opted for khakis and a plaid western shirt. But he'd wear his dress ropers instead of his regular boots. Like most men, Major was easy to dress.

Lucy noticed his extra attention to his outfit. "Do you want me to find your favorite cologne, too?"

He walked to her side of the bed and sat next to her. "Now, Miss Lucy, there's no need for that kind of talk, and you really need to do away with that pout."

"I don't understand, Major. What could be so important that you need to leave the safety of the ranch and run clear down to Austin? Plus, you won't have Duncan with you to keep watch for, you know, trouble."

Major leaned over and kissed his wife, effectively erasing the pout with a slight smile. "If it'll make you feel better, I'll take Riley and Cooper with me. Two of them are almost as effective as one of Duncan, especially if it comes down to hand-to-hand combat. Riley can whoop on 'em while Coop tells him what to do."

This drew a laugh from Lucy, and Major knew all was well in the world between them.

"You'll have to feed Riley," she said as her improved demeanor allowed her to enjoy the playful banter.

"I'm aware," he said. "They've been riding the graveyard shift, so most likely they'll sleep on the way to Austin."

"Great," said Lucy as she sat up and folded her arms. "A lot of good two sleeping beauties will do ya if danger lurks."

"Good grief." He laughed as he playfully slapped her on the backside. "I'll go find the boys if you don't mind fixin' us up with an order to go."

"Okay. I could use some time alone with the girls today, anyway."

*****

An hour later, the guys were on the road to Austin. As predicted, the boys were snoozing within thirty minutes of hitting the main highway toward the capital. Major used the opportunity to place a quick call to Duncan to let him know of his daily schedule and promised to call later that evening if there was anything of interest discussed.

The scene around the Mansion was much different from his earlier visit right after Christmas with Duncan. Fort Knox didn't have this level of military security. As they entered the grounds, they easily passed through the first checkpoint by showing their identification, but at the second checkpoint, they were stopped to confirm that their names were on the approved visitors' list.

Unaware of this requirement, Major didn't know to get the boys approved in advance, so they were forced to remain in a satellite parking area with the truck. He was escorted to the entrance on a golf cart.

After a brief wait outside the president's office protected by two soldiers in full military gear, Major was escorted into President Burnett's office alone. The president was sitting on a sofa to the left of her desk by the fireplace. She had several file folders stacked on the coffee table in front of her as well as her beloved Texas Rangers coffee mug, which emitted a faint trail of steam.

She rose off the sofa and greeted Major with an unexpected hug. The two of them had been friends for a long time, and Major could not recall ever hugging Marion Burnett. In the past, her tough, combative exterior would never allow such a showing of intimacy between friends.

Finally, she broke away and smiled. "Please, Major, excuse me. It's just, well, it's good to see an *old* friend."

Major sensed she was troubled, but he wanted her to express herself on her own terms. "Madam President, I can't imagine the pain of losing your vice president so abruptly. I'm sorry for your loss and the loss to Texas."

The president glanced past Major at the door, which had been closed. She motioned for him to take a seat.

"Major, when I envisioned a free and strong Texas, I knew that secession was the only way and that the road to freedom from Washington would be a tough one. I was wrong. Secession was the easy part. Establishing a new government and the process of governing is much more difficult than I ever imagined."

"Well, the EMP attack was a blessing and a curse in that regard," said Major. "It opened the door for this opportunity, but it also immediately put you behind the eight ball in terms of forming a new nation. It's kinda like an employee who plans on making a big move away from his existing job to do his own thing. He plans for months in advance, you know, setting himself up with office space, staff, and clients or business contacts. When the time is right, he makes his move. You didn't have the benefit of any of the set-up phase of the change. You had to make a decision. Secession was a bold move and took a tremendous amount of courage. Now you have to see it through."

The president smiled and drank some of her coffee. "You get it, Major. I'm surrounded by good folks, don't get me wrong. But they're political animals, longtime government employees. They don't understand the real world like us ranchers. You've seen it from both sides in your lifetime."

"As have you, Madam President," said Major respectfully.

"Please stop calling me that, Major. Marion, from now on, in both public and private."

Major chuckled. "Privately, yes, but publicly, never. You are the President of Texas, and everyone should afford you that respect in public."

"Okay, fine. Major, let me get to the point, and I'm not going to mince words. There are powerful forces working against me and

Texas. Monty was assassinated by a professional killer, one that has the earmarks of a military sniper. I don't know if he was a rogue operator from within Texas, maybe working on behalf of Linkletter's side of the aisle, or maybe the shooter was from another government, like Washington." The president was referring to Patrick Linkletter, the former mayor of Austin and new Senate Minority Leader of Texas.

Major sat up in his seat and leaned forward. With a lowered voice, he asked, "What has your investigation produced so far?"

"Nothing, because there hasn't been one," she replied. "Major, Austin's in disarray. I don't know who I can trust. Yesterday was a day of mourning, and tomorrow Monty will be buried at his ranch outside San Angelo."

"Why haven't you turned this over to the Rangers? Or at least to the military investigative unit?"

"I want an outsider to get the answers. I want you, Major."

Major leaned back in his chair and clasped his hands in front of his stomach. He knew deep down if this was a military shooter, like Duncan, then the trail probably had gone cold within minutes after the trigger was pulled. If the orders came from Washington, he'd never find out who was behind it. Like Duncan seeking those responsible for leaving him and Park behind on Sinmi-do in North Korea, Major would also be chasing ghosts.

If it had been orchestrated from within Texas, his opportunities to find a trail of bread crumbs was somewhat better, but the digital footprints that typically remained no longer existed since the collapse. An investigation like this would take good old-fashioned detective work via interviews, chasing leads, and thousands of man-hours. Hours he was not prepared to take away from the ranch and his family.

"Marion, I completely understand where you're coming from, and I don't blame you if a little bit of paranoia has crept in. And please, I don't use the word *paranoia* in a derogatory sense. Your vice president was just assassinated; it's logical for every president to wonder if they're in somebody's crosshairs."

"Then you'll help me?"

Major hesitated before answering. He needed to talk with Lucy and his family. He also needed to get Duncan's thoughts.

"Major?" she asked, her voice hopeful.

"Marion, I have a lot of things to consider, especially the time factor involved. You know how these things go. We don't have the benefits of computers and the internet and manpower. With what's going on in West Texas, I can't leave the ranch unattended."

"What if I provide you full-time military protection for you and the ranch? I'll let you handpick your investigative team. You can work outside of government constraints, but with full authority to do whatever it takes to find the people behind Monty's death. I'll pay you in gold!"

Major started laughing but immediately stifled his outburst when he saw that the president was serious. "Marion, here's what I'll do. You know I have to discuss this with Lucy and my family. I'll do that tonight. In addition, I will attend the vice president's burial tomorrow and interview those people who were on the ranch at the time. If you will clear my presence with the proper security personnel, I'd appreciate it."

"That's great, Major. I'll take it. Listen, there's one more thing. Monty's friends in the armed forces will be present too. See if you can strike up a conversation with them to gauge their attitude. I'm meeting with them soon to discuss where we go from here."

"I will, Marion. Listen, you have to solidify your relationships with the military. No nation is secure without an army to defend it."

Chapter 20

January 18
Lake J. B. Thomas
The Armstrong Ranch
Borden County, Texas

"Life in my village was not terrible," began Sook as she and Palmer started day two of their perimeter patrols along the east side of the Armstrong Ranch. Before they left the barn that morning, Palmer suggested they extend their perimeter and ride past the gun range toward Lake J. B. Thomas. Palmer had intended to show Sook the lake the day they went hog-hunting, but the intruders at the ranch had required their attention.

Sook continued. "There are so many different ways to fish in Korea. Near Sinmi-do, along the mountains, you can stand above the water and see thousands of white buoys. The buoys mark formations of shellfish farms. If you take your boat out a little farther, sand bars have formed where you can pull out an octopus with your hook."

Palmer listened with interest as she pointed toward a path that circumvented the thick underbrush in the woods and wound its way downhill toward the water.

"Just a mile from my village, toward China, the water was very shallow, and during the low tide, I would dig up short-neck clams. As a young girl, I would carry so many buckets from the beach to my mother. That night, she would make us *doenjang-jjigae*, a soybean stew made with the clams, mushrooms, and vegetables. We ate this often."

Sook dropped her head and became emotional at the thought of her younger days with her parents. Palmer was amazed at how well Sook kept her feelings bottled up when it came to her family. It was an unspoken understanding between the two of them that her entire family was most likely killed by American nuclear bombs.

Palmer gave her a moment to regain her composure then changed the subject to Lake J. B. Thomas, which was coming into view as the trail widened. Once they reached the banks, Palmer dismounted and tied her horse off to a fallen tree. Sook did the same, and the two girls walked to the edge of the bank where they could see up and down the muddy lake.

Palmer pointed to the left. "The muddiest part of the lake is on our property where Wildcat Creek dumps into the Colorado River. When the heavy rains come, the water rushes through the gullies, picking up mud and dirt until it reaches the lake."

"Gullies? Like the birds?" asked Sook.

Palmer laughed. "No. The birds are called gulls or seagulls. We don't have those here, but we do on the Texas beaches. Gullies are small canyons or big ditches."

Palmer led Sook by the arm closer to the water and pointed to the ravine where Wildcat Creek was located.

"I see," said Sook.

"When Pops was alive, he would call the heavy rains *gully-washers*. A heavy rain washed the gullies."

Sook burst out laughing. Apparently, she thought the concept was funny or the combination of words to create *gully-washers*. Either way, it helped her forget about the loss of her family.

"What kind of fish live in this muddy water?" she asked.

"Mainly largemouth bass," replied Palmer. "We have been in a drought for several years, and the water keeps getting filled with silt and mud. To our right, the water is deeper and the fishing is better. To maintain the fish population, Texas Parks and Wildlife restocks the lake every few years with fingerlings."

"Baby bass?" asked Sook.

Palmer laughed. "Yes, baby bass. Do you see those plants?" Palmer pointed down the banks toward a colony of cattails.

"Yes, they are interesting. What do you call them?"

"Cattails."

"Why do they call them cattails?"

Palmer laughed. She loved Sook. "It's complicated. You know, people use them as part of the flower arrangements for weddings. We have to plan a wedding for you."

"Can we get married in a church?" asked Sook.

"We'll have to see, Sook," replied Palmer. "It might be too dangerous for us to leave the ranch for—"

"Arrrggghhh!"

Before Palmer could answer, she and Sook were tackled from behind and thrown down the embankment towards the water's edge.

Chapter 21

January 18
Lake J. B. Thomas
The Armstrong Ranch
Borden County, Texas

The force of the much heavier man knocked Sook headfirst down the muddy banks, where she landed on her chest and slid toward the edge of the water. To her right, Palmer was rolling down in a tangled mass of bodies as the man who crashed into her also lost his footing and fell down the hill.

Sook struggled to gain her footing in the muck. She quickly looked around and counted three men. One was struggling with Palmer, the other was standing with his hands on his hips at the top of the bank, and the third was making his way toward her.

She debated whether to help Palmer or defend herself. The man lunging for her forced her into self-preservation mode. She couldn't help Palmer if she was injured or killed by her attacker.

Unable to get to her feet in time, Sook crawled backwards on all fours to create some distance between her and the man who was struggling to walk along the water's edge. In those seconds of the attack, her mind quickly processed and assessed her plight.

The man was clumsy, and despite his size advantage, he was unstable on the bank. Sook moved backwards until she was in a solid position and then waited for the man to make his move.

He bent over and grabbed for her ankles. Sook didn't hesitate. She kicked upward with her right foot, catching her assailant directly under the chin. It threw him off balance, but the weight of his body came down upon her as he lost his balance.

The man groaned from the kick as he clutched his throat. Sook, however, knew the job wasn't finished. With the man's legs splayed open on top of her, she stared into his face, snarled, and yelled out a guttural scream as she brought her left knee towards her chest and crushed it into his groin.

The man's face responded to the vicious knee kick. His eyes got wide, his mouth formed an O, and he quickly forgot about the pain in his throat.

Bull's-eye, Sook thought to herself.

She rolled the man off her, and he tumbled into the murky waters of the lake. Sook scrambled to her feet and rushed to Palmer's aid, who was clawing at her attacker's face. He tried to climb on top of her and pin her down. Palmer fought back. Clawing, writhing in the mud, and screaming at the man caused him to anger and lose his composure.

Just as he was drawing back to punch Palmer in the face, Sook jumped into the air and kicked him in the side with both feet. The sounds of breaking ribs could be heard, and the whoosh of air being blasted out of his lungs startled Palmer. Momentarily, she looked at Sook in shock until her attention was drawn up the bank.

"Sook, he's stealing your horse!" Palmer rolled the man with the cracked ribs off her legs with a couple more boot kicks to the back. She scrambled to her feet and helped Sook get up.

"Are you okay?" asked Sook.

"Yeah, but your horse," replied an out-of-breath Palmer, who was winded from the struggle.

"Catch him, Palmer! Go!"

Palmer started up the hill to retrieve her horse. "Sook, guard them with your pistol. Be careful!" Palmer was on her horse in a flash and began the chase through the wooded trails.

Sook reached for her gun and found her holster to be empty. She looked frantically on the ground, continuously patting her jeans and empty holster. Sook turned to where she'd wrestled the man off her, and she saw the H&K that had been given to her by Lucy.

At the same time, her first attacker saw it as well. They both scrambled up the embankment, trying to reach the gun. Her hands and nails became bloodied as she clawed her way up the rocky bank; then she lunged to grab the gun. Still lying prone on the ground, she swung the weapon around to shoot her attacker, but he knocked it out of her hand and farther up the hill.

He was much stronger than her, and now he was furious that she'd gotten the better of him earlier.

"My turn, gook!" he screamed as he tried to pin her down. He was using his weight to hold her against the rocky surface, which caused stones to stick into Sook's back.

"Nooo!" she screamed as she tried to push him off, but the man had gained control of the fight.

"Well, lookie here," he growled with a toothless grin as he stared at Sook's engagement ring. "Are you gonna be some kind of war bride? Them sure are purdy diamonds. Almost as purdy as you."

Sook continued to struggle under his grasp, but he had her pinned.

"Get off!" she shouted in his face, which resulted in him spitting on her.

"Shut up and give me that ring!" he shouted in return.

He slid his hand up from her left wrist towards her hand in an attempt to slide the ring off her finger. Sook tried to wiggle loose, but he tightened his grip on her by squeezing his thighs together.

Growing impatient, he loosened his grip on her other wrist, which gave Sook the opening she was looking for. Using the palm of her hand, she thrust her arm upwards and caught the man under the chin again. The blow wasn't powerful enough to knock him off, but it did throw him off balance. Her second punch was more forceful, this time directly to his throat.

He loosened his grip and began to roll off her. Sook didn't stop with her counterassault. In fact, she didn't stop until it was over.

Enraged, she used all of her taekwondo training to brutally kick the man in all of the human body's most vulnerable striking points. She stood and kicked him in the groin, which doubled him over. Without hesitating, she struck him in the solar plexus, that area just below the rib cage that contains the diaphragm. The man began to gasp for air.

Sook was blinded by her rage. She kicked at his Adam's apple twice and then bloodied his nose. The man was raising his arm, a gesture of surrender and an attempt to save his life from Sook's lethal kicks.

As he rose to his knees, she growled and approached him. Her last kick was lethal. With all of the force of her training coupled with rage, she kicked him in the center of his chest. It caused the man to flip backwards down the embankment until his upper body landed facedown in the muddy water.

Sook didn't need to check his pulse. She knew the blow to his heart was too much for his weakened system to endure. He was dead.

Sook turned to her attention to the man with the broken ribs. He'd attempted to crawl away, making it to the cattails before passing out. He wasn't dead, but he was certainly incapacitated. Sook retrieved her weapon and slowly approached his body. He was unconscious but breathing. She checked his clothing for a weapon and found nothing.

For a moment, she sat on the bank and stared at his body, periodically glancing at the dead man to check for a miracle resuscitation. Just as she caught her breath, Sook heard gunshots in the distance.

"Palmer!" she hollered as she scrambled up the hill towards the woods. "Palmer!"

Sook couldn't discern which direction the shots had come from, so she held her position. Frustrated that she was unable to help, she began to pace back and forth until she heard the sound of something heavy moving through the woods toward her.

Sook readied her weapon and crouched behind a pine tree. Her hands shook as she raised the pistol, not out of nervousness, but pain from being beaten against the rocky surface.

"Sook? Are you okay?" said Palmer as she entered the clearing with both horses.

"Yes!" she shouted her reply and ran towards her future sister-in-law. "Are you?"

Palmer smiled and nodded before dismounting. They tied off the horses and stood on the bank, staring at the two men.

"Are they dead?" asked Palmer.

Sook pointed to the right. "Him, no. Unconscious. Broken ribs."

"I'm pretty sure I know what the answer is on this one," said Palmer as she took a step closer to the dead man, who lay facedown in the lake. "Did you shoot him?"

Before Sook could answer, she broke down crying. In between sobs, she shook her head back and forth.

"Sook, don't worry," said Palmer. "I had to shoot my guy. I tried to warn him to stop, but he kept riding, and I was worried for you. So I just shot him to get the chase over with. Listen, it won't be the last time we have to kill people. It's the way it is now."

Sook took a deep breath and calmed herself down. "It is not his death that bothers me, Palmer. I didn't shoot him. That would have been easier for me. I violated my oath from taekwondo. I misused my skills out of anger. I lost my self-control because he wanted to take my ring. I dishonored myself by doing so."

Palmer hugged Sook and whispered in her ear, "It was self-defense. You had to protect yourself."

Sook pulled back, still adamant that she'd failed the tenets of the ancient martial art. "The battle was won. I didn't need to finish the fight. I needed to finish him." She pointed at the dead man.

"Come here," said Palmer as she led Sook to the fallen pine near the horses. They sat down and stared across the lake. From this vantage point, the bodies were below the edge of the bank and unseen. Palmer continued. "You are part of our family now, so I have to explain the code I have with Cooper and Riley."

"A code?" asked Sook.

"Yes. We traveled on the road a lot to attend rodeos all over the country. Sometimes, we'd get hurt while performing, and sometimes, especially with Riley, we'd get into fights."

Sook chuckled. "Riley is a fighter."

Palmer laughed with her. "Momma says that Riley began fighting in her belly months before he was born. She said he came out punchin', kickin' and screamin', which scared the nurses at the hospital."

"I believe this," said Sook with a chuckle.

"Here's the thing, Sook. We vowed to shield our parents from the trouble we got into because we didn't want to worry them. If something terrible happened, of course we'd tell 'em. But otherwise, we said what happened on the road stayed on the road. Understand?"

"Yes, the secrets stay between us," replied Sook as she looked down at the holes in her jeans and her bloodied hands. She wiped the blood off on her jeans and tried to pull the frayed edges of the pants together. "I had a nasty fall off my horse, but I'm okay."

Palmer began to laugh. "Yeah, exactly. A hog came out of the woods and startled our horses, which threw us both to the ground."

"Stupid hogs," said Sook, who had replaced her tears of humiliation with tears of laughter.

"Stupid hogs," repeated Palmer as she gave her sister a hug.

Chapter 22

**January 18
The Armstrong Ranch
Borden County, Texas**

It had been an eventful day for the Armstrongs, but the dinnertime conversation had been dominated by Major as he recounted his trip into Austin. Duncan had returned for the evening from Camp Lubbock with Espy in tow. After dinner, Major suggested Palmer show Espy around the ranch after they unloaded the weapons and ammunition procured by Duncan the day before. Espy had earned a level of trust within the Armstrong family and was now considered within their inner circle except for the conversation Major was about to have with Lucy and the kids.

With the table cleared and the dishes washed, Lucy fixed up a platter of oatmeal cookies and led everyone into the living room.

"I get the feeling we're about to have a family discussion," quipped Riley as he grabbed a handful of cookies from the platter. The fistful was quickly dropped when his mother smacked the top of his hand.

"Son, there's five more of us who'd like to have some of those," she admonished the man-child.

"Riley can have mine, Miss Lucy," volunteered Sook. With Palmer's help, Sook had covered some of the scratches on her chin with makeup, and she was sure to wear an oversized sweatshirt to help hide her battered arms. Lucy studied Sook once again. Palmer had warned Sook on the way back to the ranch that afternoon that it wasn't likely her mother would believe their story. *Just stick to it*, Palmer had instructed.

"Duncan, let me say again how glad I am that you could make it back to the ranch tonight," started Major. "We understand fully that your presence will be required in Lubbock, but I have something to discuss with all of you, and it requires a group consensus."

"What is it, Dad?" asked Duncan.

"Marion has asked me to investigate the murder of Vice President Gregg," replied Major.

Duncan continued. "Isn't this a matter for the Rangers, Dad, or the Texas military? I mean, they have an investigative arm too."

"You're right on both counts, son. It's highly unusual for any government to seek an outsider to investigate something of this nature, but these are unusual times. And, frankly, Marion is rightfully concerned that this might be an inside job."

"One of our own?" asked Lucy.

"It's possible," replied Major. "The fact is, many Texans were not one hundred percent on board with the decision to secede. Some may have chosen to disrupt Marion's administration by taking out her right arm, especially one with close ties to the military."

"The shooter was a pro, Dad," interjected Duncan. "Could've been military. There are guys at Bliss or Hood who could've pulled off that shot. That said, there are a whole lot more at Langley or at the DTRA in Fort Belvoir who could've done it too."

"Marion has asked me on a personal level to take an interest and help her," continued Major.

"Dad, honestly, you're not gonna find the shooter," said Duncan. "He's long gone."

"I know, son. But I might be able to determine who ordered Gregg's assassination."

Lucy leaned forward and spoke up. "What would all of this entail?"

"More than I'm willing to do," replied Major. "Without the use of the internet and access to databases, and slowed by limited communications, we're talking about hours upon hours of investigative legwork that I'm not willing to provide."

"Old school," said Cooper. "Daddy, what would you get out of it?

I mean, we don't really need the money, do we?"

"Nah, not really, son. I could probably write my own meal ticket. Marion has offered security for the ranch while I'm away, but you know how that goes. If something more important comes along, they'll pull the detail."

"Dad's right," said Duncan. "Promises made and promises kept are two different things."

Major nodded and continued. "Then there's the whole civic duty thing. When your president asks for something, especially a heartfelt favor out of fear for her own life, it's hard to say no."

The room grew silent as Major's words were processed. This was the best argument yet for his agreeing to the task.

Lucy broke the silence. "What is the next step, and when does she need an answer?"

Major squeezed her hand as he detected the concerned tone in her voice. "I made no commitments on time frame. I did agree to attend Gregg's burial at his ranch tomorrow outside San Angelo. I'll meet with his widow, talk to his security detail, and get a feel for how the shooting went down."

"Then you'll come home, and we'll discuss it?" asked Lucy.

"Yes. We'll sit down and make a decision then."

CHAPTER 23

January 19
The Armstrong Ranch
Borden County, Texas

"Where are my muscular, strong, well-built handsome young men?" asked Lucy in a raised voice as she walked through the bottom floor of the ranch house. She knew Cooper and Riley were downstairs hiding from her. She was walking down the hallway toward the bedroom when she caught a glimpse of two shadows moving quickly behind her toward the kitchen. They were trying to escape through the back door.

The sprawling home, as was typical of West Texas ranch houses, had grown through one addition after another. As families expanded with more children or the elderly returned to be cared for, living spaces with outside entrances were added on to a home's footprint.

Lucy suspected they were making a dash for the rear exit of the kitchen, so she picked up the pace. She reached the hallway exit at the side of the house and was waiting for Cooper and Riley as they backed slowly out of the house.

Cooper pulled the door shut and gently released the doorknob. Lucy could see a false sense of relief come over them as they exhaled. Just as they turned and gave each other a high five, she stood in front of them with a shovel in each hand.

"Perfect, gentlemen. How did you know this was where we were gonna start from?"

"What?" they said in unison.

Riley took the lead, as he wasn't as smart as Cooper when it came to holding his tongue. "C'mon, Momma. Diggin'? What in the world do we have to dig for?"

She walked forward and presented the boys with their shovels. "We've got a busy day, so you best stop your whinin'. We're gonna head down toward the shootin' range, near Wildcat Creek, and dig some more survival caches. Duncan is concerned that these herds of refugees might potentially overrun the ranch, and he doesn't like us keeping all of our eggs in one basket. I agree, so today, we dig."

"Momma," started Riley, risking a playful beating, "if this was Duncan's idea, why ain't he out here diggin' with us?"

"Because he needs to spend some time with his fiancée before he returns to Lubbock this morning. When you have a fiancée someday, we'll cut you some slack once in a while."

"Great," said Riley in a huff. "Just where am I supposed to find a girlfriend? I knew I should have thrown one of those buckle bunnies on the back of my horse when we left Calgary."

Cooper started laughing. "Well, you could always marry Red Rover. The way you dote over that truck, you'd think you two were madly in love!"

Riley playfully raised his shovel like it was a baseball bat and threatened to swat his brother with it.

"Enough of that, boys. Time's a-wastin'. Grab one of the feed trucks and meet me back here at the storehouse. I'll show you what I have planned for the day."

"Can I bring Red Rover instead?" asked Riley hopefully.

"Sure, that'll work," replied Lucy.

Cooper hugged his brother around the neck. "Are you sure? She'll get dirty."

"Red Rover is not a she, Coop!"

"Could've fooled me, little brother. I mean, y'all are sweet on each other and all."

"Dang it, Coop!" yelled Riley as he chased his brother around the front of the house with his shovel.

Lucy chuckled, shook her head, and walked toward the storehouse, which had been built years ago to keep excess food and supplies.

She reached the solid wooden door and unlocked the old cast-iron padlock. A rush of cool, dusty air hit her in the face as she stepped inside. She immediately walked down three creaky wooden steps until she was a few feet below the grade of the backyard. The temperature difference could be felt immediately.

Lucy fumbled for the light switch and flipped it on. Several lightbulbs suspended from the ceiling by electrical cords illuminated the space. After speaking with Duncan, she took the additional handguns they'd kept locked in their safe and brought them to the storehouse. She also added backup magazines and ammo to the pile.

As the diesel motor of Red Rover approached, Lucy walked to the corner of the building and slid out a stack of dirt-brown-colored five-gallon buckets. Then she found a cardboard box full of gamma-seal lids. Once affixed atop the five-gallon buckets, the gamma lids provided an airtight, leakproof seal to protect the contents. Unlike a regular lid, which must be pried off, the gamma seal lid had a spoked, removable lid in the middle, which could easily be removed by spinning it open. When in a hurry, they could easily grab the bucket by the handle, open it quickly by spinning open the watertight top, and expose the contents needed for survival.

"Okay, Momma, where do we start?" asked Cooper as his shadow filled the doorway. Riley was behind him, peering over Cooper's shoulder.

"C'mon down, boys, and we'll get started," said Lucy.

As she shuffled around the storehouse, gathering the items for the cache buckets, she told the boys about the history of the concept.

"When I point something out to you, place one in each of the buckets," she started. "We're gonna make a total of eight, for now, and hide them on the east side of the ranch, just in case."

"Just in case of what, Momma?" asked Riley.

"In case we're overrun," she replied. "It's just one more protective measure to take, which I learned about as I studied prepping. Back during World War Two, the French freedom fighters and resistance used them to battle the Nazi forces. America and the British supplied them with food, medical supplies, and weapons because France was antigun even back then. Only the farmers had shotguns for hunting, but the rest of the civilian population did not."

Lucy handed them the sidearms, the corresponding ammunition, and magazines. Their assembly line was started. She moved to the premade medical kits, which contained basic first aid and trauma kits.

Lucy explained further. "The North Vietnamese incorporated the concept of caches into their warfare tactics with American forces. They'd hide in the jungles, fire upon our patrols, and then hide their weapons in caches as they ran away. When our troops caught up to them, they'd shrug their shoulders and show they were unarmed. Duncan told me the Taliban and ISIS fighters did the same thing. The Americans could never determine who was a friend or a foe."

"This is different though," said Cooper. "We're adding food, these LifeStraws, batteries, and first aid kits."

"Yeah, even matches, lighters, and candles," added Riley. "Will it all fit?"

"I hope so," replied Lucy. "I'm trying to think of everything we'd need in an emergency to last us at least three to five days."

"Are you saying I'd have to eat these things for three or four days?" asked Riley, who held up an aluminum-foil package of emergency food bars. "What is this anyway?"

"There are nine high-calorie nutrition bars in there, Riley," Lucy answered. "Thirty-six hundred calories a day for three days. There'll be enough for one person for six days in each bucket."

"Ugh," groaned Riley. "I like that option better." He was pointing toward jars of peanut butter and Ritz crackers. There were also honey bears stacked like the Chinese terracotta army next to the crackers.

"Yes, one each of those, too, please," Lucy instructed. "All of those have pretty long shelf lives and can be stored in the airtight container. We'll add these to each bucket to help eliminate moisture and humidity." She picked up a ziplock baggy full of desiccant packs and showed it to the boys.

"Finally, we need to add some basic tools. Each cache will contain a flashlight, a knife, a Leatherman tool, a folding handsaw, and a hatchet. Throw in a bundle of 550 paracord and a small tarp and it should be pretty full."

"What about this?" asked Riley, holding up a roll of toilet paper.

Lucy giggled. "Absolute necessity."

"Yeah, Riley, no bug sprayer or cactus for me," added Cooper.

They finished assembling the caches by adding several more items—which focused on shelter, water, food, and defense—and loaded up Red Rover for the trek down into the canyon.

Riley enjoyed this part of the day the most because he got to take his new toy off-roading. Growing up in Texas, the boys had been buddies with guys who loved their trucks and would spend their free time looking for challenging terrain to drive them on. They'd never caught the off-roading bug, opting instead to put their horses to the test. Now that Riley had Red Rover, he was enjoying the trail from a different perspective.

"It's a little rough, but your truck does a great job on this terrain, Riley," said Lucy as she bounced back and forth on the bench seat between two of her sons. "I'm guessin' the ride back from Montana wasn't this rough, was it?"

"No, Momma," replied Cooper. "It was a different kind of rough."

They rode silently until they reached a stand of scrub oaks. Lucy pointed the native trees out. "Let's put the first one here."

They exited the truck, and Riley pulled open the tailgate. Lucy held up one finger, so the first bucket was pulled out. She had a spiral notebook and pencil, plus a tape measure she handed to Cooper.

Lucy explained her thought process. "We don't necessarily need to bury the buckets, but it will help to conceal them with rocks and dirt. We just need to hide it from anyone else who might use this path, whether to or from the house."

"We need to pick a spot we can remember and memorize, right?" asked Cooper.

"Exactly, which is why I picked this location," replied Lucy. She began to point out the landmarks that caught her eye. "There's the corner of our fence as it heads toward the river. And you see this oak?"

"Yeah, it looks like Preacher standing with his legs together, spreading his arms to the sky and talking to God," said Riley laughingly.

"It stands out, doesn't it?" asked Lucy.

"It sure does," replied Cooper. "Plus, there are all kinds of rock outcroppings and mounds of dirt to work with. So what's next?"

Lucy led the boys toward the oak tree and visually identified a straight line between the base of the tree and the corner fence post.

"Boys, using this tape measure, find the halfway point between this tree and the fence corner. Then stand there."

The guys took the fifty-foot tape and systematically measured the distance between the two landmarks. When they agreed upon a center point, Lucy called out to them.

"Okay! How many feet between the two spots?" She readied her pencil to write down the numbers. She'd already sketched out the landmarks.

"Right at a hundred feet!" Riley shouted back.

Lucy began to walk it off although she knew what she intended to write down for the distance.

With her last step, she made a mental note of the number.

"Now, boys, I want each of you to walk in opposite directions and count your paces each way. Don't take big, long man-size strides, either. Walk casually as if you were strolling down the sidewalk with a young lady on your arm."

Her sons took off in each direction, and Lucy laughed as she watched them struggle to maintain an equal stride. It was impossible to do, which was why she always marveled at the police relying upon walking as a field sobriety test. She couldn't walk a straight line, heel to toe, if her life depended on it.

Within a couple of minutes, the boys returned with their answers.

"Coop, you first," said Lucy.

"Sixteen up and seventeen back."

Lucy didn't write it down.

"Riley?" she asked.

Riley, who appeared puzzled, hesitated to answer.

Lucy tapped her pencil on the notebook. She finally tilted her head and looked at him.

"Um, eighteen and eighteen?" he responded in an inquisitive tone.

Lucy closed her eyes and shook her head. "Is that what you really got?"

"No, ma'am," he replied sheepishly. "I got the same as Coop, sort of. Both of mine were sixteen."

Cooper started laughing. "Well, then why did you say eighteen?"

Riley shot back. "Momma didn't write your steps down, so I figured you got it wrong, so I guessed eighteen instead."

"Good grief, dumb—" Cooper was about to berate his brother when Lucy stepped in.

"Look here, you two, the correct answer is twenty paces, and here's why. The average person's stride, or pace, is thirty inches. Fifty feet is six hundred inches. Six hundred divided by thirty is twenty. Twenty paces."

Lucy presented them her drawing so they could see. The cache map located the fence corner and a few of the posts in each direction. She drew a circle to represent the oak tree and then marked an X equidistant between the two. She wrote *20 paces* to represent the length from the oak to the hidden cache.

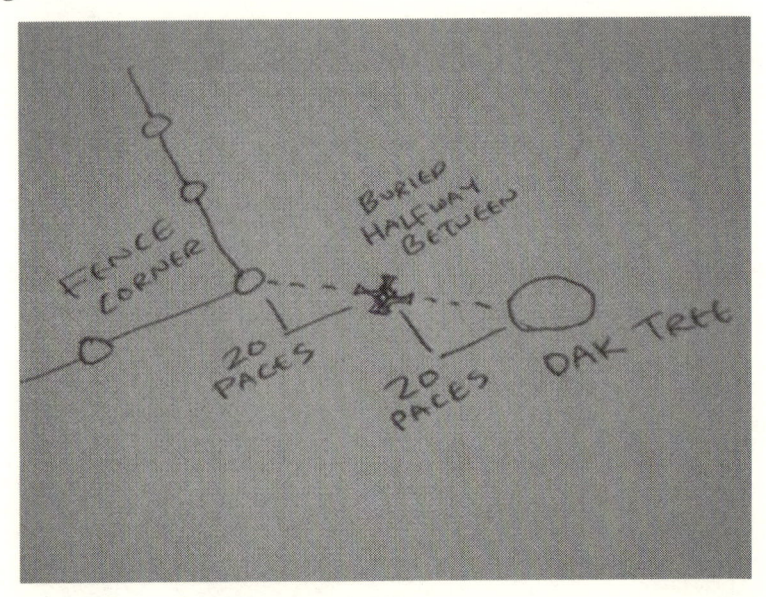

"How the heck am I supposed to figure that out in my head?" lamented Riley.

"Well, maybe you could take up bull ridin' like me. A couple of kicks to the head and you'd be able to do simple math too."

The boys continued to bicker with one another as Lucy walked away, wondering if she shouldn't have picked Sook and Palmer for this job.

Chapter 24

January 19
Lamesa, Texas

Duncan and his team at the TX-QRF were much better prepared for today's call than the proverbial Chinese fire drill, which accurately described their initial response to the crisis in Seminole the other day. Ordinarily, a newly formed unit like the one in Camp Lubbock would have extensive training sessions, advanced planning, and dry runs before being deployed to respond to a situation. Despite their initial confusion, his team had come together and done a stellar job in rounding up the refugees in Seminole without loss of life to any of the locals.

Duncan took the interim day to debrief his men and discuss ways to improve upon their response. A full day with his lieutenants and Espy helped them hone their response skills so when the emergency call came from the Lamesa Police Department, the team was assembled and geared up within thirty minutes. Now they were racing down the highway for the sixty-mile drive to the town with a population of just under ten thousand, not counting the hundreds of refugees who had begun to appear overnight.

Lamesa was a little over sixty miles from the Hobbs border checkpoint and forty miles due east of Seminole. A pack of several hundred refugees must've circumvented Seminole and come back together on Highway 180, which ran into Lamesa and then farther east to Gail, which was a little too close to home for Duncan's comfort.

He'd become concerned about the travel patterns of the refugees. After interviewing border patrol agents and compiling the notes taken from conversations with refugees, the adjutant general's office had come up with a figure of sixteen to seventeen thousand refugees who'd entered Texas illegally.

This posed problems on many levels, including what to do with the refugees when captured. Austin was still wrestling with housing the illegal aliens temporarily until a suitable means of deportation could be determined. Complicating the matter was Washington's refusal to take them back despite the fact they were American citizens.

It was a game of political chess that didn't interest Duncan. He had a job to do, and that was to round up the refugees and deliver them to the nearest state prison facility per instructions from his superiors at Fort Hood. Yesterday, the refugees taken into custody at Seminole had been transported to the Preston E. Smith Prison Unit a mile east of Lamesa. At least today Duncan could accomplish same-day delivery.

"Where's the rally point?" asked Duncan as Espy neared the outskirts of town.

"Middle of town," replied Espy. "Both the Lamesa PD and the Dawson County Sheriff's Office are within a couple of blocks of each other. They've asked us to meet them at the Dawson County Courthouse."

"Gee, Espy, why do we need to get bogged down in the middle of the town?" asked Duncan. "This place is five or six times bigger than Seminole."

"From what I gather, the county judge wanted to provide a show of force. You know, to make an impression."

In Texas, the county judge acted as the head of the court system as well as the chief administrator of the county. They acted as the liaison between their county and Austin, as well as coordinated economic development, financial expenditures, and infrastructure management.

"Let me guess, he's impressing his constituents for votes. Don't these people rest?" said Duncan dryly, showing his contempt for politicians and their grandstanding.

"I guess not," said Espy as he maneuvered through a barricade manned by local police officers. They didn't bother to stop Duncan's convoy.

"Listen, I know this isn't Mosul, but I don't like our people pinned down with limited maneuverability. Next time, let's identify a rally position on the outside of town, not one that makes the county judge's star shine more brightly."

"Yessir," said Espy as he slowly drove around the county courthouse to allow the rest of the vehicles to enter.

"C'mon, Espy. Are we part of a dang parade?"

Espy shot him a glance and scowled. Duncan smiled. He suspected Espy had heard enough of his squallin'.

Lining First Street, Austin Avenue, and Main Avenue, which encircled the courthouse, were hundreds of locals waving miniature Texas flags. The scene was reminiscent of the reception Patton's 2nd Armored Division received when it entered the small town of Palermo on the island of Sicily in the summer of 1943. Families of all ages waved American flags as Patton arrived victorious into the Sicilian capital. Hours later, the armored forces of British General Sir Bernard Montgomery, Patton's rival, entered Palermo, seeking accolades for freeing the region from the Nazis. The townspeople quickly changed their allegiance and began to wave the UK's Union Jack.

Duncan watched in amazement as a group of local officials poured out of the courthouse to greet him. One man in particular stood out as he grinned from ear to ear and proudly held his western-style gun belt sporting two pearl-handled revolvers.

"Espy, wait here," said Duncan. "We won't be long."

Duncan jumped out of the Humvee and strutted up the sidewalk to meet the entourage.

"Welcome, young man. I am County Judge David Foy, and it is my pleasure to welcome you to our little corner of the world, Lamesa, Texas."

The man extended his hand to shake, and Duncan did so briefly. His annoyance with the whole situation was building inside him. As they stood in the open, his eyes darted to the rooftops around the perimeter of the courthouse. He had no reason to believe that snipers would be present, but his instincts prevented him from letting his guard down.

"Who's in charge here?" asked Duncan brusquely.

"Well, son, I am. I'm the county judge," replied Foy.

"No, I'm referring to law enforcement. Where's the chief of police or your sheriff? I understand there's a hostage situation that needs to be dealt with."

"Well, um," Foy began to stammer, "they're at the middle school about seven blocks from here."

Duncan exhaled and looked around for a uniformed police officer. Standing several paces behind the county judge and his group were two deputies. He pushed past Foy, leaving the man standing with his mouth open.

"Deputy, has your sheriff established a perimeter around the school and set up a command post?"

"Yes, sir. It's about seven blocks west of here. I can lead you down there."

"Thank you," replied Duncan. "I need to unwind this snake of a convoy, which is stuck around your courthouse. Point me in the right direction."

The deputy looked at the number of vehicles in Duncan's convoy and then provided him directions to get back onto Second Street. He said he'd retrieve his patrol car and lead the convoy to the school.

Duncan began to trot back toward his Humvee when the county judge yelled after him, "After you round up these interlopers, you're welcome to come back here for refreshments and a ceremony!"

Duncan shook his head as he reached the truck and mumbled to himself, "Idiot."

After several minutes of maneuvering the vehicles and displacing the growing crowd of revelers, the TX-QRF arrived across from Lamesa Middle School. He ordered his men to position themselves across from the front entrance of the school and await further orders. Then he sought out the sheriff.

The deputy who led them to the parking lot across from the school pointed him in the direction of a small concrete building with a sign painted across the top, which read LMS Shop. The outbuilding was used to teach kids when school was in session, but today acted as the command center for local law enforcement.

Duncan entered the building and was greeted with a flurry of activity. Spread out across several folding tables were schematics of the middle school complex. Several sheriff's deputies were dressed in SWAT gear, including body armor and fully automatic weapons. Duncan was somewhat taken aback by the appearance of the deputies. After all, this wasn't a big city like Chicago, which would become a war zone during the apocalypse.

He was greeted by an older man with a hearty handshake and a smile. "My name is Sheriff Dawson, just like the county. My family settled these parts in the 1830s following the Texas Revolution."

"Sheriff Dawson, I'm Commander Duncan Armstrong with the Texas Quick Reaction Force. Thank you for calling—"

"Wait, did you say Duncan Armstrong, as in Major Duncan Armstrong?"

"Yes, sir, he's my father."

"Well, I'll be, son. Our families go way back. My dad and your grandfather, I guess, were old poker-playing buddies. They'd bet everything from gold to cattle to land. It's a real pleasure to meet you. How's your dad?"

Duncan smiled and enjoyed the conversation with Sheriff Dawson. They exchanged information on how the Armstrongs and the Dawsons were faring considering the recent events. Unlike the county judge Duncan had just met, Sheriff Dawson had his head screwed on straight and his feet on the ground.

"What's the situation inside, Sheriff?" asked Duncan.

"After they stopped teaching school a week or so ago, they turned the middle school into a refugee center. But it's a refugee center designed for our people, not those folks who busted through the fences. A lot of our residents inside are poor or infirm. They ran out of food early on, and the local churches stepped up to help them. As gasoline shortages began, the local meals-on-wheels program got shut down, and we had to ask those who needed help to gather in one central location."

Duncan leaned over the table and began to study the drawings. Sheriff Dawson's men politely stepped away to give Duncan plenty of room.

The sheriff continued. "Just after dark yesterday, the first wave of illegals began to enter the west part of town. At first, they were calm and respectful as they went door-to-door looking for food and shelter. However, as the night went on, they were turned away time and again. Their attitudes turned belligerent and the trouble began. Homes and garages were broken into. Local stores were looted, and a group of nearly a hundred descended upon the middle school because they were told it was a refugee center."

"Which it is," added Duncan.

"Yes, but for our people, not theirs."

Duncan nodded out of understanding, but not necessarily out of approval. He was still having difficulty accepting that Americans were the enemy.

"Sheriff, are they armed?"

"We don't know for certain. One of the church helpers escaped as things turned ugly inside, and told my deputies that they had hammers, baseball bats, and anything else you can imagine to beat someone with. So far, we have no evidence of that happening, but it could at any time."

"Have you attempted to make contact with them?"

"Not yet. We were waiting for you."

Duncan turned his attention back to the drawings.

"Where are they within the school complex?" asked Duncan. He stood to the side so the sheriff could point to the site plan.

"The gymnasium is used for serving meals, and the classrooms are set up as dormitory-style rooms. The administration offices are used for special-needs families and those who are weak but not sick enough to warrant a hospital bed."

Duncan looked up at the sheriff's deputies in their imposing riot gear. He considered his own attire, which looked like he was ready to enter Mosul or another hot spot in the Middle East. This situation didn't call for a show of overwhelming force. If the refugees were spooked, they might turn violent against the mostly defenseless residents in Lamesa.

He'd made a decision. "Sheriff, sometimes the best approach is to lie."

CHAPTER 25

January 19
Lamesa, Texas

"What do you have in mind?" asked the sheriff.

Duncan walked him through the operation. "The first step is to get your deputies out of their intimidating riot gear and into street clothes with concealed-carry weapons at the ready. They will cover all of the exits and be prepared to enter the school at the first signs of trouble.

"Second, I need the keys to the school buses parked at the back of the lot. My men are going to pull them up to the entrance to load the refugees up for resettlement."

"Resettlement where?" asked the sheriff.

"Leave that up to me," said Duncan. Duncan studied a map of the county on the wall and found what he was looking for. He told the sheriff to get his men ready and to be in position within the hour. At this point, the situation hadn't escalated to violence, and there was no sense of urgency to make a move. Duncan wanted to get all the pieces in place before they got under way.

Duncan exited the trailer and located Espy. He laid out the plan, and Espy considered it unconventional, but it might just work. He agreed to accompany Duncan every step of the way.

Before an hour had passed, Duncan received word that the sheriff's men were in place, as were the buses. With the help of a local hardware store, heavy-duty chains and padlocks were placed near the exit to the school.

"Ready?" Duncan asked Espy.

Espy took a deep breath, felt for his sidearm, which was now hidden under his untucked shirt, and nodded.

The timing was perfect, as lunchtime had arrived and it was time to feed the displaced Lamesa residents and the refugees. Since the takeover of the facilities, food had not been prepared in the temporary refugee camp.

Duncan and Espy entered the administrative office, ostensibly to use the public-address system. When they arrived, three men were holding two very frightened ladies from the church hostage. Without outwardly showing his sense of relief, Duncan was pleased to see no firearms were involved. The men, who were most likely the leaders of the illegal aliens occupying the school, were holding baseball bats and a butcher knife. Lethal weapons, to be sure, but not with the ability to kill like a gun.

"Good morning, everybody," announced Duncan cheerfully as he entered the room. He gave no indication that the men were hostile. "I take it that you are our newcomers. Welcome!"

Duncan's odd behavior immediately confused the men. They gave him a puzzled look until one of them decided to get mouthy. He stepped forward and raised his bat in a menacing manner toward Duncan.

Please give me an excuse, Duncan thought to himself.

"Who are you, motherf—" the man began before Duncan cut him off.

He raised both hands and said, "Hold up. There's no need for that salty language in front of these nice ladies from the church. I'm from the government, and I'm here to help."

"Whatchu gonna help, man? We're hungry and nobody's feedin' us. We wanna eat!"

Duncan turned serious. "Well, sir, I had no idea. I was just dispatched from Austin to get things squared away for you folks. I'm with the Texas Department of Refugee Resettlement. My job is to place you in appropriate housing, get you fresh clothes, and, of course, get you fed. You know the old saying, *three hots and a cot*."

"You blowin' smoke, boy? That sounds like prison talk."

Duncan acted apologetic and then let out a chuckle. "Oh, sir. My apologies. Bad choice of words, right?"

"Sure was," said a large man who stood off to the side with a knife. Duncan had already made his threat assessment when he walked into the room. He would be the first to go if things didn't go well.

"Again, my apologies," said Duncan. "Here's how this is gonna work. This facility is designed for folks who are disabled and elderly. Some are sick, and others simply can't take care of themselves. They're here voluntarily and have turned their homes over to the government. That was part of the arrangement for coming here."

"What's that got to do with us?" the mouthy leader asked.

"Well, you folks are able-bodied and capable of contributing to the community," replied Duncan. "Their vacant homes will now become your new homes. Under the Refugee Resettlement Act and the corresponding treaties signed between Texas and the United States, you may remain U.S. citizens or apply for a specially created dual Texas citizenship. If you do so, then you'll be able to receive additional benefits such as weekly stipends, transportation, and larger gasoline rations."

"Man, is this for real?"

"It's for real, my friend, and that's why I'm here. Would you fellas mind helping me get started?"

The leader of the three turned to his comrades, and they both shrugged. Fortunately for Duncan, these useful idiots were a few bricks shy of a load.

"Yeah, man, we'll help," he finally responded. "But me and my buddies want first dibs on housing. I mean, this was all our idea, and we deserve a better cut than them others."

Duncan shrugged. "Doesn't matter to me. Why not? You help me, and I'll help you. That's the way government should work, right?"

"Yeah, right."

Duncan turned his attention to the two ladies who were being held against the wall by their captors. "Do you use the PA system when addressing your refugees?"

"Yes, sir," one of them responded nervously. She nodded toward the mouthy guy. "This gentleman uses it all the time."

"Excellent!" Duncan exclaimed as if he'd just observed a kid pin the tail on the donkey. Playing this role was making him nauseous. He just wanted to kill these ass clowns and call it a day. But then he wouldn't get to see the look on their faces when he showed them their new home. "Sir, would you mind making the announcement to your friends and ask them to assemble near the front foyer of the school. We have buses waiting. Also, please tell them to keep their families together. We wouldn't want their little ones to get separated."

"Okay," said the man. He set his baseball bat on the desk and cued the microphone to speak over the public-address system. "Listen up, this here is Clarence again. I've got some good news. The guy is here from the—what did you call it again?" He moved the microphone closer to Duncan.

Duncan smiled and spoke into the mic. "The Texas Department of Refugee Resettlement."

The man nodded and returned to his task. "Anyway, they're gonna give us homes to live in and some food rations to start. Also, if we wanna become Texas citizens, or even U.S. and Texas citizens, that's okay. Then they'll get us jobs and welfare payments and maybe even a car."

He released the microphone button and looked to Duncan for approval.

Duncan raised his eyebrows and smiled. He encouraged the man to continue. "Keep goin', you're doin' great."

"Anyways, I need everyone to go quickly and quietly to the front of the school. They've got buses waitin' to take us to our new homes and, hey, make sure you keep families together. You don't want to stay locked up here, do you?"

Pleased with himself, he set down the microphone and smiled. "Well, mister, I certainly didn't expect this, but I knew you Texans would eventually do right by us. Let's go."

"After you guys," said Duncan. "I'll let you lead the way."

As they passed by Espy, he stepped back to give them plenty of room. He grinned and winked at Duncan.

Duncan took a moment and whispered to the women, "I need you two to stay calm, okay? Please come with me and find the others who run this facility. Make sure that none of the newcomers stay behind. If you can't identify them with certainty, find me by the front entrance. Got it?"

They both nodded rapidly and headed for the door. Espy gave them a comforting smile and waited for Duncan to join him.

"All right, let's be cool about this," instructed Duncan. "When we get to the foyer, I need you to touch base with our drivers and their partners who'll be guarding these people. Once we're clear of the school, I'll have our team ready along the route to chain the rear emergency exits of the buses closed so nobody can bust out the back. When they see their final destination, things will get ugly."

"Yes, sir, Commander. That was amazing."

"We've got a long way to go before declaring success, Sergeant."

Espy beamed at the reference. It was the first time Duncan had referred to him by his new rank.

Loading the group into the buses went off without a hitch. To expedite the trip, Sheriff Dawson's deputies closed off the streets leading to the east of Lamesa. Duncan wanted to get the four school buses clear of town before the refugees realized he'd pulled the ruse.

As they turned left off Akron Street, Sheriff Dawson's men were waiting to place the chains and lock around the exterior handles of the rear emergency exits. This was the most dangerous part of the operation—the final mile down County Road 19 to the Preston E. Smith Prison, the refugees' new home.

Three meals and a cot, just as promised.

Chapter 26

January 19
Preston E. Smith Prison
Lamesa, Texas

Named for former Texas Governor Preston Smith, the prison outside Lamesa was capable of housing twenty-three hundred inmates plus several hundred more in their expansion cells on a temporary basis. Duncan had not spoken directly with the prison, leaving that task up to Sheriff Dawson to clear it with the local warden, Lester Jackson.

"Commander, I've got about thirty seconds before these people explode," said a frantic lieutenant over the comms.

"There, Espy," said Duncan, pointing toward a tall set of chain-link gates, which opened as they approached. A contingent of prison guards stood in a semicircle as the buses pulled in. By the time they pulled to a stop, there was a full-blown riot on each bus.

Duncan's men slowly backed out the doors with their weapons raised. People were hanging out the buses' windows, flipping off anyone they could make eye contact with, and shouting obscenities at the tops of their lungs.

As Duncan's lieutenants joined his side, several were wiping the sweat off their brows despite the mid-thirties temperatures. While the first part of Duncan's plan had worked, he doubted he'd try to implement it again.

"Who's runnin' this circus act?" bellowed a voice from behind Duncan. He turned to see a very large black man approaching his group.

Standing nearly six feet eight inches tall, the prison warden towered over them as he arrived by their side.

"I'm Commander Duncan Armstrong with the Texas—"

"Yeah, I gathered that," Jackson interrupted. "Do you think you're just gonna drop this mess off on my doorstep? I don't think so."

"Warden Jackson, I'm just following orders from Fort Hood," started Duncan. "Our directive is to round up any refugees and deliver them to local law enforcement or, in the alternative, the nearest state prison."

"Look here, Commander. I know about that so-called directive, but this is my prison. I've got animals at various levels of classification in there. This ain't a hotel for women and children, the poor, or the downtrodden."

Duncan tried to reason with the man. "Warden, my understanding is that the refugees will be moved as soon as Austin and Washington can reach an agreement on logistics for their return to the States. That should happen—"

"Bull crap! I don't know what you people have been smokin', but no government moves that fast. What am I supposed to do with all of them? Put them in general pop? How many ya got, anyway?"

"A little over two hundred," Duncan lied. The actual head count was three hundred eighty-three. He just wanted to wash his hands of the problem and get back to Camp Lubbock. In his mind, his job was done.

The warden chuckled. "Our regular inmate capacity is maxed out at two-two-three-four. We were full up *before* the two buses arrived from Seminole yesterday. I had to move men out of the luxurious G-1 accommodations into the G-3 units. That went over like a ton of bricks. Those inmates were used to living in dorms and working outside the fence with only periodic, unarmed supervision. We had to drag them into the general population kicking and screaming."

He stopped and walked toward the buses. A woman began screaming at him and threw a shoe in his general direction. Another attempted to spit on him from twenty feet away but fell woefully short.

"Warden, I wish had a—" started Duncan before getting interrupted again. He was getting irritated with the warden at this point. While he understood the man's frustration and that he needed an outlet to vent to, Duncan was tired of being the punching bag. Now he knew how Espy had felt earlier.

"I think you need to do another head count, soldier," said the warden rudely. Duncan stepped forward and was about to escalate the war of words when Espy came to the rescue.

"Warden Jackson, would it help if we removed the women and children from the prison? I see that you have a fairly large visitation center over there. If we brought in cots and bed linens, could they be housed separately?"

"I suppose that's an option," he replied. "Normally, this facility runs on four hundred employees, two-thirds of which are non-security. My manpower levels have been cut in half because people stopped showing up for work. If I could segregate the men into the G-level dorms, and the elderly, women and kids into the rec center, as we call it, my manpower problems go away. You gotta understand, I'm taking on a tremendous responsibility here. I can't open up these people to murderers, rapists, and violent criminals. I could never sleep at night if something gawd-awful happened."

Espy had effectively gotten to the crux of the matter. The warden was genuinely afraid for the safety of the refugees and didn't want something to happen while on his watch.

"Warden Jackson, let me tell you what I can do," started Duncan. "If you can handle separating the refugees as just proposed, I'll get beds, bedding, clothing, and especially more food for the refugees and your inmates. Also, I will make it abundantly clear to Fort Hood that you can't take on a single new refugee until they move these others out. I just need one favor in return."

"What's that?" he asked.

"There are three troublemakers—the ringleaders. They terrorized two old ladies for hours while they led the takeover of the middle school. They belong with the worst of your worst. Can you make that happen?"

"You bet, commander. Point 'em out and we'll introduce them to their dee-luxe penthouse. The boys will be thrilled to get some fresh meat."

Duncan patted Espy on the back and whispered into his ear, "Well done. Get me HQ on the phone at Fort Hood. Let's see if I can keep this promise."

Before Espy could make the call, the satellite phone rang in his ear. He handed the phone to Duncan.

"Sir, we have another situation."

Duncan shook his head in disbelief.

"The hits just keep on comin'."

CHAPTER 27

January 19
The Gregg Ranch
West of San Angelo, Texas

The mood was somber as Major arrived at the Gregg place outside San Angelo. It was not a long drive for him to take from Armstrong Ranch, through Big Spring and then southwest toward Sterling City. He considered having Riley and Cooper tag along, but Lucy had chores for them to do, and Major felt like it would be unprofessional for him to arrive with family members in tow.

Major was impressed with the number of military personnel present at the funeral. He was aware of Gregg's popularity with the officers and soldiers who fell under his command over the years. The contingent present today was an overwhelming show of respect for a man who'd had a long illustrious career in the U.S. armed forces.

From the Texas perspective, Major was aware that President Burnett would not be attending for security reasons, but Adjutant General Deur was there on behalf of the administration. After the burial, Deur approached Major near the entrance to Mrs. Gregg's home, where they chatted for a moment. The president had instructed Deur to assist Major in lining up interviews with everyone present the day of the shooting.

Major expressed his concern for meeting with Mrs. Gregg during this highly emotional time, but Deur assured him that the widow was more than willing to cooperate. Like the loved one of any deceased, she was searching for answers.

Deur led Major up the wide set of stairs entering the home, and once inside, Major removed his black felt hat by grasping it by the crown and holding it against his belly so the lining didn't show.

Mrs. Gregg was sitting in her husband's study alone, staring at his military honors and memorabilia. She wore a black dress with a shawl around her shoulders. She held a dainty white handkerchief in her hand, which she used periodically to dab her wet eyes.

"Mrs. Gregg, we're sorry to intrude," started Deur. "Would you have a moment to speak with this gentleman? He's the investigator I spoke to you about."

She nodded and motioned toward a chair across from her. "Yes, of course. Please have a seat. I apologize for my sniffling. I thought the crying would be over, but I was wrong."

Major shook her frail hand and settled into the chair. "I fully understand, Mrs. Gregg. Your husband was a great man, and he will be missed by many."

She nodded and managed a smile before looking down to the handkerchief again. Major turned to Deur, who'd taken up a position next to the window.

"Um, Kregg, would you mind leaving us alone for a moment? Please shut the door so we can have privacy, too. Thanks."

Deur frowned at being dismissed but followed Major's directive.

Once the door was closed, Major began. "Mrs. Gregg, I don't work for the government other than I'm an old lawman who happens to be an acquaintance of the president. She's asked me to look into the death of your husband and report directly to her."

Mrs. Gregg's interest was piqued, and she became more involved in the conversation. "Why?"

"Ma'am, I'm going to have to be blunt about this," Major began to answer. "Are you sure you're up for this today?"

"Yes, please," she replied. "I thought this investigation should have started yesterday. The killer has probably gotten away at this point."

"I have to be honest, ma'am. You are correct, and the likelihood of catching the shooter is very slim. At this point, our best bet is to find the people responsible for hiring the shooter and bring them to justice."

She began to fiddle with her handkerchief again and then suddenly pushed it into a spot between the chair's arm and its cushion. Major sensed she was fully engaged now and ready to get down to business.

"I'm sorry, but no one has told me your name," said Mrs. Gregg.

"I apologize, ma'am. My name is Major Duncan Armstrong, formerly in charge of Company C of the Texas Rangers. My ranch is north of here, just past—"

She sat up in her chair, and her eyes widened as if she'd seen a ghost. She began pointing at Major but was unable to speak.

Finally, she found her voice and began to stammer. "M-M-Monty. He knows you. That's it. I couldn't remember because I was so distraught. He'd just been shot, and I was trying to help. I was covered in blood and in shock, but he whispered to me. I couldn't remember what he said, and I've stayed up for two nights trying to remember. You-you."

Major reached out and took Mrs. Gregg by both hands to calm her nerves. She'd become agitated, not out of fear, but as if she'd experienced an epiphany.

"Ma'am, it's okay. Would you like me to get you a glass of water? Do you need a moment?"

"No!" she said with a raised voice. "Now I remember. Armstrong. He said your name. Did you know my husband? I mean, personally?"

Major took a breath and responded, "Yes, ma'am. We met at the capitol building one day when my son and I were visiting with the president. He sat in on a conversation we were having about border security. Why? Please, Mrs. Gregg. What did your husband whisper to you?"

She looked Major in the eyes and replied, "He said, 'Tell Armstrong it was Yancey.'"

Major released her hands and fell back in his chair. His mind immediately raced to his suspicions about Gregg's involvement with Yancey as it pertained to Duncan's mission.

Was Gregg referring to the extraction being called off? Or did Gregg suspect Yancey was behind his assassination? Or perhaps both?

Before Major could speak, she continued. "This means something to you, doesn't it? Do you know Billy Yancey?"

Major hesitated before responding. He had to be very careful with his answers and further questioning of Mrs. Gregg. She might be able to read into his questions what his mind was processing.

"Only once, at the secession celebration in Austin. We spoke briefly. What is your family's relationship to Yancey?"

Mrs. Gregg, fully coherent now, relayed to Major everything she could recall about Gregg and Yancey's relationship, including the late-night meetings behind closed doors in their home. Of all the associates Gregg worked with, Yancey and one other man with the CIA were the only ones that came to their home for anything other than social occasions.

Another forty minutes had passed when a knock at the door interrupted them. Major had learned enough to form a working theory behind the assassination of Montgomery Gregg. All fingers pointed at Billy Yancey, and the motives were twofold—eliminate a witness to the failed assassination attempt on Kim Jong-un and the aftermath involving Duncan, or to punish the decorated general for his involvement in the secession.

As they said their goodbyes, Major turned to Mrs. Gregg and whispered a question into her ear. "Other than working for the CIA, did your husband ever allude to what Yancey specifically did?"

"Yes," she replied unemotionally. "Whenever the United States government wasn't satisfied with the outcome of an election, it was Yancey's job to flip the script."

Major looked at the previously frail woman, who now appeared to have a new sense of purpose. He thanked her again and promised to be in touch.

As he walked out into the bright sunshine and donned his hat, he mumbled to himself, "Now we have a third motive, one that leads to folks way above Yancey's pay grade."

Chapter 28

January 20
The Mansion
Austin, Texas

The next day, Major left the ranch once again. This time he was bound for Austin to meet with the president. If his hypothesis was correct, and he had no reasons to believe otherwise, then the investigation began and ended with Billy Yancey, unless there was a more nefarious purpose behind Gregg's assassination, such as undermining her newly formed government. During their brief phone conversation, in which they agreed he should talk to her about the details in person, she also told him that she'd scheduled a meeting with the top generals from the former United States military. She invited Major to sit in and observe. He considered that a good idea because it would give him an opportunity to study their demeanor outside of the emotional surroundings of a funeral, just in case the military was behind the assassination for some reason.

"Hello, Major," greeted the president as he arrived at her office.

They spoke in private for a moment about his interviews at the Gregg ranch and his theories. They both agreed that the worst-case scenario was the third one raised by Mrs. Gregg's final statement. If Washington was trying to undermine her government to force her to concede some kind of failure, she'd have a tough time fending them off.

Before the topic of his continued involvement in the investigation arose, the president's chief of staff interrupted them for the meeting in the large conference room with her generals.

For the first thirty minutes, a constructive back-and-forth

conversation occurred between President Burnett and her military leaders. Major was impressed with the president's ability to hold a sustained conversation with the career military officers. Words like *tactics*, *strategies*, and *campaigns* were bantered about, and from Major's limited knowledge of the levels of warfare, it sounded as if the president had convinced the generals of her dedication to the Texas military.

After the meeting, the group milled around and spoke to one another about their commands, troop levels, and the overall attitudes of those within their charge. Major was approached by several of the top commanders to discuss Duncan.

Word had gotten back that he'd proven himself at Seminole, and yesterday's operation at Lamesa was considered to be tactical genius. All of them expressed an interest in moving Duncan up the ladder and incorporating him under their commands. Major warned them that any position his son was offered that took him farther from home would have to be approved by Miss Lucy, who was a far worthier opponent than they might be willing to take on.

Throughout the conversations, Major impressed himself with his ability to engage in conversation with these leaders on a political level. Like in Washington, at least in theory, a civilian-run government retained control over the decisions of whether to go to war, whom to fight, and with whom to become allies.

Beyond the logistics of the battlefield, government, Major said, should be responsible for the purse strings and the societal issues involving the use of the military. However, once the decision was made to fight, it was the military commanders, and their vast experience on the battlefield, who should determine the tactics and strategy to be implemented.

After the meeting broke up, Major and the president had a light lunch in her office. After finishing his second glass of sweet tea, Major excused himself to use the restroom. When he returned, President Burnett sat on her couch in front of the fireplace. Spread out before her were a dozen file folders, each with a large red stamp on the front that read CONFIDENTIAL.

"Marion, I guess I should be going," started Major as he entered the room. He glanced down at the folders and quickly averted his eyes out of respect. "Besides, it looks like you have matters to attend to that don't involve yours truly."

She fell back onto the sofa and sighed. "Vice president candidates."

"Any front-runner?" Major asked.

"Yeah. None of the above."

The two laughed, and Major sat in the chair across from her.

"Marion, we kinda got interrupted earlier before I could finish. If this character Yancey is behind Gregg's death, and I'm leaning strongly in that direction, I'm not sure we could prove it. Even if we could, he's probably untouchable. I doubt Washington would extradite him to Texas."

She managed a smile. "They'd laugh in my face if I asked."

"Probably so. Which leads me to my point. I was on the fence about handling this investigation anyway because I have an obligation to the ranch and my family. Even if I did, the conclusions reached would be the same. Honestly, the best advice I have is to watch your back and be aware of anything that occurs that appears out of sorts. As always, you know I'm available to you as a sounding board if you need one."

The president leaned forward, pushed the file folders in a neatly arranged pile, and slid them to the corner of the coffee table.

"I know, Major, which is why I called upon you in the first place. I really don't know where I go from here other than deal with any crisis as it arises. I just don't want to be the basis of that crisis."

Major stood and helped the president off the couch. They shook hands, and Major gave his final words of advice before he left.

"Marion, every day you occupy this office, think of the power you've been given as the president of this great republic. Then ask yourself if what you're doing is right. Is it right by your principles? Is it right by Texans? And is it right by God? If you can look yourself in the mirror and answer yes to those three questions, then you'll have the courage to endure any challenge."

Chapter 29

January 20
The Armstrong Ranch
Borden County, Texas

"It's good to see ya back at work, boss," said Preacher jokingly. He knew Major was probably in agony over the events of the last two days. He hated traveling away from the ranch, but that paled in comparison to his distaste for rubbing elbows with politicians, even a friend like the president.

"Yeah, yeah," started Major. "I'm glad to be back in the saddle where I belong. My face hurt from two days of smilin' and talkin'."

"I bet," said Preacher with a chuckle. "You know I'm just ribbin' ya."

Major laughed as he mounted his horse. "Preach, I don't know what you have planned for the day, but I sure would like to do some good old-fashioned ranch work. Do we have any fences to mend? Cattle to rustle? Heck, I'll shovel manure out of the stalls and then probably roll around in it like a hog just to get to feelin' like my old self."

"Whoa, was it that bad?"

"Nah, not really. It's just that part of my life is over, you know? I traded in my bolo and dress khakis years ago. I don't think I'm cut out for it anymore."

"Good to hear because have I got a job for you," said Preacher in a playful tone.

Major's sudden look of shock tickled Preacher. He began roaring in laughter.

"You're gonna make me shovel horse manure, aren't you?" asked Major with trepidation.

"I should, boss, just 'cause you put the thought in my mind," replied Preacher as he mounted up and whistled at the ranch hands to ride over from the barn. "How'd you like to join me and the boys on a little cattle drive? We're dividing up the herd and moving some out east."

"Is something wrong?"

"Nope. Miss Lucy referred to it as a preventive measure in case we run into trouble. There's a ranch on the other side of Wildcat Creek that was abandoned after it was foreclosed last summer. It's small, but its fences are solid."

"Yeah, I remember," said Major. "The old Diamond Fire place. We looked into buying it at foreclosure, but the bank was being stubborn on their price."

"Still empty, and I'm pretty sure the bank would take one of them bags of quarters you got for it."

"No, thanks. We'll just take it over for now and give it back when all of this is over."

Preacher grabbed the reins of his horse, dug in his heels, and took off at a gallop, leaving Major scrambling to catch up. He hadn't driven cattle in a while and looked forward to helping the boys out. He had a lot to process after the last two days and was anxious to have some quiet time riding along to organize his thoughts.

The cattle at Armstrong Ranch was their most valuable resource other than the people who lived there. The Armstrong family's ability to buy quality calves, fatten them up on feed that created a healthy adult, and sell them at a nice profit had sustained them for over a century.

Preacher was an old hand at organizing the team necessary to drive cattle. The process was relatively straightforward. Move these massive animals from point A to point B without chaos erupting in the form of defections from the herd or a stampede.

All of the ranch hands were quality horsemen and expert wranglers. It was invariable that strays would wander away from the herd. The challenge was not only to bring them back but prevent the others from following the wayward soul.

Preacher had charted out a path that led them down the same path carved into the ridge overlooking J. B. Thomas lake that Lucy and the boys had used to hide the survival caches. The terrain wasn't treacherous, but it was narrow, which resulted in the herd being spread out. This created a challenge for the wranglers.

The day before, Preacher had separated thirty steers from the rest of the herd. The group of eight men, with the addition of Major, could easily handle moving a small herd of this size, but the narrow path presented a challenge. They'd need to keep on their toes to pull it off.

Preacher shouted his instructions as they got started. "This is a little different from normal, boys. You gotta look at this like keeping thirty schoolkids walking in a straight line down a sidewalk. All it takes is one to get curious and stray from the path. When that happens, the rest of our curiosity seekers will follow the leader off a cliff."

They continued to ride as they reached the back gate, which opened up to the trail.

Preacher continued to give advice. "Remember, keep this low stress. Shouting won't do us any good because it'll just get 'em agitated. Riders in the back, move up along any steer that looks like it wants to wander or isn't keeping up. They'll get the message and fall back in line."

The herd was moving at a methodical pace now, and Preacher was pleased. He gradually fell back and let Antonio take the lead. He joined Major at the rear.

"Somethin' happen in Austin, boss? You look flummoxed."

Major started laughing, which caused the cattle at the rear to become startled. He stifled his laugh and looked over at his old friend. "Flummoxed? That's a lot of word, Preach. Have you been playing Scrabble with Palmer?"

"Nah, I was reading a book and saw the word used to describe a guy's face. I pictured it to look like the way your face was a minute ago."

"Makes sense, although I'm not sure flummoxed is the right word. How about preoccupied? That better describes it."

Preacher shrugged and sat up in his saddle a little to look toward the front of the herd. So far, so good. "I like flummoxed better. Anyway, what's gnawin' at ya?"

"Preach, it takes a lot of *cajones* to order the assassination of a high-ranking public official," Major began in reply. "Gregg had made a few enemies back in Washington, and I believe they were gettin' even."

"Maybe the fella had it comin'?" asked Preacher.

"Yeah, probably. That's what Duncan thinks, anyway. My concern is something more sinister might be going on. That bullet may have been sending a message to Marion."

"You mean as in *the next bullet is coming for you* kinda message?"

Major nodded. "Yessir."

"Okay, so what's it all mean?" asked Preacher.

"I don't rightly know, Preach. Whoever is pullin' the strings on this whole thing hasn't made their next move yet. I suspect we'll know it when we see it. All I can say is this. Our responsibility is to this little part of the world and the people who rely upon us to keep it safe. Anything bigger is beyond our control anyway."

PART THREE

Texas is at War

Chapter 30

January 20
Just Before Midnight
Lubbock, Texas

Holloway had adopted an abandoned warehouse on the southeast side of Lubbock as his staging area for tonight's attack. By seven o'clock that evening, his entire team was in place, and although they were small in numbers, they were powerful in their intensity. Holloway walked through the group, stopping to check their gear and offer words of encouragement. He thought back to the young recruits who'd come through Bagram Airfield in Afghanistan to train for war.

Many of them weren't born when the 9/11 attacks took place. When these impressionable soldiers arrived in this strange land of rocks and desert, the fact that the world was dangerous and evil existed in certain groups of people, had barely seeped into their worldview.

Holloway's commandos were different. They had grown up in a country led by dictators and brutal regimes. They were taught at an early age not to respect the authority of the state, but to fear it. They were unlike American children, who were admonished to wear helmets and knee pads while riding their bikes or, later in life, were promised safe places in college if they didn't like the way another student spoke to them.

In America, the so-called millennials abandoned the saying *sticks and stones might break my bones and words can never hurt me* in favor of a hypersensitive society in which every perceived slight became an emotional crisis.

North Korean kids and young adults were hardened in a way Americans could never understand. A misspoken word or a simple misunderstanding could result in entire families being sent to prison work camps for the rest of their lives, or execution in front of an entire village to make a point.

While his commandos had lived in America and enjoyed the spoils afforded its citizens, they hadn't forgotten their roots and the hardships that led them to this point. Under Holloway's tutelage, they'd chosen the path of evil, and tonight they were going to use their training to inflict harm on a city of unsuspecting Texans who had dodged the apocalyptic bullet in the form of the EMP.

"In a few minutes, we will begin our attack," started Holloway as he walked to the center of the spacious warehouse where the commandos were hidden with their vehicles. His voice boomed through the metal building and was easily heard by his men, who inched forward to encircle their leader. "You know your assignments and your targets. Once we inflict our initial chaos, the next target will be the prize. There are a few things I want to remind you about as we prepare for this battle.

"The enemy will be caught off guard and may appear confused or unprepared at first. Do not mistake their apparent incompetence as a sign of weakness. They are good fighters. I also believe they are led by a seasoned military warrior who should be feared.

"When engaging our enemy, I want you to pay attention to detail. Stay alert at all times, and take nothing for granted. We will be outnumbered and cannot afford to lose a single man.

"Be aware of your surroundings. Look for fallback positions and rally points if you get overrun. Communicate with the other men in your team. Hand signals when possible, vocally as a last resort.

"Each of you is a valuable asset to this operation and possesses special skills to accomplish our purpose. I have divided you into teams with that in mind. Remember each other's strengths and weaknesses when you enter the battle. Unlike our enemy, you have trained in the streets. You've done battle in cities and towns. They have not. They've studied in classrooms or within the confines of a military base. Maybe some have spent time in the Middle East, as I have, but nothing there has prepared them for an attack on their homeland. Take advantage of their inability to comprehend what's happening and strike lightning fast, as you've been trained!"

Holloway raised his rifle in the air, and his men began to shout *victory* in English, or *manse*, the North Korean equivalent, which honored Kim Jong-il. Holloway didn't care where they drew their inspiration from, as long as they did their job like warriors.

Earlier that morning, he and General Lee had reviewed the operation for the final time before the North Korean leader left for his own target located southwest of Fort Worth. At four minutes past midnight, all teams would initiate their attacks and not stop until the entire ERCOT power grid was taken off-line. The two leaders exchanged words of encouragement and wished one another luck as they parted ways forever.

For two days, Holloway and his top lieutenants had conducted surveillance around the three substations, which connected Lubbock Power & Light, or LP&L, to the ERCOT grid. Using stolen iPhones they'd taken from unsuspecting Texans they'd ambushed, Holloway's men photographed the substations and their surroundings in detail. Upon return to Patricia each evening, they'd shared the photos with other members of their team so they'd become familiar with their targets.

Holloway deployed three teams to each of the substations designed and built to integrate LP&L into the ERCOT system. In order to cut off energy to Lubbock and most of the Texas Panhandle, all three substations needed to be taken off-line. Otherwise, the newly designed system would simply transfer power from one to the other to pick up the slack.

The design, as implemented by the power companies, was an ingenious approach to allow continuous power to consumers in the event of one or even two failures. However, the ERCOT engineers never envisioned a simultaneous attack on all three.

From his position across from Camp Lubbock, Holloway communicated with his men who'd positioned themselves outside the

North, Wadsworth, and New Oliver facilities of LP&L. Holloway wished he had more rocket-propelled grenades. As it was, he had to hide his possession of these three RPGs from General Lee because they had been taken from his soldiers after his men killed them.

He would be judicious in their use, hopefully saving one for the proverbial rainy day.

Holloway checked his watch. It was almost time. Throughout Texas, North Korean commandos were in position to initiate their attacks using a combination of stealth techniques to enter the facilities, explosives to bring down the critical infrastructure to transmit energy across Texas, and automatic gunfire to destroy the transformers designed to convert high-voltage power to the lower voltage used in every home and business in the country.

When their assaults on the Texas power grid were complete, all of the new nation would experience the collapse endured by Americans and the apocalyptic world of darkness it created.

It was four past midnight. It was time.

Chapter 31

January 21
Comanche Peak Nuclear Power Plant
Near Glen Rose, Texas

General Lee was a soldier, but he was also a student of terrorism. Spending the last decade in Canada and digesting American media had given him a different perspective on the art of war. Gone were the days when two mighty armies lined up across from one another to battle over territory. Insurgency warfare was successful, utilizing preplanning, patience, and surprise to inflict damage upon the enemy. He was about to embark on a battle that would accomplish what Dear Leader's bombs could not—knock the arrogant Texans down to their knees.

He'd handpicked these men weeks ago for their proficiency in the use of explosives. Together with the rocket-propelled grenades, he would attack the crown jewel in the ERCOT power grid—the Comanche Peak Nuclear Power Plant located thirty miles southwest of Fort Worth.

Comanche Peak was one of two nuclear power plants in Texas, the other being located near the Gulf Coast of Texas. Comanche Peak, with its four fully operational reactors, provided power to the Dallas-Fort Worth area with over a million homes.

Just as important, its strategic location within Texas made Comanche Peak a strategic cog in the wheel of power lines traversing the country. Bringing it down, together with the massive transmission lines surrounding the plant itself, would be a devastating blow to ERCOT's ability to distribute power.

The task would not be an easy one. In addition to the size of the sprawling complex, there were as many as three hundred employees working shifts at the plant at any given time, although the numbers were substantially less after midnight.

Security personnel manned an entry gate to the most restricted parts of Comanche Peak and were supplemented by patrols who drove around the facility in small white pickup trucks with yellow lights flashing continuously. During the early evening, when nighttime set in, Lee was appreciative of the flashing lights, which allowed his team to keep tabs on the roving patrols at all times.

Geographically, the location of the power plant presented a challenge for him. It was situated on a peninsula that jutted out into the Squaw Creek Reservoir. Using the lake water to cool their reactors was the primary reason for the design, but it presented a problem for any attacker, terrorist or otherwise, to gain access.

The long entry road to the plant prevented Lee's men from getting close to the facility by vehicle. Breaching the facility and strategically placing explosives was out of the question. Fortunately, he had other weapons at his disposal.

An infantry squad in the Korean People's Army included two Type 69 RPG operators carrying one launcher and three grenade rounds. The Type 69 was a shoulder-launched antitank grenade launcher designed by the Chinese and sold to North Korea. A clone of the Russian RPG-7, the weapon had significant firepower and was portable.

The problem for Lee was its limited effective range of under a thousand feet. The reactors at Comanche Peak were positioned well away from the facility's entrance, and therefore a frontal assault was out of the question. However, he had another option.

Across the Squaw Creek Reservoir was a wooded area with several high points that looked down upon the nuclear power plant. The location was ideal for other reasons. The four targets, the nuclear reactors, were situated on the end of the peninsula nearest this part of the lake. Further, after the attack was completed, Lee would have an easy exit out of the area to regroup with his men before they found their way toward his next group of targets.

The eighty-five-millimeter warhead was certainly capable of inflicting sufficient damage to cause the destruction of the containment building that housed the control rods and the uranium fuel. Secondary rounds would be focused on turbines, generators, and transformers that connected the containment building to the cooling towers.

Lee checked in with his demolition experts. Power lines departed the facility in two directions strung atop transmission towers capable of supporting the high-voltage conductors and the lines themselves. These structures were designed to withstand intense weather like hurricanes and tornadoes, as well as being rammed by vehicles, whether intentionally or by accident.

While in America, awaiting this moment to unleash their hatred, the Lightning Death Squads had accumulated weapons of war, including dynamite. The powerful explosive was often used in drilling and blasting operations for road construction, mining, and quarrying.

Isolated incidents of dynamite being stolen from construction sites occurred over the years and were rarely solved. Fortunately for the government, the use of the stolen dynamite never materialized. In many of these occurrences, Lee's commandos were responsible for the theft.

His men identified two consecutive transmission towers away from the nuclear power plant to destroy, which would result in a domino effect of collapsing towers in both directions. By destroying both the plant and its means for carrying electricity, one of the most populated areas of Texas would lose power and its ability to effectuate repairs on Comanche Peak for months if not years.

Lee checked his watch. It was four past midnight. It was time.

The operatives who were assigned to the massive power line towers were instructed to detonate the TNT affixed to the tower's base when they observed Holloway's first volley of a rocket-propelled grenade into Comanche Peak.

He tapped his gunner on the shoulder, and the first RPG was launched. A whoosh of fire blasted out of the rear of the launcher, warming the faces of Lee and his secondary shooters. Before the rocket made contact at the nuclear power plant, Lee ordered the next man to be ready.

A spotter observed the detonation.

"One hundred feet to the left. Adjust sights!"

The next gunner modified the presets on his infrared night-vision sights accordingly.

"Ready. Fire!"

Once again, the sound of the rocket-propelled grenade cut through the night sky, now flying silently toward its target until the explosion filled the center of the system of pipes, power generators, and transformers that made up the connection between the cooling towers on the left and the containment building on the right.

The spotter shouted, "Direct hit," but no one could hear him. His voice was muted by the intense explosions that occurred on both sides of the Comanche Peak peninsula as the transmission towers and power lines were blown off their concrete platforms.

Like mighty oak trees cut down by lumberjacks, the towers' steel strained under the pressure as its stability was taken away by the blasts. Slowly, the towers began to topple until the four marked for demolition fell toward the ground, dragging down power lines and towers on each side of them as well.

Lee approached his spotter. "What about the containment building?"

"Still standing, sir. Adjust sights forty feet to the right."

Lee gave the directive to his next gunner. Tension surrounded the commandos as he made his adjustments, took aim and fired.

Whoosh!

Once again, the fire thrust the RPG toward its target. Now the power was out at the facility, and it was immersed in darkness except for a few vehicles' headlights and the never-ending yellow emergency lights on the now stationary patrols.

They waited to hear from the spotter.

"Direct hit on the containment structure. Building walls breached, but interior intact. One more, sir. Exact same location."

"Same gunner. Fire when ready!" ordered Lee.

The commando remained in his position as the launcher was reloaded.

"Ready," he announced. "Firing!"

Lee pulled out his binoculars and watched the RPG as it sailed toward the target. He was the first to see the results of their efforts.

The inside of the containment building with its reactor and uranium-filled control rods disappeared in a bright-white explosion. Lee put away his binoculars and smiled. Then he mumbled to himself, "Now you will live like we do."

Chapter 32

January 21
Lubbock, Texas

At this hour, there was no traffic around Lubbock, especially in the relatively low population area surrounding Camp Lubbock. Nonetheless, Holloway and his men took great precautions to avoid detection. Throughout the evening, his men got into position. Directly across Regis Street several ranch-style homes overlooked Camp Lubbock. His catlike commandos systematically infiltrated these homes and quietly killed their occupants using their knives and professionally trained bare hands.

Holloway had no illusions as to whether he'd be successful in his plans. Relying upon the diversions created at the substations and another surprise he had for the good people of Lubbock, he was hoping on a mistake by the young warrior who'd disrupted his hijacking of the fuel truck back in Arizona.

"Payback's a bitch, pal," muttered Holloway as he lowered his monocular and focused on the reports coming in from his four units around the city.

One of the great advantages afforded the United States military was the superior audio-visual equipment provided to their soldiers. Not only could members of a unit communicate directly with one another, but the visual footage sent back to their commanders on the ground, and in the States, gave the U.S. a substantial advantage over its adversaries.

Holloway felt fortunate to have a handful of satellite telephones at their disposal considering the impact the EMP had had on most electronics. To keep him abreast of their progress, one of the riflemen assigned to shooting out the transformers at the substations doubled as his communications man in the field.

Holloway phoned each team in succession, receiving details of their maneuvers and doling out advice as needed. All three units assigned to the substations around Lubbock were instructed to make their move precisely at four past midnight. The first of his RPGs would be used as a diversionary tactic while causing disarray at the same time. They were awaiting his orders.

Holloway stood alone on the northbound lane of Interstate 27, watching the activity take place at Camp Lubbock. It took seven minutes following the initial attacks upon the substations for the power grid to collapse in the city, but it required another ten minutes for the soldiers stationed below him to react.

Trucks were assembling, and men in full combat gear were scrambling to get into position to be deployed. Holloway waited patiently for the Texas Guardsmen to leave the facility. His hope was that only a skeleton crew would be left behind to defend their armory. If his plan was successful, his team would be met with little resistance.

One unit at a time began to pull out of the camp. They turned either left or right depending upon the substation they were responding to. He'd calculated the time for them to travel to each of the substations, stage their units, and await further orders. Just as the guardsmen arrived at the remote LP&L facilities, he'd draw out the remaining soldiers with an RPG attack on the Lubbock County Sheriff's Office.

He studied his watch and received confirmation of success from the substation teams. By design, they were instructed to return to Camp Lubbock to assist in the assault upon the armory, but their indirect route would avoid running head-on into the responding guardsmen. The additional minute or two was worth the advantage the extra manpower afforded him.

Anxious, Holloway checked his watch again and referred to his notes to confirm his calculations. He telephoned the team positioned on a rooftop across from the sheriff's office. From their close proximity, the RPG would inflict maximum damage upon the town's sole source of law enforcement, as both the Lubbock Police Department and the sheriff's office had been consolidated under one roof.

Holloway gave the order. He closed his eye and listened.

In the quiet of the night, the explosion sounded massive. Holloway grinned and turned to watch a plume of smoke rise into the sky, illuminated by the fire created by the powerful RPG. After admiring his handiwork, he turned his attention back to Camp Lubbock, awaiting the anticipated overreaction in the form of more troops leaving to respond to the explosion.

It never came.

CHAPTER 33

January 21
Camp Lubbock
Lubbock, Texas

Soldiers returning home from combat duty often experience night sweats, vivid dreams, and sleep apnea as a result of living through the horrors of war. Not every veteran was wired the same, and luckily for Duncan, he wasn't haunted by the nightmares of his time in battle or the assassinations he'd carried out on behalf of his country.

The fist rapping on his door was different from a light knock indicating his oh-six-hundred wake-up request. His subconscious was screaming at him—*trouble!* He shot up on his cot and looked for the glowing red display of the LED clock behind his desk.

It wasn't visible. Duncan blinked and quickly rubbed the sleep out of his eyes, trying to gain his night vision in the darkness. The evening's new moon provided no ambient light through the windows.

The knocking continued, now accompanied by an urgency-filled voice. "Commander, we have a situation, sir. Commander Duncan? Sir?"

"Yeah, come in," replied Duncan. He slept in his fatigue pants and a tee shirt. He fumbled under his cot, looking for his boots, when a young soldier unfamiliar to Duncan entered the room. Duncan opened his eyes wide to make out who he was.

"Sir, we have a power outage," the young man explained as he took a step inside.

"Soldier, has Sergeant Esparza been notified of the situation?"

"Yessir, he sent me to wake you," the young man replied. "Sir, the outage is citywide."

Duncan found his way across his office toward the window that overlooked Regis Street and the main entrance to the base. There were no lights on anywhere. He looked skyward and saw stars.

Suddenly, bright lights filled his windows, causing him to immediately close his eyes and turn away. The sound of generators being started provided an explanation.

"Get me some type of portable lighting—a lantern, flashlight, or candles. I don't care. Find Sergeant Esparza and send him to me immediately."

"Yes, sir!" the messenger saluted and spun around as he quickly exited through Duncan's door.

Duncan's mind raced. Power outages occasionally occurred in normal times, but the sudden loss of electricity when the weather was clear and demand low was suspicious.

Using the lights that now filled his office from the front gate, he walked back to his cot and powered up his satellite phone. That ruled out another EMP.

Duncan finished dressing and strapped on his weapon. He then approached a box in the corner of the office, which contained over a dozen rolled-up maps of the region within his command. In addition to road and topography maps, he recalled one map labeled ERCOT.

In the limited light, he pulled the maps out and spread them across his desk until he found the one he was looking for. Frustrated, Duncan eventually swept everything off his desk onto the floor by his cot and rolled open the map of the substations, transformers and power lines that made up the LP&L system.

Espy entered his office. "Commander, I have teams ready to respond. I do not believe this is a typical power outage. Our street patrols reported seeing sparks flying near the North substation in addition to automatic gunfire."

"Like California," Duncan mumbled as he identified the North substation on the map. The soldier returned with a portable Coleman lantern and set it on Duncan's desk.

"I agree, sir," added Espy. "Your orders, sir?"

"Dispatch three teams to each of these locations," replied Duncan as he pointed out the LP&L substations that connected their utility to the ERCOT power grid. "Sergeant, I want constant radio contact with our men. This might be part of something bigger."

"Bigger, sir?"

"Just a hunch. Go, and get back here ASAP," replied Duncan. He then turned to the young man who had awakened him. "What's your name, soldier?"

"Private Page, sir."

"Private, I need you to locate the officer on duty for the armory. I know it's closed, but someone is assigned twenty-four seven. Bring them to my office now."

"Yessir."

The men left Duncan alone with his thoughts.

I warned everyone who'd listen that North Korean operatives were planning something. How could I ignore my own advice? I should've placed patrols or even a sentry rotation on these substations. But there are thousands of these things around Texas. You can't guard them all.

Duncan second-guessed himself and the failure to see this coming. It was a logical step for any invading force to disable critical infrastructure like power and communications. He'd underestimated the DPRK. It was a ballsy move to take on the United States, even in a grid-down scenario. But to attack Texas, a new nation but with an inherited standing army, took some kind of crazy arrogance. Yet here he stood, in the dark.

Through the chaos of shuffling feet in the hallways outside his office, he could hear Private Page's voice escorting the duty officer assigned to the armory for the evening. As they entered his office, he immediately recognized the flirty corporal he'd encountered the other day.

"Commander, this is Corporal Herrera," Private Page announced as they entered.

"Yes, we've met. Corporal Herrera, I have an important project for you and Private Page. Are you two up for it?"

"Yes, sir!" she said with conviction, although Duncan detected apprehension in her voice. Still, he needed her to be confident and carry out his orders.

"Good. First, Private, find Sergeant Esparza and tell him to meet me in the armory. You meet me there as well. Go!"

Duncan turned to Corporal Herrera. "Come with me. Do you have your keys? To both entry doors?"

"Yessir. Do you mean the emergency exit too? It stays locked unless we're receiving a shipment of weapons from Fort Bliss, sir," she asked.

"Well, we're about to make a few adjustments, temporarily."

Duncan led the way to the armory and waited while Corporal Herrera unlocked the steel doors. The biometric locks were still functioning because of their battery backup power packs, but the old-fashioned skeleton key system still worked in this older facility.

"It will be hard to see without lights, sir," said Corporal Herrera.

"We'll get some more lighting in a minute, Corporal. We don't have much time. Please follow me."

Duncan wound his way through the rows of weapons and ammunition until he reached the red illuminated EXIT sign. "Please open this door, Corporal."

"Yes, sir. Let me disable the alarm first." Corporal Herrera entered a series of codes into a keypad and then opened the door. A wave of cool, fresh air rushed in from the outside. As they exited the building, he heard Espy's voice call for him.

"Commander, are you in here?"

"Back here, Sergeant. Hurry!"

Espy and Private Page ran through the armory, with the young private stumbling when he caught his hip on a container holding one of the newest weapons in the military's arsenal, the XM25 airburst grenade launcher. Like the new shotgun Duncan had procured the other day, this bullpup-designed grenade launcher had been taken out of its experimental phase and was used when engaging enemies behind cover.

Duncan walked into the utility yard behind the armory. The large open space was obscured from the outside by twelve-foot-tall block and masonry walls. A large double entry gate faced the airport side of the armory. A few Humvees were parked inside the utility yard together with two eighteen-wheelers, which were used to transfer supplies from Fort Bliss to Camp Lubbock.

"Listen up. I'm about to ask a lot of you," started Duncan. "Sergeant, I need you to assign two more men to Corporal Herrera for this task. I want the four of them to clear out the armory as much as possible."

"Sir?"

"You heard me, Sergeant," replied Duncan, who turned his attention to Herrera. "Corporal, you know our arsenal better than I do. I want you to start with our most lethal military-issue weapons and corresponding ammunition. Antitank weapons first, followed by machine guns, automatic rifles and so on."

"Sir, the whole armory?" she asked.

"Yes, keep filling both trucks equally until I say stop," answered Duncan. He looked at the vehicles scattered about the utility yard and then turned to Espy. "Sergeant, find the logistics duty officer and have him locate the keys to these big rigs. When they are filled, or after I give the order, I want to back them up so that the rear doors of these trailers make direct contact with a block wall. Don't lose the keys. Got it?"

Duncan took one last look around the yard, and then an explosion rocked the downtown area, causing all of them to instinctively duck.

Chapter 34

January 21
Camp Lubbock
Lubbock, Texas

Duncan and Espy raced back through the armory, leaving Corporal Herrera and Private Page in a mad scramble to load weapons into the trailers of the eighteen-wheelers. Espy peeled off to locate the logistics officer while Duncan ran outside to the front gate.

He immediately felt exposed and in danger. Duncan felt for his sidearm but realized it wouldn't be enough if an assault on Camp Lubbock was imminent. He approached the guarded entrance and addressed the duty officer.

"Do you have any signs of activity whatsoever? Vehicular? Pedestrian? Heck, dogs barking. Anything?"

"No, sir," she replied. "We were startled when the lights went out and immediately raised our threat awareness level. After logistics fired up the genny, we took defensive positions behind the barricade."

"Are perimeter patrols still in place?"

"Yes, sir, although they're slated to go off duty at one a.m."

"Hold your entire team in place until further notice," said Duncan. "Can you determine where the explosion came from?"

"Yes, sir," she replied. "I grew up in Lubbock. There's no doubt something hit the police station or the courthouse. Maybe even the sheriff's office on the far side. It's hard to tell except you can still see smoke in the air."

Duncan looked to where she was pointing and saw a trail of dark smoke that turned lighter in color as it rose into the sky. A reddish glow appeared from time to time, indicating a fire was burning out of control.

"Commander!" shouted Espy from the entrance to the administration building. "I've got a Lubbock LEO on the line requesting assistance."

Duncan ran toward Espy, who met him halfway across the parking lot. Duncan took the phone while Espy waved one of their lieutenants out of the building to join them.

"This is Commander Armstrong. Go ahead."

Duncan listened to the distressed sheriff's deputy explain their circumstances. As he did, the sound of automatic gunfire could be heard in stereo—louder through the satphone and a little fainter through Duncan's other ear.

"Hang on, Deputy. We'll send a team to assist." Duncan signed off and turned to his two officers. "Assemble a team to assist the Lubbock Sheriff's Office. They've taken a hit from what sounds like an RPG. We need the men in full kits with body armor."

"How many, sir?" asked the lieutenant.

Duncan rubbed his forehead to remove the beads of sweat that had accumulated despite the near freezing temperatures. The clear sky and cold temps had combined to cover their vehicles with frost.

He turned and looked toward the city and then to the surrounding residential area. Duncan thought he caught a glimpse of glowing red taillights along the interstate above them, but he turned his attention back to the task at hand.

"Lieutenant, take eight men in four of the Humvees with fifty cals attached. One driver and one gunner. Find the source of the small-arms fire and light it up. No need for pleasantries or formalities. Blast them and get back here. Understand?"

"Yes, sir." The lieutenant ran back to the building, leaving Duncan alone with Espy in the middle of the parking lot. Espy handed Duncan his rifle.

Duncan took another look around and started walking with Espy back to the front entrance. "Espy, this has all the markings of a broader attack. They took down the grid, and now they're assaulting local governmental buildings, including law enforcement."

"Do you think we're next?" asked Espy as he glanced around Camp Lubbock nervously. "We've deployed the bulk of our people to the substations and now the sheriff's office."

Four Humvees roared past them toward the front gate, squealing their tires as they exited onto Regis Street.

Duncan continued his assessment. "How many men do we have left?"

Espy conducted a mental head count and relayed the results to his commanding officer. "Four working the armory detail. Four each on the front and rear gates. Eight more on patrol, assuming you assign everyone to maintain security until *this*, whatever *this* is, is over."

Duncan turned as two patrol vehicles merged at the front gate and spoke with the duty officer who hailed from Lubbock. She was giving them orders, likely advising them of the circumstances at the sheriff's office nearby.

Duncan summarized their total defensive capability. "Twenty, plus the two of—"

He was unable to complete his sentence when the unmistakable sound of an RPG sailing through the air caught his attention.

Espy shouted, "Incoming!"

Both he and Duncan hit the ground and crawled under an M35 transport truck, and an RPG struck the main entry gate, instantly killing the eight security personnel who were congregated there and obliterating the entry road and fencing on both sides of the gate.

"Hold 'em off, Espy! I'll be back!"

Duncan ran for the main entrance to the building as vehicle lights lit up their perimeter and began racing toward the facility at a high rate of speed. Automatic gunfire chased Duncan inside, the high-powered rounds chewing up the asphalt behind every stride he took.

Espy began to return fire, but he was outnumbered on all sides. Duncan didn't stop to help. He needed to get to the armory.

He ran through the nearly empty space into the back entrance. Corporal Herrera was closing up one of the truck's trailers, and the other truck was almost loaded.

"You've got to hurry!" shouted Duncan. "Get them parked, grab your rifles, and meet us in the lobby. Full kits, people. We're under attack!"

Duncan ran back inside and stopped at his office, which was now alit with an orangish glow from the fire burning at the main gate. He quickly put on his protective gear, which included body armor, additional magazines, and his knives.

He searched frantically for the satphone, which had been swept onto the floor earlier. He dropped to his knees to pick it up just as gunfire tore through the windows, spraying bullets into the walls and raining shards of glass throughout his office.

Shouts filled the air as the remaining soldiers on the base gathered in the main hallway of the administration building, which also housed the National Guard recruiting offices.

Pointing at two of the security patrols, Duncan shouted his orders. "You two, cover Sergeant Esparza and get him inside with us. Everyone, stay away from the windows."

Duncan's orders had barely left his mouth when more gunfire raked the exterior walls and tore through the glass openings, prompting the soldiers to turn away from the flying glass.

His men exited the front door in a low crouch and began shooting in the direction of the approaching vehicles, effectively laying down cover fire for Espy to return inside. Once the entirety of his unit was in place, Duncan doled out their assignments.

"Page, Herrera, Esparza, you three are with me. The rest of you spread out and cover all the entrances to the buildings and cover any windows that are low enough to enter from outside. Go!"

Chapter 35

January 21
Camp Lubbock
Lubbock, Texas

Holloway's plan was working to perfection, but he knew his time was limited. He had to assume that the local command had recalled their people from the substations. That gave him about thirty minutes to take control of the armory, load his trucks, and prepare to fight their way out. It was an extremely risky move, but the chaos created by the combination of attacks around Lubbock gave him a big enough window of opportunity to see it through, with a little luck. Luck was often beyond a person's control. But decisions were always in a person's hands. Good decision-making, coupled with preparation, could create both luck and opportunity.

He was aware that he'd lose a lot of men during this operation, but that didn't matter at this point. His future didn't include military-style assaults on armories and National Guard facilities. He was prepared to go back to being an opportunist, taking advantage of the weak in order to better his lot in life.

As a result, there would be a few sacrificial lambs among his men, but he'd protect his loyal, hard-core gangbangers from Fullerton for their future endeavors.

His plan divided his team to conduct two separate facets of the operation. The initial assault using pickup trucks and automatic weapons was designed to draw the bulk of the remaining troops to the front of the buildings. If his men could penetrate the building and engage the enemy, all the better. Even if they couldn't, they were instructed to keep the heat on and draw the attention of the soldiers holed up inside the facility.

Meanwhile, he and his most trusted men would breach the rear utility gates of the complex. Based upon his reconnaissance of trucks coming and going through Camp Lubbock, the armory was most likely within the protective walls behind the main building.

The armory was the prize. His small group of thugs would have the weapons and ammo necessary to fight off any military force if they needed to defend the ranch, which Holloway intended to acquire next. He just had to find the right spot.

Holloway waited patiently for the third part of the assault on Camp Lubbock to take place. His RPG attack on the main gate had succeeded in taking out a third of the defenders of the facilities.

The second wave using the pickup trucks to barge through the chain-link fencing caught the Texans off guard and forced them to huddle within the supposed protective walls of the main building rather than take the fight to his men where they were most vulnerable—in the open fields surrounding the complex. Driving them inside also enabled him to position his part of the operation at the rear gates to access the utility yard and the armory.

He rolled down his window and listened, trying to tune out the automatic-weapons fire that filled the air. Then it happened. The unmistakable sound of one of the massive four-door Ford pickups crashing through the plate-glass entrance of the main building. His commandos would now directly engage the enemy, who would naturally focus their efforts on the greatest threat.

Holloway dropped the transmission into low gear, and with his left foot on the brake, he revved the motor. The mighty Ford truck coiled like a cobra, ready to leap out of its basket and viciously bite its prey.

As he released the brake, the truck lunged forward and rammed into the solid wood gate, which was no match for the three hundred ninety-five horses under the hood and the four hundred pound-feet of torque in its rear end.

Holloway and his passengers were thrown backward against their seats before steadying themselves to do battle. Two other pickups followed them through the opening as they fanned out, weapons ready to shoot anything that moved.

They wheeled into the parking lot, and his men jumped out, positioning themselves near the steel door that entered the armory.

In addition to Holloway, eleven of his best were by his side, prepared to kill anything that moved and fill the trucks with the most powerful weapons available. With a little luck, as the battle raged on at the front of the building, Holloway and his commandos would get a satisfactory load of advanced military weaponry and sneak into the night.

Holloway summoned his top demolition man to the armory door. He efficiently placed sufficient Semtex and charges on the door hinges to compromise the steel structure, allowing them access.

"Stand clear," the commando shouted as he readied the detonation device. All of Holloway's men sought cover on both sides of the entry to avoid the blast.

The explosion was deafening, and effective. The steel succumbed to the Semtex blast, leaving the door hanging from the frame by its locking mechanism. It was no match for the kick from the muscular Holloway, who pounded it into the dark armory with one leg.

As his men poured into the space, they fanned out in all directions, preparing to be engaged by gunfire. Although they weren't shot at, they could hear the gun battles raging in the main building. With the inside of the armory eerily still and pitch black, Holloway moved deeper into the building with his men in tow.

The sound of a vehicle behind them in the utility yard grabbed their attention, causing them to spin around and look toward the blown doorway—which had just been blocked with the back end of a massive wrecker.

Chapter 36

January 21
Camp Lubbock
Lubbock, Texas

During all of Holloway's maneuvers in the utility yard, Duncan was watching along with Espy, Page, and Herrera from a hidden position behind a military tow truck designed to assist broken-down troop transport vehicles. With the other security door locked, Duncan had the attackers trapped inside, which enabled him to help his men who were holding down the administrative building.

"Page, Herrera, cover these openings. If you see any movement, even it's a dang rat scurrying by, you shoot it."

"Roger that, Commander!" exclaimed Private Page, who immediately moved to the driver's side of the truck and dropped to one knee to cover the openings.

"Yessir," said Corporal Herrera. Without hesitation, she drew her sidearm and trained her sights on the area under the wrecker where a man could shimmy through, but not quick enough to avoid getting killed.

After Duncan issued his orders, he joined Espy near the gate. "Did you make contact with the teams?"

"Yes, sir," he replied. "I've recalled the three units deployed to the substations, and they are en route back here. What should I do about the detachment sent downtown?"

"Let them help protect the civvies," said Duncan. "Let's lend an assist to our brothers inside and hold down the fort until the cavalry arrives."

Duncan and Espy bolted out of the utility yard and rounded the corner, staying close to the wall. Five pickup trucks faced the building. Only two sets of headlights were still illuminating the building, but it was sufficient to give Duncan a view to the entrance. Some of the attackers lay dead in the grass near their trucks while others had never made it out of the front seats.

"Looks like we've notched a few kills," whispered Espy as they approached the first window.

"Espy, we've got to watch out for friendly fire," admonished Duncan. Entering a firefight in the close confines of a building, without the benefit of night vision and comms, was suicidal. He wanted to help his men, but he wasn't interested in them killing their commander by mistake.

"You're right, sir," said Espy. "We can't go in there and announce our presence either. The hostiles will identify us and take us out. Either way, we're on the wrong end of this battle."

Duncan inched forward to the first window to try to get a look at what was happening inside. The hallway was darkened, and he couldn't hear any signs of activity. He threw himself back against the wall out of frustration.

"Espy, this is what a rock and a hard place looks like," he finally said to his loyal aide. "We've got the bogies trapped inside, and help is on the way. We need our people to hold down the fort without us."

"That sucks," Espy said in frustration. "I feel like I wanna do something to help our guys."

"Well, we could help them with a distraction," said Duncan. "Let's work our way behind these trucks and shoot out the front tires. It might draw some of them out in a panic only to find their means of escape has been compromised. We'll pick 'em off as they do."

"Yes, sir," added Espy. "Even if it doesn't draw them out, they'll know they're trapped inside with no means of escape. That turns many a soldier into a state of panic."

"Which leads to deadly mistakes," added Duncan. "Let's get started."

Using the commandos' pickup trucks as cover, they quickly moved from one tailgate to another, shooting out the front tires as they went. As they did so, apparently drawing the attention of all involved, the gunfire inside the buildings ceased. Within several minutes, they'd turned the corner of the administration building entrance when they caught a glimpse of two men crawling out of Duncan's office window.

Throwing caution to the wind, Espy raced toward them with his weapon raised, keeping the North Koreans in his sights. They swung in his direction but were immediately ripped into by Espy's deadly aim.

Duncan finished shooting out the tires, and the two men found a spot behind the truck that had crashed through the front entrance.

"You take the Cedar Avenue side of the buildings, and I'll take Regis Street," ordered Duncan. "Our guys will know better than to come through those windows."

"Hey, the gunfire is dying down," said Espy. "They're saving their ammo until they have a clear—"

Another explosion rocked the night, forcing the two men to the ground.

"Where?" asked a stunned Espy.

"The utility yard! Come on!" shouted Duncan as he leapt out of his crouch and ran along the back side of the disabled pickups.

"What about the front?" asked Espy as he was slow to react.

"Forget it for now," Duncan said as he continued running with his rifle at low ready. "We've gotta help Herrera and Page!"

Espy hustled to follow his commander, periodically glancing at the front windows for any attackers attempting to escape.

Duncan ran along the tall wall that surrounded the utility yard when he heard the sound of doors slamming and the attackers' trucks starting.

They're escaping!

Out of breath from carrying his extra gear, Duncan sucked in fresh air and pressed forward in a race to beat the pickups to the rear gate. He heard them on the other side of the wall as they accelerated.

They were pulling away, but he ran as fast as he could, hoping to get off a few shots to stop them.

He was losing the race. The trucks were well ahead of him now, and he caught a glimpse of them as they bounced through the adjacent fields and hit Cedar Avenue, causing their tires to squeal as they made the transition from dirt to asphalt.

Duncan fired wildly in their direction, but they were out of range as they headed northward in the direction of the airport. He bent over and rested on his knees to catch his breath when Espy caught up to him.

"Sir, the other teams will be here shortly. Should I send them in pursuit?"

"No, let's take care of the ones we have trapped," replied Duncan, and then a feeling of dread came over him. "Dammit. Herrera and Page."

Duncan got his second wind and raced into the utility yard, where smoke was pouring out of a gaping hole near the wrecker. The blast he'd heard must've been made with the same type of explosives they'd used to break in, only this time they'd created a new exit.

Espy raced past Duncan to where the body of Private Page lay near the blown-out wall. Espy felt for a pulse and lowered his head. Duncan immediately peeled off to the other side of the wrecker, which had been lifted up in the air and moved over several feet.

Corporal Herrera was lying on the ground in a pool of her own blood. Her face had been ripped open by flying debris, and she had a shoulder wound, which Duncan quickly applied pressure to.

"Herrera, are you with me?" asked Duncan. He heard Espy's phone ring behind him.

"Yessir. It caught me by surprise. They didn't try to get out, and then the wall exploded, and I was knocked to the ground. I lost my weapon and tried to draw my sidearm, but they shot me from under the wrecker. I'm sorry, Commander."

Duncan grimaced as he used his shemagh to wipe the blood from the pretty young woman's face. Once upon a time, the miracles of plastic surgery could restore her beauty. As he'd just learned, Texas had just entered a new period in which *once upon a time* was truly for fairy tales.

Chapter 37

January 21
Camp Lubbock
Lubbock, Texas

After an hour-long battle with the North Korean commandos, Duncan and his men finally regained control of their facility. He didn't second-guess his decision to chase after the fleeing pickup full of men. They would have been miles away by the time his teams returned to Camp Lubbock, and there was no guarantee the attackers intended to continue north. Besides, he needed to help his own men and prevent anyone else from escaping.

"What did the medic say about Corporal Herrera?" Duncan asked Espy as he took a seat in his office. Two privates had just completed sweeping out the broken glass and making the space usable for their commander.

"She lost a lot of blood, but we have a seasoned combat medic," replied Espy. "He used Celox to stop the bleeding and was pleased to report the round went through and out the back side of her shoulder. She suffered minimal damage to her muscles although her range of motion might be limited after she heals."

"What about her face?"

"They're gonna take her to the University Medical Center when the sun comes out. He hopes they have backup generators operating and a plastic surgeon available to work on her. He didn't say much other than that."

Duncan shook his head in disgust. Anger began to swell inside him, but he needed to finish hearing Espy's report. "Casualties?"

"Commander, we lost the eight personnel at the front gate and another four inside the building after the frontal assault. We didn't lose anyone at the substations or the sheriff's office."

Thirteen of his own, dead. He would second-guess his decision making for days and weeks to come. For now, he wanted to focus on what they'd found out about the commandos.

"Espy, what was the final body count on the North Koreans?"

"Seventeen, sir. We have two captives, one of whom took a bullet to the thigh. The other surrendered willingly."

Duncan nodded his head continuously, contemplating what to do next. He had a pretty good idea of what was in store for his captives, but he needed to contact Fort Hood and his superiors.

"Espy, have you coordinated a conference call with the brass?"

"I tried, sir, but there's chaos from one end of the country to the other. The information I received from my counterpart at Hood was that similar coordinated attacks took place on transformers throughout the ERCOT system. I was told the entire grid was taken down, and they expect it will be long-lasting."

"Any other attacks on armories like ours?" Duncan asked.

"No, sir. Of course, information is still slowly coming in to QRF command, but it appears all the other operations were quick hits and clandestine. Only two power plants involved explosives. All the others were relatively straightforward attacks on substations, following the same MO as here in Lubbock."

"No reported armory attacks?" asked Duncan again, this time with a curious inflection in his voice.

"No, sir. I'm kinda surprised by that, sir."

Duncan studied his aide in the low light provided by the lantern. "What's your opinion, Espy?"

"Well, and again, I realize my contact at Fort Hood said information is still streaming in, but why did they take down our grid and attempt to hit the armory? Also, looking back at how it happened, there was extensive planning and recon employed."

"Agreed," started Duncan. "They timed it down to the minute. They knew how far away the substations were. They assumed we'd keep back a basic security contingent and utilized an RPG attack to force us to respond. They even knew where the back entrance to the armory was."

"They've been watching us for some time," interjected Espy.

"I believe so, too. Have you separated the prisoners as I requested?"

"Yes, sir. They are bound and gagged, sitting in adjacent rooms alone. I've not allowed any contact between them and our personnel. As you can imagine, sir, I'm having trouble keeping them alive, if you know what I mean."

"Fully," quipped Duncan. "Did you retrieve the things I asked for?"

"Yessir. They're on the table behind the injured prisoner. He's not aware of what is behind him."

"Let's go," said Duncan as he pushed himself out of his chair. He opened the snap on his holster and removed his sidearm, placing it on the corner of his desk as he walked around it. He also removed his shirt, which had his name and rank embroidered on the front, tossing it on his cot.

The two men walked down a dark hallway leading toward the mess hall. He instructed Espy to clear that section of the complex of all personnel. Further, Espy was to stand guard outside the doors and make sure nobody attempted to eavesdrop on Duncan's interrogation.

Just as Duncan was about to enter the room with the injured prisoner, Duncan calmly whispered in Espy's ear, "Do not come in this room no matter what you think you hear. And when this is over, you'll forget it. Are we clear?"

"Yes, Commander," replied Espy.

Duncan lowered his voice further, and he squinted his eyes as he spoke. His mouth was inches away from Espy's ear. "I'm no longer your commander, Espy. I quit."

He left a shocked Espy standing alone in the hallway as he entered the first interrogation room.

Chapter 38

January 21
Camp Lubbock
Lubbock, Texas

Duncan Armstrong possessed many skills, including a stone-cold heart when necessary. Over time, he'd perfected the art of torture. The highly effective waterboarding method was not one of his favorite tools. Its strength relied primarily on the psychological fear of the tortured prisoner. A captive could prepare himself mentally and fight waterboarding sessions for days or even weeks. Duncan was too impatient for that.

He wanted answers, now.

He entered the room and didn't say a word for several minutes, both to intimidate the prisoner and to give Espy time to clear the hallway. Per his request, candles flickered in the corners of the room flanking the door, thereby casting a large shadow of Duncan on the wall across from the bound man.

Duncan was ready to begin. He walked around the desk, which contained the tools of torture. Each of the devices and instruments were designed to systematically inflict more pain on the prisoner until he agreed to answer Duncan's questions. Then it would be up to Duncan, the interrogator, to discern if the man was telling the truth.

Duncan towered over the seated commando and stared him down. The prisoner's tough exterior came from years of training. Kudos to the North Korean for not buckling under already from the leg wound he'd suffered. He'd been shot in the top of his thigh, and his pants were soaked with blood.

One of Duncan's men had used a combat tourniquet above the

wound to keep him from bleeding out. That same tourniquet would *accidentally* break loose if the prisoner didn't cooperate, go into shock from Duncan's other techniques, or die during the *conversation*.

Duncan pulled one of his knives out of his pocket and inserted it between the gag affixed to his prisoner's face and mouth. Duncan made no attempt to avoid cutting the commando in the process, causing a fairly deep wound to be carved into his cheek before it reached the bone. The prisoner winced as blood streamed down his face, but his angry eyes remained locked with Duncan's.

"I thought that might make it easier for you to speak. Tell me what I want to hear, and I'll get the medic in here to treat the wound. Simple enough, right?"

The man stared back and didn't respond.

Duncan leaned forward and yelled, "Right?"

"Screw you!" the prisoner responded and spit in Duncan's direction but missed his face as Duncan quickly avoided the attempt. He did provide the prisoner a punishment for his effort.

Duncan drew back his right arm as if he were going to slash the prisoner with his knife. The man's eyes followed the weapon and never saw the second knife being retrieved from Duncan's pants. With a quick move, Duncan drove the circular butt end of the knife into the man's nose, causing cartilage to break and blood to fly across the prisoner's face.

"Next time, I'll use the other end and rip that nose right off your head!"

The prisoner tried in vain to reach his shoulder to wipe the blood off his face. He finally opted for shaking his head, and with a considerable painful effort, he exhaled through both nostrils to clear his airways of blood.

"There, feel better?" asked Duncan sarcastically. "Thank you for letting me know you speak English. Let's start talking, gook." Duncan used a word he despised, but it was necessary for a torturer to humiliate his captive as well as threaten them with increased pain.

"Like I said," the prisoner growled as he snorted more blood out of his broken nose, "screw you!"

Duncan immediately rammed his fist into the man's leg wound, causing him to scream at the top of his lungs in pain. Duncan now knew the man had a threshold for pain that could be overcome. He just needed to push the right buttons.

"Whadya want from me? I know nothing!"

"Your English is pretty good, gook. Where ya from?" Duncan began to circle his prisoner, causing the man's head to swivel in an attempt to follow him. After walking around the table, Duncan returned around the other side with a pair of Vise-Grip locking pliers.

The man's eyes grew wide, and he began to babble. "California, man. I'm from California. I don't know these guys. I just kinda hooked up with 'em in a bar one night, and everything went bad."

"Oh, so you're not part of their group, just an innocent bystander. Just along for the ride? Is that what you want me to believe?"

"Yeah, man. It's totally true. I'm not even North Korean like those others."

"Liar!" shouted Duncan as he adjusted the pliers to the proper width and immediately clamped them on the man's nose, squeezing the handle to lock them tight.

The man let out a bloodcurdling scream and began to shake his head wildly from side to side in an attempt to force the Vise-Grips off his crushed nose. The harder he shook, the more painful it became as the locking pliers smacked both sides of his face.

"Please. Take it off. Take it off. I'll tell the truth."

Duncan nodded. "Fair enough. Hold your head still."

The prisoner began to cry, and he held his head perfectly still, waiting for Duncan to remove the pliers. He didn't expect what happened next.

Rather than releasing the locking mechanism on the handle, Duncan just ripped the pliers off the man's nose. The shock of the brutal pain caused the man's eyes to widen and his mouth to shout in agony. He immediately began to scream for help. He begged anyone to please rescue him from this maniac.

But nobody came to his rescue. In fact, by the level of noise this guy was making, the entirety of Camp Lubbock could hear even if they weren't in the hallway with Espy.

"How many are with you?"

"Over twenty, maybe less now."

"Who's your leader? And what's his rank?"

"His name is Holloway, but he doesn't have a rank. We're not with the commandos. I mean, we were, but we all were part of a gang in LA. Holloway is former military. U.S. Army, I think."

"What's his first name?"

"Man, I don't know. Seriously. He's never said his first name. All I know is he hates the Army because they wouldn't let him fight after he lost his eye."

Duncan stopped pacing as he digested this information. He continued with his questioning.

"What commandos?"

"The Lightning Death Squads. There are thousands of them in the States now. Maybe tens of thousands, I don't know. Several hundred of them snuck into Texas."

"What are they doing?" asked Duncan.

"Tonight was about taking down the Texas grid. Outside of that, I don't know what they have in mind."

Duncan lowered the back of his fist onto the man's gaping wound on his leg, which was beginning to bleed again.

"I swear!" the man screamed between screams of agony. He renewed his pleas for help from anyone who could hear. "Is there anybody out there? This dude's crazy! Help!"

"Next question. Do you have a base of operations? A camp of some kind?"

The prisoner hesitated and began to look wildly around the room. He continued to avoid answering the question when Duncan, who had been circling his prey, came around the back of the desk with a box of Epsom salts. He began to pour it over the gash in the man's cheek and the rest of the box into his leg.

The initial burn of the salt in the man's wounds caused him to squirm, but Duncan's gripping the man's leg wound and rubbing the salt into his bloody flesh caused him to scream in agony.

"Answer me!"

"It's a little town. I don't know what it's called. There's no stoplight and a high school nearby. It's an hour or so south of here. Nobody was there when we arrived, so we just moved in."

Duncan rubbed more salt into the man's wound and then struck him with his right fist in the jaw, knocking him unconscious before the force of the blow toppled him over in his chair.

His job was done here.

He calmly walked into the hallway and pulled the door closed behind him. He wouldn't discover until later when the sun rose and he found a mirror that his face was covered with the man's blood, as were his hands and arms.

Duncan exhaled and avoided eye contact with Espy, who had stepped back to the opposite side of the hallway to give Duncan plenty of space.

He immediately approached the second prisoner's room and quietly entered. He closed the door behind him and walked in front of the man who hadn't been injured and had willfully surrendered.

As soon as he came fully into the view of the captive, the man began screaming for help. He pushed his feet off the ground in an attempt to get away from the menacing Duncan.

"I'll talk. I'll tell you everything. Please don't kill me. I swear. Just ask!"

Ten minutes later, Duncan was satisfied with the results of the interrogation. He left the man in his chair, bawling like a baby, with his pants soiled from both his own urine and feces.

Duncan exited the room, and a horrified Espy stood waiting.

"Sir, did you learn anything?" he asked hesitantly.

"Yup, sure did," said Duncan as he began walking away.

"Sir, did you really resign?" asked Espy as he walked briskly to catch up with Duncan.

"Nah, just for a little while. C'mon, I'll tell you what I learned."

Part Four

Welcome to the Apocalypse

Chapter 39

January 21
Patricia, Texas

Holloway led the three-truck entourage at speeds exceeding one hundred miles an hour as they traveled away from Lubbock back to their base of operations in Patricia, seventy-five miles south. After he took a few side roads to be comfortable they weren't being followed by the Texas Guardsmen, he roared down the highway without concern of detection.

None of the members of his team who accompanied Holloway had been wounded except for the near-concussive headaches inflicted upon them from the blast inside the armory. He resigned himself to the reality that most likely the frontal assault teams either perished or were captured in the ill-advised raid upon the National Guard armory.

Frustrated, he pounded the steering wheel repeatedly, drawing the attention of his men, who looked at him as if he were becoming unhinged. Holloway opened his fist and held his hand in the air, indicating that he was in control and there was no need for concern about his mental stability. His men had hitched their horses to his wagon instead of General Lee and the rest of the Lightning Death Squad commandos. He needed to continue to maintain their respect.

Nonetheless, Holloway was still angry with the outcome and vowed revenge on the Texan who'd outsmarted him. Their maneuvers were like an intricate game of chess, and his adversary had set the perfect gambit, a trap, which had almost ensnared him. Holloway vowed to seek revenge, but for now, he had much bigger concerns.

Most likely, some of his men had been taken alive and forced to sing like canaries. He doubted the Texans cared for things like Geneva Conventions or United Nations mandates on prisoner treatment. His adversary was probably extracting the information about him and their temporary base at that very moment.

"Gentlemen, we'll have a couple of hours' head start at the most," started Holloway. "We'll start at the old cotton gin where we left two men to guard the fuel truck and the bulk of our supplies. There's no time to return to the houses. We've got to get packed and ready."

"Yes, sir," replied his top lieutenant, who was beside him in the front seat of the truck. "We have five pickups. If we fill them with fuel, we can leave the tanker behind. It'll be close to empty anyway."

Holloway took a deep breath and exhaled his anger. It was time for the next phase of his operation. "Okay, what about the food trailer? I don't want to be slowed down by that rig."

"Same thing, sir," his right-hand man responded. "After providing General Lee's men equal portions to last them three days on the road, we have enough food for a week. We can divide it up easily between the five trucks, sir."

"Anything else? Is the high school emptied of provisions?"

"Yes, sir. That was one of the tasks I assigned the men to do while we were gone. The other was to create the appearance of a stalled car just to the west of town with evidence it belonged to us."

Holloway was intrigued and curious about his lieutenant's actions without consulting him. *I hope it was a good idea, or you're gonna hear what I think about it.*

"Explain," he growled.

"Assuming that the soldiers chase after us and either find our base on their own or through weaklings who gave in to questioning, I wanted to lead them in the wrong direction when they continue their search. I instructed our guys to drive one of the old cars a mile outside town and leave it in park with the motor running to keep the engine warm. When our pursuers come upon it, they might feel the motor as hot, and it should send them in the wrong direction."

Holloway thought the idea was stupid so far, but he decided to indulge the man in the last ten minutes of their trip back. "What makes you think they'll associate the car with us?"

"They'll find the stolen food truck and gasoline tanker first. When they fan out through the town, they'll find this car. Inside, I've instructed our people to leave a map indicating the route to a phony rally point. I had them write information on the map in Korean, sir."

Nice touch.

"Why send them west? Maybe I wanted to go back that way?"

"Sir, you once said to me that you'd never go back," he responded.

"I meant I'd never go back to LA," interrupted Holloway. He recalled an alcohol-fueled conversation back in Roswell, New Mexico, in which Holloway had reflected upon their days in the Fullerton Boyz gang and what a mirage LA truly was. Behind the glitz of Hollywood, Venice Beach, palm trees and pretty girls lay an underbelly of slime, a world that, if exposed, would knock the luster off the City of Angels.

"Sir, I remember exactly what you said," his lieutenant continued. "You said *at the end of the day, the sun doesn't set over Venice Beach, it just gives up and drops into the ocean with an evil hiss.*"

Holloway smiled and shrugged. He had said that. Holloway was impressed with the young man's analytical approach. Maybe he should have involved him in more of the planning.

"Okay, maybe you're right, and that might apply in this situation as well. Do you have a suggestion as to where we should go?"

The young man eagerly responded, suddenly excited to have an opportunity to voice his opinion without fear of derision or repercussions.

"Sir, your stated goal is to find a large ranch and settle down. This part of West Texas is wide open and will most likely provide you with many options to suit your needs."

"Hold up a second," interrupted Holloway. "Were you a real estate agent or something?"

"No, but I used to bang a girl who was."

Holloway started laughing, and the young man's frank response eased the tension in the cab of the truck. Holloway checked his speed, which hovered around ninety now. He checked his mirrors and saw the two sets of headlights behind him keeping up the pace.

"Okay, go on," he instructed his young realtor.

"If you move near the more populated areas like Dallas, Austin, San Antonio, or the coast, large ranches will be difficult to find. Also, it's most likely the government will use their military forces out of Fort Bliss and Fort Hood to protect the larger cities, making it difficult for us to do business."

"So far, so good. Keep going."

"If we stay in this area, we'll have small to midsize cities that are relatively unprotected. Look at Lubbock, for example. That contingent of guardsmen could barely protect their own base, much less the whole city. Remember how we got these trucks? We were able to make several trips without being caught."

"Good point. So where do you suggest?"

"Sir the next logical place the Texas Guard will search for us is straight out of town, following the highway to Midland. They don't have the manpower to search every Podunk county road in the area. Plus, they don't have the time. With the grid down, they'll be recalled to their own base to help Lubbock. Do you remember how quickly LA collapsed after the EMP? It was a matter of hours, not days."

They were approaching Patricia, which meant they'd be scrambling around to vacate the premises. He needed his new brainstormer to get to the point.

"Okay, which way do we go?"

"I suggest we head east on the road leading past the high school. There's a big lake about fifty miles away. With the grid down, we're gonna need a source of water. Where there's a lake, there's a house with a well. Even if it isn't a ranch, we could take over a neighborhood or even claim all the land around the lake. Either way, if we can't find what you want, we'll make it one way or the other."

By hook or by crook.

Chapter 40

January 21
Camp Lubbock
Lubbock, Texas

Duncan and the rest of his team were surrounded by a mess of death and destruction. Every window was blown out. The walls and doors were riddled with bullets. Dead bodies were strewn about. But that did not dampen the spirits of those lucky few who had been chosen by Duncan to accompany him as they used the information from the hostages to chase down this guy named Holloway who'd orchestrated the attack on Camp Lubbock.

He and Espy discussed the possibility that Holloway might try a counterattack, assuming the base would mount a good old-fashioned posse to hunt him down. Out of an abundance of caution, they delayed their departure from Camp Lubbock and stood guard around the perimeter while the dead bodies were removed.

His guardsmen were placed in body bags. Duncan hoped to find a way to get through to their families in light of the circumstances. Otherwise, he'd arrange for a memorial service that afternoon and create a cemetery within the confines of Camp Lubbock to honor them.

The dead commandos were loaded into the back of a utility truck and hauled a mile off base into an open field, where they were covered in gasoline and unceremoniously burned.

With the facility in shambles, he'd have to determine whether they'd remain at Camp Lubbock or find a more suitable location. One of his lieutenants was also a local resident and promised to come up with several alternatives that would suit their needs.

The biggest issue was the protection of their weapons and ammunition stockpiles. Weapons had been a valuable commodity before the grid went down. Now they would be highly sought after by men like Holloway who'd emerge as a result of Texas's entry into an apocalyptic world.

Through his interrogations of the prisoners and backtracking his footsteps since arriving at Peach Springs in Arizona, Duncan was able to determine that he and Holloway had crossed paths several times. It all made sense to him now—the encounter on the highway at Winslow and the subsequent events in New Mexico in which U.S. military vehicles carrying North Koreans were observed traveling toward Carlsbad Caverns. Duncan and Holloway had followed virtually the same path to converge here at Camp Lubbock.

Duncan was ready to end this, so he was prepared to put his efforts into hunting the man down. He personally wanted to kill Holloway by slicing his throat open until the evil drained out of him.

After the bodies were disposed of, Duncan conducted one final security assessment before they headed south. He and Espy led the convoy of Humvees and a single troop transport toward Lamesa, the town Duncan had spent an entire day in just forty-eight hours ago. His frustrations grew after he'd determined Holloway's hideout based upon the interrogations. He wished he'd known this platoon-strength group of North Korean commandos had been barely a dozen miles away from where he'd diffused the hostage situation at the middle school.

In any event, he was hot on their trail now and was ready to destroy Holloway. Just a few miles outside Patricia, he pulled the convoy to a stop.

"Sir, is there something I can do?" asked a puzzled Espy. "Do you need to advise the men?"

"No, Sergeant. I need to take care of something," replied Duncan, using Espy's rank instead of their less formal means of conversation. He turned around to the private guarding the handcuffed prisoner. "Private, remove the prisoner and join me outside."

Duncan exited the Humvee, as did Espy with his weapon at low ready. The private pulled the man out of the Humvee and stood him in the middle of the road. Duncan pulled his sidearm and pointed it at the man's head, who immediately urinated in his pants, again.

"Private, take him in front of that road sign, unlock his cuffs, and then recuff him to the sign with his arms behind his back."

The private looked in Espy's direction, who nodded for him to proceed.

"Sir, may I ask—?" questioned Espy before Duncan cut him off.

"It's become a family tradition, Sergeant."

Once the man was cuffed, Duncan holstered his sidearm and knocked his feet out from under him, where he collapsed on his tailbone with a thud.

"Please don't kill me!" the man begged. "I told you everything you wanted to know."

"I'm not gonna kill you, but I'm certainly not gonna keep you alive either," snarled Duncan in the man's ear. Duncan spun around and headed back for the Humvee.

Espy followed him, looked back toward the prisoner, who was begging to be released, and then circled his hand in the air to advise the other guardsmen to get ready. The engines fired, and the convoy lurched forward—four Humvees, three with fifty-caliber weapons mounted on top, together with a deuce-and-a-half troop transport. The vehicles, carrying twenty-four guardsmen seeking revenge, pulled into the small town of Patricia, Texas, population zero.

Chapter 41

January 21
The Armstrong Ranch
Borden County, Texas

Lucy and Preacher huddled around the kitchen table as Major completed his phone call with Duncan. The description of the evening's events was harrowing, even though Duncan provided Major the abbreviated CliffsNotes version. He was en route to where the North Koreans had been hiding practically right under their noses. Major twirled the satellite phone on the table, exhaled, and motioned for Lucy and Preacher to sit down.

"It's bad, isn't it?" asked Lucy calmly, although her demeanor had changed from when Duncan's call came through. She and Major had been asleep when the power grid went down, so they were unaware of what had happened. It was five in the morning when the phone rang, an early morning call that sends shockwaves through any mother's body who has a son or daughter in the military.

"Yeah, on several levels, potentially," replied Major. "Big picture first. Just after midnight, North Korean military forces, trained commandos according to Duncan, attacked substations and power-generating plants across Texas. He doesn't have the details from his superiors yet because I imagine Austin and the military are in a frenzy."

"How does he know?" asked Preacher.

"Camp Lubbock was attacked by as many as two dozen North Koreans as part of the coordinated strikes on the grid. In Lubbock, they destroyed the three electrical substations that connected their utility to ERCOT. Then, while Duncan's men were responding to the assault on the substations, they fired rocket-propelled grenades into the sheriff's office and then at the front gate of Camp Lubbock."

Lucy grabbed the phone away from Major so he would stop nervously spinning it on the table. She didn't want the noise to wake up any of their kids.

"Honey," she began, "where is he going right now?"

"Duncan interrogated two hostages after they repelled the attack. The men said they were hiding out in a small town with nothing more than a crossroads, a high school and a cotton gin."

"Patricia," muttered Preacher. "Everybody always wondered why they built Klondike High in the middle of nowhere like that. Patricia's Farmers cotton gin is there too."

"That's just an hour from here," said Lucy as she rubbed the hair from her now ashen face. "They could be coming here next. Major, we have to get ready."

"I have to agree with Miss Lucy," added Preacher. "Duncan and his men are fixin' to flush the vermin out of their hidey-holes. The easy routes would be to head back to the border, where they'd run into the arms of the military, which is still rounding up refugees. Or they could head south toward Big Spring to get on major highways and disappear in a flash."

"Or they come straight to our place," added Lucy.

"Okay, okay," started Major, trying to calm everyone, including himself, down. "Duncan's after them much quicker than they probably anticipated. He'll probably take them out in Patricia. By the way, I don't use the term *take out* loosely. He has no intentions of taking prisoners."

"Nor did they, it appears," said Preacher.

"Very true," continued Major. "That said, we need to be ready. The first order of business is to warn the patrols of the situation. We need to place extra emphasis on the western and southern fences from the Reinecke Unit, past the guard tower, and over toward the river. One thing we have going for us is the fact that there isn't a direct road from the ranch to Patricia. You really have to know how to zigzag on the county roads, some of which are just hard-packed gravel. It would be a slow getaway, and I hope, under the circumstances, they'd take the easier routes to the west or south."

"I'll take care of the patrols," said Preacher. "Can we use the girls, too?"

All eyes were on Lucy, who had shielded Palmer and Sook from guard duty for the more dangerous side of the ranch. She finally gave her reply. "I have confidence in both of them, so yes, they can assist. But don't put them on the front line, you know, the guard tower or the western fence. How about pull Antonio's men from the barnyard and let the girls handle that? They'll be able to quickly respond from there if necessary."

"All right," said Major. "The next thing we need to do is get the generators cranked up. Preacher, tell the ranch hands to eat their perishable foods as quickly as possible. For those who have generators, starting at eight o'clock this morning, run them following a four on, four off basis until their refrigerated foods are gone. We'll be doing the same here. Also, make sure they charge their radios, power tools, and rechargeable batteries while the generators are running. We can manage our fuel this way while not losing any food."

Lucy nodded. "I'll get the generators ready for our refrigerated and frozen foods also. Major, should I prepare the bunkers just in case? I worry about the women and children if the ranch comes under attack. Honey, they're defenseless."

Major thought for a moment and knew Lucy was right. He wasn't entirely comfortable with hiding everyone in one place for a situation like this. The bunkers were impenetrable to nuclear attack, but marauders could find ways to cut off their air supplies or use fear to force them out if they located the hatch, by relentlessly pounding on it.

"Okay, get it ready, but it's a last resort, Miss Lucy. I'd rather take them to the east woods and some of the vacant houses around the lake if we have time. The key is to get ready."

The three of them pushed away from the table when Preacher asked, "Have y'all considered asking Duncan to come home? His gun is like five of ours."

Major sighed and reached for Lucy's hand. He squeezed it and replied, "I've thought about that every moment since the phone rang earlier. His being away has been stressful enough. I never imagined we'd be fighting the North Koreans on Texas soil."

"Honey, I agree with all of that, but at what point do we decide to be selfish and take care of our own instead of risking everything for Texas?"

Major closed his eyes and shook his head. He wished he knew the answer.

Chapter 42

January 21
The Mansion
Austin, Texas

President Marion Burnett stood alone in her dark office, staring across the cityscape of Austin, which sat in complete darkness. Only the generator-produced lighting around the Mansion's perimeter could be seen after the ERCOT grid collapsed. She'd been awakened by her assistant after explosions at the Comanche Peak nuclear facility had been reported to Fort Worth law enforcement. They in turn contacted the National Guard, but by then, the word of the coordinated assault on the ERCOT grid was known throughout Texas.

She was not quite in shock, but a state of despair had overcome her. Her office, cold from lack of heat, caused a chill to overcome her, and her mind immediately went to her counterpart in Washington, President Alani Harman. She now knew how the U.S. president had felt when the EMP struck. Disbelief, confusion, despair, and desolation were all appropriate characterizations of the wave of emotions that had overcome her in the last hour.

A gentle tapping at her office door and then a slight opening flooded her room with light. The voice of her chief of staff followed the entry of the yellowish glow.

"Madam President, you can turn your lights on. The generators have been operable for some time."

"I know," said the president. "I just wasn't ready for it."

"Okay, um, Madam President, Adjutant General Deur is here to speak with you. He says it's urgent."

"Of course it is," she said sarcastically. Burnett took a deep breath and exhaled. She felt alone. "Sure, turn on the lights and send him in. I need coffee, too, please. It's time to pull up my big-girl panties." Burnett laughed at her last comment, a phrase that was a throwback to her younger days.

Her chief of staff flipped on the lights, surprising Burnett's vision and forcing her to close her eyes momentarily. When she opened them, Deur had entered the room along with two of his aides, including an attractive woman Burnett had seen before.

"Good morning, Kregg," she greeted the entourage as she made her way to her desk.

"Good morning, Madam President," said Deur. "I have with me Colonel Sanderson with the Texas Quick Reaction Force headquartered at Fort Hood and Pauline Hart, deputy adjutant general in charge of clandestine affairs."

The president returned the salute of Sanderson and then reached across her desk to shake hands with Hart. She took a closer look at the woman and recognized her. "I think we've met, have we not?"

Hart replied, "Yes, ma'am. It was at the Christmas Ball here in the Mansion year before last. I'm Kregg's sister-in-law."

"Yes, I remember," said Burnett. She looked over to Deur and then back to Hart. "Pauline, I apologize if I'm speaking inappropriately, I don't profess to know everyone who works in third- and fourth-tier positions within my government. Did I hear correctly? You're the head of clandestine affairs?"

"Yes, Madam President. My last position with the United States government made me uniquely qualified for the position Kregg needed filled."

"Plus," interrupted Deur, "as my family, I know I can trust her."

The president shrugged and motioned for all of them to sit down. Her chief of staff arrived with coffee, and the comforting aroma had an immediate calming effect.

"Okay, Kregg, how bad is it?" asked the president.

"Madam President, there are many details to fill in, and I promise you a comprehensive report as soon as I gather information from across the country. What I can confirm is that the ERCOT electrical generating and distribution network has been compromised. Based upon initial reports, while the impact on the system is not nearly as devastating as the electromagnetic pulse attack on the U.S. power grid, we suffered a comparable failure."

"North Koreans did this?" she asked.

Deur nodded to Hart, who provided the response. "Yes, Madam President. Eyewitnesses and members of the QRF team in Lubbock have confirmed that the attack was planned and carried out by North Korean operatives known as the Lightning Death Squads. These are special ops soldiers trained by Kim's regime to counter our Delta and SEAL teams. I plan on debriefing the commander at Camp Lubbock, who interrogated two commandos after the attack on their base."

Colonel Sanderson sat up in his seat. "I was instrumental in the hiring of Commander Armstrong and know this young man to be levelheaded. I would trust his assessment implicitly."

The president looked to Deur. "Major's son?"

"Yes, ma'am. He was suggested for the position because of his proximity to Lubbock and his experience in the U.S. military."

"What measures have we taken as a result of this blindside?" asked the president.

"Our response will be overwhelming and comprehensive," said Deur. "The military has deployed troops to the major population centers as an early show of force and control. As the sun rises across the country and Texans learn of the attacks, we want them to know their government is ready to respond."

"Your first order of business is to establish control so people don't get out of hand," interjected the president. "My earlier martial law declaration covered this, right?"

"If I may, ma'am," started Colonel Sanderson, "the TX-QRF will handle crowd control and population outbursts in the smaller cities while lending a hand to local law enforcement in protecting the remaining critical infrastructure, such as water utilities."

"Are they still operating?" asked the president.

"To an extent," replied Sanderson. "Gravity-fed water towers are constructed at a height sufficient to pressurize a small town's water supply for a period of time based upon its capacity and the town's usage. Most of the water towers exceed six thousand gallons in capacity that, if allocated properly, can supply water to most towns for two weeks."

"Two weeks," said the president. "Then what?"

Deur took back over the conversation. "That's part of what we'll need to address, ma'am. In addition to keeping calm in the streets, we need to undertake a widespread educational program to teach people how to survive without our critical infrastructure. Based upon the extent of the damage inflicted upon ERCOT, it will take many months or even years to restore power to all parts of Texas."

"What about the enemy? What are we doing to hunt them down?"

"It's difficult to ascertain their goals at this time," replied Hart. "After the nuclear attacks and counterattacks, it's doubtful that the Kim regime would have the military wherewithal to deploy an occupying force in North America. An invading army would most likely seek to kill ninety percent of the target country's citizens and enslave the rest in some manner. To wipe out the entire population would leave them with a Pyrrhic victory at best."

"What are they doing here?" asked the president.

Deur responded, "This appears to be more of an insurgency action designed to prevent recovery and destroy the will of the people, both in America and Texas. In January, food storage levels were starting to dwindle while alternative fuel resources like oil and coal were already in short supply."

"May I add one more thing?" asked Hart.

The president gestured for her to go ahead.

"Throughout the Southwestern United States and Texas, there is a substantial population of illegal aliens that might turn against the citizenry of both countries. Old hostilities might create new alliances, much like an angry fifth column. Madam President, the axiom *the enemy of my enemy is my friend* has been around for a long time. I would advise you to be aware of an uprising from this segment of the populace."

"Great, we get to refight Santa Anna," quipped President Burnett.

"In my opinion," Colonel Sanderson added, "the North Koreans are trying to make a point. Their fight with the United States—and by prior association, Texas—is based upon pride and principle. U.S. foreign policy beat them down for decades. In their mind, a level playing field has been created although their country has been leveled by our nuclear weapons. For these Lightning Death Squad commandos, they consider themselves a *moral force*, using the term of Carl von Clausewitz, the Prussian general who wrote about war in the early 1800s. They fight based on ideology, not out of a sense of duty pursuant to the orders of their commanders."

President Burnett shook her head and rolled her eyes. "How do you defend a country against insanity? Terrorists taught us that people are willing to die for their religious beliefs. These commandos are willing to die and inflict death upon others because of their allegiance to a dictator and his ideology."

"Yes, ma'am," said Colonel Sanderson.

"Well, we Texans have somethin' for 'em," continued President Burnett before she paused to take a big gulp of coffee from her Rangers mug. "We'll show them that we're Texas strong, from the youngest among us all the way to the occupant of this office. Here's what we're gonna do."

CHAPTER 43

January 21
Vealmoor, Texas

"Do you see that ranch over there?" asked Holloway as he pointed off the road to the Slaughters' Lazy S Ranch. "That would have been perfect except some moron burned the house to the ground. It has barns, maybe a dairy building, and lots of fenced land. It would've been just what I was looking for."

Holloway slowed as they approached an apparently deserted town. Vealmoor had dwindled in population from a couple of hundred in the sixties to around fifty at the time of the collapse. Isolated from the rest of Texas by virtue of its remote location, within weeks of the EMP attack, all of the inhabitants fled for the homes of relatives in larger, more populated cities, where they could count on government assistance to feed their families.

Holloway threw his left arm out the truck's open window and made a fist indicating for the other vehicles to slow down as they approached the intersection of the two county roads in Vealmoor. A handful of one-story homes, a couple of closed-down businesses, and a church filled up the remainder of the intersection.

"Let's catch our breath and study the map," said Holloway. "I could use some chow and a change of clothes too."

He jumped out of the truck and spoke to each of his men, who remained in their trucks. He pointed out homes for them to clear and occupy until he was ready to move on to their next destination. He ordered them to keep their trucks hidden and not to leave the houses unless there was trouble. Although this area appeared completely deserted, he didn't want to be discovered by the National Guard if they came through.

Holloway occupied the nicest of the properties situated on the corner. The older ranch-style home was surrounded by a fence, was pristinely landscaped, and had a propane tank, which might provide a source of heat. With a little luck, he thought to himself, he might be able to extract some hot water out of the water heater to wash the stench off his body.

After taking the time to clear the home and rummage through its closets and cupboards looking for things of value, he located a water hose and drained the warm water into a bathtub down the hall, where he soaked until the water cooled.

While he relaxed, Holloway reflected on what had brought him to this point, and his mind wandered to books he used to enjoy as a kid about the gangsters of the twenties and thirties. From the big city mobsters like Al Capone in Chicago to the rural bank robbers like Bonnie and Clyde, he often dreamt of life on the run, eluding the law and hiding out in desolate places like this one.

He toweled off and was pleased to find clothes that fit him in the farmer's closet. He was ready to transition once again from life as a soldier to that of a criminal opportunist, a vocation he enjoyed a lot more. With law enforcement in total disarray thanks to the efforts of his North Korean friends, his job as a marauder would be much easier. He was looking at himself in the mirror and imagining himself in a normal life when something caught his attention through the bedroom window.

A tan-colored Humvee was parked at the intersection barely fifty feet from the house. He frantically scrambled to grab his rifle, and he ran to the front of the home to get a better view. He pressed his back against the wall and moved the curtain to one side.

"I'll be damned," he muttered as he squinted his eyes to confirm what he saw. "If it isn't that pretty soldier boy. Are you lost, kid? Hey, where are your buddies?"

Holloway stretched his neck to look behind the Humvee to see if more vehicles were part of this patrol. Nothing came, and then Holloway got excited.

"My turn!"

Without putting on his shoes, he ran toward the rear of the house and out the back door. He raced across the coarse grass to take up a position at the back side of the barn. Just as he reached the barn, he heard the rumble of the Humvee as it continued eastward past the house. The driver accelerated just as Holloway reached the back of the barn with his rifle raised.

A stand of mature, leafless pecan trees blocked his line of sight to the truck as it roared away from him. Frustrated, he repeatedly slammed his fist into the side of the small red barn before walking to the edge of the chain-link fence to watch the Humvee disappear from sight to his east.

He took another glance back toward Patricia and finally returned inside. Resigned to the fact that he'd lost his prey, he flopped down on the couch and considered his options. If he loaded up the guys and gave chase, he might be successful in killing his nemesis, but they would surely radio for reinforcements in the process, which would give away Holloway's position. Perhaps it was better for them to get a false sense of security and continue on their patrol. Eventually, they'd have to return to Lubbock and they'd confirm that this area was clear.

He made a mental note to review the map and study where this county road led and what options the Humvee had in returning to Lubbock. If they readied themselves, the driver might come back through this intersection. If they did, Holloway would have somethin' for them.

Chapter 44

January 21
The Armstrong Ranch
Borden County, Texas

Duncan had Espy stop the truck for a moment as he got out to shake hands with Antonio and two of the ranch hands. He warned them to be on the lookout for the North Korean commandos. Antonio was very familiar with the areas surrounding Patricia and nearby Vealmoor. He assured Duncan they'd increase their awareness to protect the ranch.

As Espy drove along the hard-packed gravel driveway leading to the barns, Duncan reflected on the condition of the ranch. Even for late January, the lack of cattle and activity was disconcerting. Granted, he'd been away for the majority of the last eight years, but to view the bleak surroundings saddened him. Perhaps it was the reality setting in that Texas had joined the apocalyptic world around them. Regardless, he tried to shake off his sense of foreboding as the low lights emitted from the ranch house came into view.

The Humvee pulled to a stop, and before he could open the door, his family was bounding down the stairs off the front porch, led by Sook, who was going to be the first to get a hug from their returning warriors.

He hoisted her up in his arms and twirled her one-hundred-twenty-pound frame in a circle. Sook had gained weight since her arrival at the Armstrong Ranch, and most of it was in the form of muscle. Between her work around the ranch and her taekwondo training with Palmer, she'd become much more athletic.

After the two finished their reunion, Duncan hugged his mother.

His brothers got their usual manly bro-hugs. Standing on the porch, observing the joyful return, were Preacher and Major who stood like bookends, arms folded, holding up the tree-skinned porch posts.

"Come on, everyone," shouted Miss Lucy. "Let's get out of this night air. Boys, I have some leftover cowboy stew for you guys. I made sausage out of the last of the hog meat stored in the refrigerator together with all the vegetables I had. We're trying to clean out the fridge, so I threw the recipe book out the window on this one."

"Hey, Riley, was it good?" asked Duncan jokingly.

"Dang straight! I woofed down two bowls."

"C'mon, Duncan." Preacher laughed. "He's the last one to ask. He's like that Mikey kid on the old Life cereal commercials."

"I remember those commercials," added Major.

"Of course you do, old-timer," said Lucy with a laugh and a gentle pat on her husband's chest as she passed him on the porch.

Duncan and Espy removed their gear and then were directed to sit by the warm fire, where they were promptly flanked on each side by Sook and Palmer. It was clear that Palmer, who'd feigned restraint when she greeted Espy, was clearly smitten with Duncan's aide-de-camp.

While Lucy warmed them a bowl of stew atop their wood-burning stove, which sat in the corner of the kitchen, Major lit more candles to increase the lighting in the living room. Duncan and Espy recounted the events of earlier this morning together with their search of Patricia for the North Koreans.

After an exhaustive search looking for clues, their only lead was the stalled vehicle heading toward the New Mexico border with the map covered in Korean writing. Duncan retrieved the map and handed it to Sook so she could interpret the markings.

She held the map so it could be read in the light of the fire. Espy told the Armstrong family how well-respected Duncan was by everyone in the unit because of his levelheaded approach to the attack and his individual bravery. After he finished, Sook took the floor.

"This map has been written by three people," she began, pointing to the *Hangul*, the alphabet of the Korean language put into use in the fifteenth century. "Every Korean has their own handwriting style. Women are more precise; men are often sloppy or incorrect. These markings that cover most of the map are to designate specific locations. These symbols mean *truck*."

Duncan interrupted. "We disabled half a dozen new Ford King Ranch models that surrounded Camp Lubbock. The trucks that got away were also Fords but looked more like F-250s. I believe these were stolen and used to transport the North Korean commandos to Patricia after the attack on the Hobbs checkpoint."

He looked at Sook and smiled, so she continued. "The second set of markings are directed toward this location." She looked to Duncan for assistance.

"That's Patricia," interjected Duncan. "This means that an advance team, led by this guy Holloway we just told you about, has been hiding out in Patricia for a couple of weeks or more."

Duncan went on to lay out his theory that he and Sook had crossed paths with Holloway on at least two occasions since their arrival in Arizona. He relayed what he'd learned from the two prisoners, being careful to use the word *questioning* rather than *interrogation* or *torture*.

At one point, as he relayed his findings, he glanced at his mother, who stared a hole through him. Lucy gave him a slight smile, as if to say, *I know how you got this information, and thank you for sparing your mother the details*. He provided her a wink in return.

"What are the third markings?" asked Cooper.

"These arrows point toward the west with the words *home base* written over here," replied Sook. Once again, she handed the map to Duncan and pointed out where the Korean symbols for *home base* were located.

"That's Carlsbad Caverns. The prisoners told me that was where they waited until all of the commandos arrived from Mexico to join them in the attack. I don't believe they would go back there."

"Why not, son?" asked Major.

"Dad, whoever planned this assault on our grid and Camp Lubbock, whether it was Holloway or Lee, was an astute tactician. The plan was well executed and went very well for them until they decided to attack our armory. It's my belief that Holloway did that on his own. He may have gone rogue, or it was some sort of prize he was awarded by Lee for his efforts. I won't know until I look into his eye and force it out of him."

"Eye?" asked Palmer inquisitively.

"Yeah. Holloway only has one eye. To make matters worse, he never wears a patch, choosing instead to let his gruesome socket intimidate people around him."

Major, who enjoyed following the trail of a criminal on the run, continued. "Well, you have the abandoned car containing this map pointed west. You have markings on the map as a clue. Did you follow up on the possible lead?"

"I did, Dad, but with only one Humvee. I really thought it was all too convenient."

"Duncan, there is one more thing," interrupted Sook. "This writing is the same as the arrows and base camp."

"What does it read?" asked Duncan.

"Stupid Texans."

She handed the map to Duncan, who quickly folded it up and threw it on the coffee table. "Well, we'll see about that, won't we?" he asked rhetorically.

Lucy took the guys' empty bowls and offered them more, but they declined. Duncan expressed their regrets, but the two of them needed to return to Camp Lubbock to help with repairs or a possible relocation. Before they took off, they discussed the ramifications of the power outage and the fact Holloway's group was still at large.

"Surely, they wouldn't stick around, right?" asked Preacher. "You fellas were hot on their trail."

"Logically, I'd agree with you, Preach," said Major. "From what Duncan has described, this bunch is as unpredictable as they are capable. We shouldn't underestimate them."

"I agree, Dad," added Duncan. "What sickens me about the raid on Camp Lubbock is that not only did we lose a lot of good people, but my team's numbers were decimated. I had plans to station a unit here at all times if things got bad for some reason. With the grid down and these thugs at large, things are bad, and I'm unable to free up any manpower to help the ranch."

Major reassured him. "That's all right, son. Don't sweat it. I believe Holloway and his men left the area. It would have been the smart thing to do. If he was, in fact, ex-military, as your prisoners stated, he would know that your unit would be looking for revenge. I wouldn't stick around if I were him."

"Okay, then I have one more thing," said Duncan. He took a deep breath and quickly debated saying this in front of Espy but decided to be transparent about his thoughts. "Should I quit the TX-QRF to help protect the ranch?"

"Wow, that's a tough one, son," said Major.

"Dad, if I stay on, my hands are gonna be full all the time. My time at the ranch will be limited because of the grid being down. Holloway and his commandos will be the least of my worries. Cities like Lubbock and Amarillo were on edge before ERCOT collapsed. People are gonna lose it when they learn the power isn't coming back on for a long time."

Lucy spoke up. As always, her voice, her vote, trumped all others. "Duncan, you agreed to take on this job, and you should see it through, at least in the short-term. As Espy has conveyed to us, you have an excellent relationship with your unit, and they need you right now. More importantly, Texas does too. Don't get me wrong, I love you and I'd feel safer if you were home with us. At the same time, I know you, Duncan. You are an unselfish man who'll do what it takes for God and country. Finish your job, and then make this decision. Now is not the time."

The decision to defer was made by the Armstrong matriarch.

Duncan and Sook rose off the hearth together and immediately hugged Miss Lucy.

"I love you both," Lucy whispered into their ears. "I will take care of this young lady, please know that."

"I do, Momma," said Duncan.

The three of them held their embrace, and Duncan assisted in wiping off the tears created by the emotional moment.

Finally, Duncan prepared to leave, but he passed on a few final words to everyone.

"Every time I left the ranch when I was deployed or sent on a special op, I knew it would be hard on me and you guys. Y'all may have noticed that I never said goodbye. I tried the first time I left for the Middle East, and you have no idea how hard it was on me."

"Us too, son," added Major.

"So new rule of engagement, okay? Let's just say *see ya later*. How's that sound?"

"Yeah, see ya later!" shouted Lucy as tears still seeped from her eyes.

"*Adios, amigos*," said Espy laughingly.

"After a while, crocodile!" added Palmer.

"Gotta go, buffalo!" yelled Cooper.

Duncan gave Sook a quick kiss and grabbed Espy by the arm. "We gotta get out of here."

Everyone was laughing as they continued throwing goodbye sayings at Duncan and Espy.

"Take care, polar bear."

"Got to truck, baby buck!"

Duncan and Espy couldn't contain their laughter as they put on their combat kits and picked up their rifles. As Duncan flung open the door to make his escape, another saying flew in their direction. It was from Preacher.

"Don't let the door hit you in the—!"

"Hey! *No mas! No mas!*" begged Duncan as he and Espy pushed one another in their desperate attempt to get to the Humvee.

Chapter 45

January 21
The White House
Washington, DC

"Thank you all for providing me this detailed assessment of what has transpired in Texas today," started President Harman as she addressed the contingent from the Pentagon and Langley, who'd piecemealed together a report of the North Korean attack on the Texas power grid. "I understand your job was made difficult by the lack of cooperation from your counterparts in Austin. Thank goodness there are still members of our former military who are willing to be candid with you."

After everyone filed out, only Chief of Staff Acton remained and the designated representative from the CIA for this briefing, Billy Yancey.

"Mr. Yancey, I understand you have some additional insight into the events in Texas today?" asked a curious President Harman. She looked at her watch and saw that it was approaching ten p.m.

"I do, Madam President," replied Yancy. "Although my role within the agency has changed dramatically after the grid collapse, I've still managed to retain my expertise in analyzing other nation's governments. I have some suggestions that might interest you."

"This sounds like a conversation that is best conducted over a drink, gentlemen. Also, away from the prying ears of snooping staffers."

She rose from her chair, and the trio made their way to the Oval Office. Once inside, Acton closed the door behind them and immediately approached the bar. He filled the president a glass of wine first and then poured whisky in the remaining two glasses.

The president took a generous sip of wine and began. "I can only imagine what's going through Marion's head right now. Listen, when the EMP hit, I was caught off guard, and it was a total shock to my system. Marion's in a tougher spot. She was dealing with the secession, followed by food shortages, and then the borders collapsed on a couple of occasions. This must be a lot for her to handle."

Acton resisted the urge to point out that all of these crises were of Burnett's own doing, but he bit his tongue. The purpose of this casual conversation was to manipulate the president into moving in the direction he wanted. Yancey, as an impartial advisor who was in the White House by happenstance, was a perfect bird to chirp in the ear of the president. If Yancey could help lead her to make certain decisions, without Acton being accused of bias, then the evening would be a win-win.

"It is, Madam President," started Yancey. "As you know, the CIA has a history of regime change that dates back to the 1940s. Our most recent efforts in Syria took two decades to effectuate, but we were finally on the brink of collapsing the Assad regime when the EMP changed everything."

"How does this apply to Texas?" asked Acton, trying to force the conversation where he wanted it to go.

"Well, typically, regime change involves overthrowing a tyrant or dictator in favor of a political opponent that has a pro-democracy point of view. It doesn't always work out, but the CIA's covert involvement in the politics of other nations has a decent track record."

The president stared at Yancey over the top of her glass as she drank. Acton saw this and became nervous because he thought Yancey was coming on a little too strong.

Acton faked incredulity. "Are you advocating overthrowing the Austin government?"

"No, no. Of course not," Yancey backtracked, clearly picking up on Acton's tone. "Actually, what I have in mind is a way to help President Burnett out of a bad situation and perhaps create a result that might elevate President Harman to the levels of Lincoln."

The president perked up at this response. Now she appeared engaged and intrigued. Although she wasn't speaking, Acton knew she was thinking.

"Based upon your experience in these circumstances, what do you suggest?" asked Acton, the former attorney who remembered how to phrase a question for maximum impact.

"It's possible President Burnett is in over her head and today's events have pushed her to the edge of the cliff," started Yancey. "I'm not suggesting a regime change in any sense of the term. Maybe the more appropriate terminology is a *reset*."

"What does that look like?" asked the president.

Finally, Acton thought to himself. *She's receptive.*

Yancey made the pitch. "The end game is to bring the nation back together, just like Abraham Lincoln did following the Civil War. Offer President Burnett a path to returning Texas to the United States without repercussions to her or those who assisted in the secession effort."

Acton took a chance with the good cop, bad cop routine. "She's a traitor, Mr. Yancey, and so are those who stood with her as they turned their backs on America in her time of need. Texas is getting a taste of what we've endured. I don't think we should allow the treasonous opportunists any chance at redemption."

Acton paused and waited for a response from the president. She finished her glass of wine, and he jumped out of his chair to refill it.

"Thank you, Charles. However, I think you're being too hard on Marion. While I disagree with what she's done, I'd much rather everyone swallow their pride for the good of the country. If a path could be devised whereby we accomplish this *reset*, as this gentleman proposes, I think it should be considered."

Yes! Yancey had pried the door open, and now it was time for Acton to get on board the bandwagon. He delivered the president her second glass of wine.

"Madam President, as you know, I've been quite vocal about my opinions toward President Burnett and the Texans in general. That said, I could be persuaded to let bygones be bygones for the good of the country. We'd have to offer a few things and ask for some concessions on her part."

Yancey broke in. "Let me interject something here. I'm a former Texan and have met President Burnett in person on a couple of occasions. She is larger than life in Texas, so saving face will be the most important aspect of all of this. You will need to promise her—and anyone, for that matter, who participated in the secession movement—complete immunity from prosecution for treason or any other crimes that the folks in the DOJ might concoct."

"Blanket pardons?" asked the president.

"There is precedent," replied Acton. "Lincoln issued an amnesty order during the Civil War for all Confederates who agreed to return their allegiance to the Union. President Trump could have immediately ended the Mueller investigation by issuing a blanket presidential pardon to anyone involved in the alleged collusion with Russia, as well as the myriad of investigations that sprang out of the special prosecutor's far-reaching tentacles."

President Harman laughed and took a big gulp of wine. "Well, Trump made a mistake by not doing so. That investigation dogged him for the four years of his presidency and gave our campaign plenty of ammo to shoot. In our war room sessions back in 2018 immediately after the midterms, we literally prayed for the investigation to continue so the media would have a bone to go after."

Acton nodded and smiled. "Not that I care, but the stepping down of his attorney general and the appointment of the special counsel ruined his presidency. He had to fight the media daily and never could overcome the stigma even though the premise for appointing Mueller in the first place was completely bogus."

"They never did find any sort of collusion, did they?" asked Yancey.

Acton leaned back and finished his whisky. "Nah, of course not, but it didn't matter. The public thought it existed, and as a result, the three of us are sitting here instead of wondering where our next meal is gonna come from."

"Okay, back to the matter at hand." The president wanted to hear about Yancey's proposed tactic.

Yancey laid out the initial steps, or at least those the president would be aware of.

"The first thing you should do, Madam President, is make a phone call to Austin. Reach out to President Burnett, provide condolences, and offer to help in any possible way. Try to soften her with a spirit of cooperation. After all, both Texas and the United States are in the same situation now. Convince her that together, we can pull through this. But apart, both nations may fail."

Acton interrupted. "If she begins to ask about details, then relay what we've discussed but try to keep some things close to the vest. Propose a summit between high-level officials of the two administrations to open up the dialogue."

"Spirit of cooperation," mumbled President Harman. "I like that. First thing tomorrow morning, I'll make the call. Let's bring the country back together again."

CHAPTER 46

January 22
Camp Lubbock
Lubbock, Texas

It was the day after the attack on the power grid and Holloway's attempt to raid the Camp Lubbock armory. Duncan and his men worked around the clock to clean up their facility and make sure it was secured against a follow-up attack.

Duncan's request to his superiors for additional troops to be assigned to his unit, or at least designated to respond to unrest in Amarillo and Lubbock, was denied. The bulk of the Texas military forces were diverted toward larger metropolitan areas like Dallas, Houston, San Antonio, and El Paso, which were in a state of utter chaos. Commanders at Fort Hood were at a loss as to how they should quell the riots and the many uprisings throughout the city, which shared the Texas border with Juarez, Mexico.

"We're on our own, Espy," said Duncan as the two men found a moment to take a break. With the interior of Camp Lubbock cleared of debris, they set about the task of securing the windows. First, they covered the openings with eight-millimeter plastic and duct tape. Next, sheets of one-inch plywood were taken from a local lumber company to cover the windows. What they sacrificed in natural light was replaced with ballistic protection against any subsequent attacks.

Duncan's concern for a repeat of yesterday's assault was replaced by concern for the crowds that had gathered around Camp Lubbock made up of local citizens demanding answers. Camp Lubbock was the only representative of the new nation's government in the region and was now looked upon as the primary law enforcement entity after the sheriff's office had been destroyed by the rocket-propelled grenade.

Thirteen deputies and Lubbock police officers had perished in the blast and subsequent fire. In addition, the Lubbock County sheriff advised Duncan that many of his deputies had quit or simply disappeared. Rather than serve and protect the community, they'd opted to protect their families. After hearing this news, Duncan wondered if they'd made a smarter choice than he had.

Lucy's words made the difference. He and Espy were both prepared to resign their positions with the TX-QRF if there was a direct threat to the ranch and its occupants. Lucy had convinced them to return to Lubbock and put Camp Lubbock back together again. However, between Fort Hood's denial of additional personnel and the attrition rate for local law enforcement, Duncan began to wonder why he had to be the upstanding citizen. After all, he thought to himself, hadn't his country abandoned him in a time of need?

Espy didn't respond, opting instead to lean his chair back against the wall, propped on its two rear legs. Duncan could see how exhausted his new sergeant was.

"Espy! Are you awake?" Duncan teased his aide-de-camp and now close friend. Although he and Espy didn't have the working relationship that Duncan had developed with Park, the two of them seemed attuned to each other's movements when in battle. Park had been better at covert operations, but Espy was an excellent soldier.

"Yeah, yeah," Espy grumbled as he brought his chair down on the floor with a thud.

"Seriously, you obviously lied about how long you slept last night," admonished Duncan. "Go hit the rack for a while. The camp is under control, and I need to spend some time in the armory with a couple of the lieutenants. With our numbers down, we need to make sure our two four-man response units have the best equipment packed in their Humvees and ready at all times."

"We need the same thing," added Espy as he stifled a yawn. "I'm talkin' night vision, comms, stun grenades, several weapons options, and body armor."

Duncan stood up from his chair and walked toward the door. He waved at Espy as if to sweep him out the door as well. "On your feet, Sergeant. Get some rest, and I'll pick the gear out."

"Sir, yes, sir," said Espy with a grin. "I'm not gonna argue. I feel like the walking dead."

They strolled down the hallway toward the armory, and just as Espy reached his office/sleeping quarters, his satellite phone rang.

Espy answered and made mental notes from the caller's news. Duncan stood patiently by as Espy completed the call.

"What?" he asked his aide.

"A crowd of residents broke into the Walmart, and they're carrying out anything they can get their hands on. Apparently, there's fighting in the parking lot, as some people are waiting for others to do the heavy lifting by getting the loot outside, only to face an angry mob who wants to take their stuff when they reach the outside."

Duncan huffed and shook his head. "Sounds like a law enforcement problem to me. Looting, robbery, and B and E are all cop problems."

"Those were the cops," Espy said dryly.

"The cops called us to bust a bunch of looters?" Duncan asked in disbelief. "They do realize we're the military, right? We break things and kill people. We don't do crowd control and arrest looters."

Espy replaced the satellite phone into the holder attached to his belt. He exhaled before he spoke. "Actually, sir, under the martial law directive from the president, our duties include tamping down societal unrest."

Duncan shook his head in disgust. He, too, was tired. His men were not properly equipped to react to a real crisis, which in his mind involved large groups of armed men taking hostages or firing upon governmental facilities like sheriff's offices, National Guard complexes, and power grids.

He gritted his teeth and patted Espy on the shoulder. "C'mon, you and I can handle this alone."

"What? I mean, sir, are you sure?"

"Espy, grab one of the Humvees with a Ma Deuce attached. Make sure we've got plenty of ammo."

Espy stopped in his tracks and studied Duncan. Duncan scowled as he stared at his young sergeant. Duncan was sure yesterday's interrogation sessions were still fresh in Espy's mind. It was possible that Espy thought he was becoming insane.

"Espy? Are you gonna bring the truck around?"

"Sir, um, should we talk about our ROE?"

Finally, Duncan couldn't hold back. He laughed and put his hand on Espy's shoulder. "I'm not gonna massacre all the civvies. Is that what you're thinking?"

Espy stammered all over himself. "Well, no, sir, or I don't know, maybe."

"I'm only gonna scare the bejesus out of them. By the time I'm finished stitching the front of Walmart with a hundred fifty-cal rounds, they'll all scatter, leaving a big mess behind, but we will have fulfilled our obligation to tamp down the unrest."

"Sir, won't that cause an uproar and bring a lot of attention to our methods?"

Duncan smiled and nodded. "I hope so. Let them be afraid. Maybe they'll stay home from now on."

Chapter 47

January 22
Near Armstrong Ranch
Borden County, Texas

It was just after dusk as Holloway gathered his reconnaissance team back together following a day of surveillance around the Armstrong Ranch and the adjacent Reinecke property where the Slaughters were living. That morning, after a good rest for his team, he had taken one truck and a few of his top guys to follow in the same direction the military Humvee had driven the day before. To his surprise, just ten miles away was a large ranching operation, which piqued his interest.

From a safe distance, Holloway and his men used their long-range optics to study the property. They took the day to walk around the ranch until they ran into the Colorado River. Then they returned in the other direction until they came upon the Reinecke property turned Slaughter ranch.

He considered employing his commandos' abilities to sneak into the oddly configured dairy operation, kill all the inhabitants, and stake his claim. After additional recon of the big ranch, he decided this small makeshift dairy ranch could wait.

He returned to Vealmoor and brought the rest of his men, who were distributed around the western and southern perimeter of the ranch. He also studied the map and showed another team the route to place themselves on the north side of the river, where they could make observations and report back their findings.

All of his men were told to return to the small town they'd occupied after dark and were reminded to avoid detection. Holloway sensed this was the prize he'd been waiting for, and it had been just beyond his fingertips the whole time.

In addition, based upon the roads in the area, he began to think that his adversary from the Texas Guard was connected to the property. If he was right, then this would be an opportunity to inflict some pain upon the guy who'd killed so many of his men. Even if the guy was unconnected to this particular ranch, then Holloway might've found a home.

He lingered on the slightly elevated hill overlooking the western fence of the property as he tried to study their perimeter patrols. While they were frequent and the riders appeared to be armed with rifles, he didn't expect they'd be a match for his trained commandos. He applauded the ranchers use of guard towers, but he laughed when he saw that those who manned the tower rarely used binoculars to survey their surroundings.

"Nothing is a piece of cake, but this operation is pretty close," he remarked aloud.

Holloway left, and he gathered his men inside a large Quonset-hut-style prefabricated metal building to review their findings. Within an hour, they had created a fairly accurate map of Armstrong Ranch, including building placement, distances between structures, and manpower levels.

They found several cans of paint and a four-foot-by-eight-foot sheet of plywood to use as a map. The map was hung on the wall of the building for everyone to refer to as they exchanged observations. Using nails and some colored electrical wiring, he assigned his men to precise points of attack. Their communications were limited, so they would have to rely upon visual and audible signals to advance.

By midnight, the group had used the benefit of their years of training both in North Korea and in the U.S. as criminals to concoct the perfect plan to overrun and commandeer Armstrong Ranch.

Tonight, they'd rest. Tomorrow, they'd conduct additional surveillance to confirm their approach. By early evening, they'd attack and conquer.

CHAPTER 48

January 23
The Armstrong Ranch
Borden County, Texas

West Texas was all Preacher knew. He had been born and raised in the Midland-Odessa area, with a strict disciplinarian of a father and a librarian in the local middle school for a mother. The oldest of six children, Preacher, born Caleb O'Malley, had been a tough kid growing up. He was the consummate big brother, constantly helping his siblings and, when necessary, defending them from their bullying classmates in the schoolyard.

The combination of living under his father's thumb and the family's strict Southern Baptist upbringing had transformed young Caleb O'Malley into a protector of his fellow man. After graduation, his family couldn't afford to pay his way through college, so Preacher took a part-time job at a local meat-packing warehouse and attended classes at Midland College, where he majored in religious studies.

When an opportunity arose to work at the Midland Baptist Church on a part-time basis, he was the first in line to be interviewed. He was hired to work in their bus ministry and later as an assistant to the youth pastor. Between his studies in his final year in college and his time spent around the church, both on and off the clock, Preacher had become a highly respected man of God.

With a college degree, his fate became uncertain, as he had to transition from part-time employee of the church to a full-time, responsible adult. Mount Zion Baptist Church in nearby Big Spring provided the answer.

An older church located in the heart of Big Spring, its preacher had pushed back against the trend to ask for more money from his congregation in order to build a bigger, better church. The regulars at Mount Zion lived at or below the poverty level. Most of the families had two or three children more than they could afford. Husbands routinely got into trouble due to drinking and drugs. Wives were abused. Kids ran away only to come home again after harrowing experiences on the road. It was a sign of the times in America.

As new Baptist churches sprang up around town, the flock fled to the more opulent sanctuaries. When the preacher of Mount Zion suddenly passed away from colon cancer, the congregation was like a herd of sheep without a shepherd.

Until Caleb O'Malley arrived. With the powerful endorsement of the church elders at Midland Baptist and the support of the Southern Baptist Convention, Caleb O'Malley became a full-fledged preacher.

His congregation grew from less than twenty to a regularly packed house in the small church, which held forty-some congregants. He got to know them all personally. He was there to officiate their weddings and baptize their children. He was there to counsel couples before marriage and provide guidance as marriages fell apart. Preacher O'Malley had fulfilled his dream of helping people and presenting the gospel to all who'd listen.

Then the fateful day came when he got too personally involved and let his anger get the better of him. Despite the great things he'd done as a preacher at Mount Zion, he forced himself into self-exile and a life on the Armstrong Ranch.

Preacher rode alone that morning along the fence rows of a ranch he'd spent more than half of his life expanding, attending to, and calling home. The Armstrong family was his family. The ranch hands who resided at Armstrong Ranch were his family. This high-desert flatland full of tufts of dried-up tumbleweed thistle packed against barbed-wire fences that rested below the cobalt blue sky was his home.

It was a place where he could breathe. He could look at the sky at night and gaze upon a million stars. During the day, he tended to his flock—people and cattle alike. At night, he continued to read the word of God, among other things. He never once reflected on his life and wondered what might have been if not for that night when he'd rescued a young family from the terror of an abuser. God had a plan for him, and he was not one to argue.

"Hey, Preach, wait up!" Major shouted from a distance. His horse was trotting across the pasture in between the few dozen cattle that still milled about in this section of the ranch. Preacher had divided the herd so that forty percent were being held on the east side of the ranch and the remainder were scattered about the remaining parts of the ranch west of the house.

"Mornin'." Preacher greeted Major with a tip of his hat. "Everything okay?"

Major pulled up alongside his old friend. "Oh, yeah. Thanks to you, everyone is settled into a routine, fully understanding that we live in a different world now."

Preacher pointed up ahead to a doe, which grazed alongside the cattle. The men rode at a safe distance, taking a moment to admire the beautiful animal rather than making her this evening's meal.

"Same world, no electricity," said Preacher with a chuckle. "Oh, I can't really say the same world. It's more like the Wild, Wild West now."

"Ever since the EMP hit the rest of America, it seems like the rule of law has been thrown out the window. Law enforcement still exists, and our military has played a very active role in controlling people, yet lawlessness is everywhere."

Preacher adjusted himself in the saddle. "How does it all end?"

"Whadya mean?"

"You know, do you reckon we'll have to live the rest of our days defending perimeters against hungry, desperate thieves and North Korean soldiers? Is there a point where the lights come back on everywhere, and folks go back to shoppin' at Walmart and watchin' high school football on Friday nights?"

Major sensed Preacher's melancholy mood. "Have you been readin' dystopian books again?"

"Yeah, Revelations."

Major laughed. "Come on, Preach! It's not the end of the world. Yeah, things have changed for the worse. A world without power is horrifying for some, but if there is any group of people capable of surviving under these circumstances, it's the folks on this ranch. I believe we can thank you for that in many respects. You've taught us how to live old-school, in the ways of self-reliance. It's one thing to read about it in a book. Practicing the old ways of doing things was the smartest thing we ever did. I thank you for that."

"I know, boss. It's just that I don't understand people. Since the EMP, we've had several occasions when we've had to shoot at our fellow men and kill them. The first time it happened, we took them to the sheriff and found him murdered. Now, somewhere out there, a herd of hungry refugees could be heading this way or, worse, a couple of dozen North Korean commandos."

"That's true, Preach, but we might also be left alone to raise our cattle, tend our crops, and watch these young families grow to the point when they're taking care of us instead of the other way around."

Preacher nodded his head. "I reckon."

The two men rode along in silence when the sound of a helicopter flying in the distance caught their attention. They stopped their horses in the middle of the tall grasses and shielded their eyes from the late morning sun. The noise grew louder as it appeared to turn in their direction.

"Boss, do you reckon the North Koreans have choppers too?"

"I don't know, but I sure hope not 'cause this one's coming straight for us."

Chapter 49

January 23
The Mansion
Outside Amarillo, Texas

After the Airbus ACH helicopter with the Texas flag emblazoned across both sides of its cabin and tail boom landed near the barns, it seemed everyone on the ranch arrived to determine what was happening. Two men in suits emerged and introduced themselves as being with President Burnett's security detail. They delivered an emergency request from the president for Major to come to Austin.

Major huddled with the family inside the ranch house to speculate about the summons and to discuss whether they could do without him for the rest of the day. They all agreed that the invitation was too intriguing to pass up and they'd be fine while he was gone. After a quick change of clothes, Major strapped on his gun belt and holster. "Don't leave home without it," he said jokingly. Hugs and well wishes were exchanged; then he was off to Austin full of apprehension, but somewhat excited.

As the helicopter entered the city limits, Major noticed the substantial increase in military activity on the streets. Obviously, a lot had changed since he'd met with the president five days ago about Gregg's death. The power outage meant an increased enforcement of the president's martial law declaration, but from the masses of people congregating in the vicinity of the capitol, the military had their hands full.

After they touched down within the perimeter security of the Mansion, Major was escorted off the helicopter by two uniformed military police. The helicopter quickly took off and headed out of the city once again. Major immediately wondered if there were more people being summoned to meet with the president.

After the thumping of the helicopter's powerful rotors faded into the distance, the roar of people's voices could be heard yelling throughout downtown Austin. It was impossible to discern whether they were chanting in unison or simply screaming, hoping to be heard by someone. Major could only characterize the tone as one of desperation as his fellow Texans sought answers and help.

Major waited nearly an hour before the president was prepared to meet with him. Her chief of staff apologized repeatedly for the delay and offered him lunch and drinks on several occasions. Finally, the president exited her office to invite Major inside.

"Major, I am so sorry for keepin' you waiting. I was just blindsided with a phone call from one of our generals at Fort Bliss. A little over an hour ago, several explosions tore a hole through our southern border wall big enough to drive a tank through. Before our people could respond with a sufficient show of strength, thousands of Mexicans poured into Texas and are now infiltrating El Paso. It's a war zone down there, Major."

"Well, Marion, it certainly isn't much better out there," started Major as he pointed toward her windows. Then his eyes glanced downward toward the coffee table that separated them the last time they spoke. It still had a stack of file folders on it, although the pile was dwindling. "The streets of Austin have changed a lot since I was here last. I imagine your military resources are taxed to their limits."

"They are. People want answers, and the truth may not be best for them, yet. Lack of food was a problem before, and I promised folks that if they'd pull together, things would get better by the spring. Then this happened."

"How can I help?" asked Major.

"There has been a new development, which is the reason I whisked you away from the ranch."

Major chuckled. "A development other than the loss of power and an invasion of Texas by North Koreans? I can't imagine anything more dramatic than that."

"I appreciate your sense of humor, Major. So try this on for size."

Major leaned back and got comfortable. "I'm ready."

"Yesterday, I got a call from the President of the United States. She wants Texas back."

"Come on, seriously?" asked Major.

"The conversation didn't start that way," continued the president. "She sounded like any other world leader, none of whom called, by the way, offering condolences and assistance, etcetera. We went back and forth discussing the ramifications of the outage and the presence of North Korean soldiers on our soil when she just blurted it out."

Major finished her thought. "She wants Texas back."

"Right. She's offered pardons, concessions, accommodations. Pretty much anything you could imagine. She even invoked Lincoln during the conversation."

"Wow," said Major.

"There's more. She played the woman card too. You know, 'first women as presidents came together to restore the union and save the country.' I was waiting for her to offer up one of her pink knit hats."

Major wasn't sure what to say. Had the president flown him all the way from Borden County to vent. "What's your gut feeling?"

"Truthfully, Major, she couldn't have timed her phone call any better. This is clearly the low point of our republic's short history. We accomplished a lot by seceding without ramifications. I rallied Texans to support me in that endeavor, and many did. Now, President Harman is asking me to admit defeat and return to the U.S. I don't know if I can do it."

"Is there a real benefit? I mean, they don't have power either. Wouldn't it be easier for Texas to take care of their own rather than sharing what few resources you have with the U.S.?"

The president leaned forward and asked, "Major, what would you do?"

Major thought for a moment and responded, "Marion, Sam Houston said he had one maxim and that was to *do right and risk the consequences.* You and I, like Sam Houston, are Texas patriots. The blood of this republic runs through our veins like our ancestors before us. Sweat, tears, and, yes, bloodshed have been the legacy of the Burnetts and Armstrongs in West Texas. Our kind of patriotism exists because families like ours need a higher cause to rally around. That cause is Texas."

"Major, I did the right thing in restoring this republic."

"Yes, you did, Marion. I believe secession was inevitable because Texans have never responded well to oppression, even in the form of an overbearing federal government. Your courage to bring Texans together to reclaim their independence was remarkable, and you should not turn your back on them or this republic."

President Marion Burnett then did something that Major thought she was incapable of. She shed a few tears. He wasn't sure what to do. The president was one of the toughest women he'd ever known. From her days in business as she brought the Four Sixes Ranch to glory and throughout her battles in the political trenches, a show of emotion and vulnerability was out of character. He was seeing another side of his old friend, which proved she was human.

"Well, thanks a lot, Major. You made your president cry."

They both began to laugh as President Burnett regained her composure. She leaned forward on the edge of the couch and reached for the stack of file folders. She searched for one in particular, pulled it out, and handed it to Major.

"You have a file on me?" Major was surprised.

"Major, Monty Gregg was a vice president to me in name only, God rest his soul. I could never trust his advice for fear he was trying to manipulate me. He was not a sounding board in a time of crisis for the same reason. I used him for his connection to the former U.S. military, and he used me to stick a needle in the eye of Washington and to expand his résumé."

"Marion, I don't think I understand."

She continued. "The last time you were here, I had a dozen options for a successor to Monty. I was looking for experience and someone who might fit a particular political demographic to assist me in my future reelection effort. Frankly, at the time I didn't have a sense of urgency and engaged in quite a bit of tire kickin' as I went through the process."

"The attacks changed that, I assume," interjected Major.

"To an extent, yes. Although I'd reached a decision the night before. I've come to appreciate the value of loyalty. Experience can be learned on the job. Political capital can be earned through deeds and actions. But loyalty can only come from someone you've known for most of your life. Somebody who would have your back regardless of what you faced. Somebody like you."

Major looked down at the file marked CONFIDENTIAL. *Is she asking me to be her vice president?*

"Marion, are you talking about me?" he asked and then hesitated. "As your vice president?"

"Yes, Major, if you'll have me as your boss."

His eyes grew wide and he glanced around the room. Then he burst out in uncontrollable laughter. The president was caught off guard by his chuckling and then joined him.

"I'm not kidding, Major. I need you. Texas needs you."

Major finally controlled himself as he realized he might be insulting his president. "Marion, I would have no idea how to be vice president of Texas. Heck. I don't even run my own ranch, Preacher does. And you know Miss Lucy, if I even suggested I'm running that household, she'd chase me out the front door with a broom or a shotgun."

"You sell yourself short, Major," she shot back. "For one, Lucy and Preacher respect you, and that's why your ranching operation and household run so efficiently. During your command of Company C, the letters of praise for your efforts filled another file folder, which is sitting over there on my desk."

"That was a long time ago," said Major, who was growing nervous as he realized the president was serious. He felt like a girl who'd just been asked by her boyfriend to get married and she contemplated accepting so she didn't hurt his feelings.

"No, not really. Then there was your interaction with the top brass of our military both here and at Monty's funeral. I heard nothing but words of praise from them concerning your demeanor and knowledge of the challenges faced by Texas."

"Just talk," said Major, who began to squirm in his seat.

"Did you not hear yourself a moment ago?" she asked. "You spoke with passion and conviction in convincing me to turn down Washington's offer. If I didn't know better, Sam Houston himself was sitting across the table from me."

"I wasn't trying to convince you one way or—" started Major before being interrupted.

"Exactly! Unlike Monty, who was always pushing an agenda, you spoke from the heart in a way that was honest and therefore convincing. That's why you're the perfect man for the job!"

Major sat back against the couch and set his file folder back on the coffee table. His mind raced as it moved from conflicted to honored to dread at having to discuss the topic with Lucy. He'd need to hide the brooms and shotguns.

"Marion, I'm extremely flattered, and I respect the fact that you've given this a lot of thought. But—"

"Nope." She stopped him from continuing. "I don't want to hear what you have to say after *but*. If you truly respect what I've been going through here and the considerable amount of thought I've put into this offer, then at least do me the courtesy of discussing it with Lucy and your family. All I ask is that you get back to me in the next few days. I've got attorney generals, adjutant generals, and army generals harping in my ear about continuity of government. I told them to keep my fanny safe and all will be fine. Nonetheless, they've got a point."

Major rose from his seat, anxious to get out of the Mansion and find some fresh air on the front lawn. This was an opportunity of a lifetime but would be a big change for his family. He had a lot to think about before he got home.

Chapter 50

January 23
Outside Amarillo, Texas

Duncan and Espy led the convoy as it sped northbound on Interstate 27 toward Amarillo. Four Humvees led the way with a single troop transport struggling to keep up with the faster vehicles. Initially, Duncan had assigned a TX-QRF unit to Amarillo, but after he'd lost so many men during the raid, he chose to consolidate his forces at Camp Lubbock and respond as necessary to the outlying areas.

"Let's go over it again, Espy," said Duncan to his loyal sergeant.

"Overnight, two garbage trucks traveling at a high rate of speed crashed through a section of fencing west of Kerrick along US 385. A couple of thousand refugees overran the military patrols there and flooded the small communities in the area, like Stratford and Cactus."

"Apparently the refugees didn't get the memo," said Duncan with a chuckle as he gripped the wheel a little tighter. "Texas is no better off than they are. Might as well go home, people."

"No kiddin'," said Espy. "Anyway, a couple of hundred arrived at Cal Farley's Boys Ranch earlier and have apparently been terrorizing the kids and adults alike. That's when we got the call."

"Tell me about Boys Ranch."

"It is an actual town set up initially to help kids who've had a rough go in life. Some of the kids are orphans, others have psychological issues and personality disorders, while a few have been ordered there by the court system because they're considered a danger to themselves or others."

"The last thing these kids need is the aggravation of a bunch of desperate people harassing them. Are there any reports of weapons being used?"

"Not yet."

"What about local law enforcement?"

"A sheriff and one deputy, sir. Do we have a directive on what to do with the refugees that we round up?"

"Catch 'em, deliver them to the local county jail, and the military will take it from there," replied Duncan.

"Fine by me," added Espy. "I don't want any more scraps with prison wardens or their inmates."

They rode along in silence until they reached the Hollywood Road exit on the south side of Amarillo. Duncan veered off the ramp and stopped at the traffic signal, which was no longer working. The intersection, which was once bustling with activity at the Love's truck stop and nearby McDonald's, was deserted. Activity in this part of Texas had come to a screeching halt.

"Weird, isn't it?" asked Duncan rhetorically. "I mean, before the power grid was taken down, people moved about but not that much. Now, there's nobody."

"Just those two on bicycles," noted Espy.

"Where could they be going?"

The men watched as the cyclists pulled into the truck stop and drove around to the side of the building. They parked their bikes and approached a fenced-in utility yard. They opened the gates and stood for a moment with their hands on their hips.

"Dumpster diving," replied Espy.

"I guess it's a sign of the times," said Duncan as he pushed through the intersection, convoy in tow.

Chapter 51

January 23
The Armstrong Ranch
Borden County, Texas

Cooper and Riley ambled along the western fence line on their beautiful chestnut horses as the sun began to set over the horizon. Another day of patrolling the perimeter together left them weary from boredom. Gone were their lives of preparing for rodeos and traveling with their sister to venues all around North America. Even the off weeks had provided them the opportunity to practice their sport in between doing chores around the ranch.

"Can you believe Slaughter wants to pull his men from the security detail?" asked Riley.

"Pretty ungrateful, if you ask me," replied Cooper. "We took them in when they had nothing and were desperate. Daddy made a deal with them that was extremely fair. We promised to feed them, get 'em set up with their dairy operation, and they promised to lend us their boys to help guard the ranch."

"Not to mention, you and Duncan saved their lives that day."

"That's true also. All I can figure is they got spooked about this whole North Korean thing and decided to protect their own."

"Well, its BS, Coop, and everyone knows it. They wouldn't have *their own* to protect if it wasn't for Daddy takin' them in."

They continued riding along, making small talk as they went. Riley, who was typically emotional, was contemplative on this late afternoon.

"Coop, what are you gonna miss the most about the old way of life besides our rodeos?"

"Everything, but really, I guess nothin'," said Cooper with a laugh.

Riley joined him and then added, "That ain't much of an answer, Coop."

"Well, heck, Riley, I guess I really haven't stopped to think about it. My whole life was ridin' bulls and hangin' out with you and Palmer. We didn't go out clubbin' or to baseball games or the movies. Palmer didn't go shoppin' at the mall with her girlfriends. Heck, she had fewer girlfriends than I had."

Riley started laughing. "I think she's sweet on that Espy fella. I'm okay with it, are you?"

"Yeah, I think so. I haven't really hung out with him, you know? He's not a cowboy, but he seems interested in what life on the ranch is all about. Duncan likes him. A lot, in fact. I guess that's good enough for me."

Cooper paused and then asked his brother, "What are you gonna miss, Riley?"

"Food," he replied bluntly.

Cooper pulled off his hat and playfully swatted at his brother. "I knew you'd say that. Momma's doin' the best she can."

"Oh, I ain't complainin'. It's just that when you take away your options, you suddenly realize how good you used to have it."

Riley paused as something caught his eye, but then he continued. "I've got another question for you. When do you think this is gonna be over? How long will it be before Texas, and America too, will be normal again?"

Cooper was quiet for a moment and then responded, "I've thought about this, and I kinda talked to Momma about it too. It may take a year just to get power restored and who knows how long to get back to a normal life."

"Coop, a lot of folks are gonna die of starvation and such, aren't they?"

"They already were. This is just gonna make it happen faster. And to top it off, we've got these commandos runnin' around out there somewhere. Don't we have enough disasters to deal with that are beyond our control without having to worry about them?"

Riley shrugged as the two continued their ride along the fence. "Do you remember when we were kids working with Pops around the ranch? We were down by Wildcat Creek and a momma pig charged us out of the brush."

Cooper nodded as he responded, "Yeah, we were just young'uns. You grabbed me for protection, and I was about to wet my pants. Pops just stood there, pulled out his six-shooter, and dropped that crazed hog dead in her tracks."

"He sure did. I remember what he said, too. Do you?"

Cooper recalled his words. "*Boys, this is our world. Beautiful and terrible things will happen. Don't be afraid.*"

The boys allowed the words to sink in, quietly applying them to the new lives they were embarking upon, when suddenly, terrible things began to happen.

THANK YOU FOR READING *FIFTH COLUMN*!

If you enjoyed it, I'd be grateful if you'd take a moment to write a short review (just a few words are needed) and post it on Amazon. Amazon uses complicated algorithms to determine what books are recommended to readers. Sales are, of course, a factor, but so are the quantities of reviews my books get. By taking a few seconds to leave a review, you help me out, and also help new readers learn about my work.

And before you go…

SIGN UP for Bobby Akart's mailing list to receive special offers, bonus content, and you'll be the first to receive news about new releases in The Lone Star Series, The Pandemic series, The Blackout series, The Boston Brahmin series and The Prepping for Tomorrow series—which includes sixteen Amazon #1 Bestsellers in thirty-nine fiction and non-fiction genres. Visit Bobby Akart's website for informative blog entries on preparedness, writing, and his latest contribution to the American Preppers Network.

www.BobbyAkart.com

Made in the USA
Middletown, DE
02 July 2018